THE PRODIGAL SONS

LaQuanda S. Washington

2018

Copyright Material

Scripture references can be found at https://www.biblegateway.com/.

Printed and Published by
Kingdom Haven Publishing, LLC.
kingdomhavenpublishingllc@gmail.com

ISBN: 978-0-9988913-2-3

Acknowledgements

I dedicate this book to my mother for instilling the love and reverence of God in my brothers and I since we were children.

I could not comprehend back then, why we needed to attend Sunday Service, Noon Prayer on Wednesdays, Friday Night Services, Revivals and Shut-Ins but I get it now.

I am so grateful for those long bus rides from our home in Northwest, Washington DC to Capitol Heights, MD, and the amazing teaching that we received under the leadership of Apostle Albert Venson, Sr.- Founder & General Overseer of the True Deliverance Church of God Ministries.

R.I.P. Apostle Albert Venson, Sr.

Proverbs 22:6 King James Version (KJV)

Train up a child in the way he should go: and when he is old, he will not depart from it.

LUKE 15:24

"FOR THIS SON OF MINE WAS DEAD AND IS ALIVE

AGAIN; HE WAS LOST AND IS FOUND…"

CHAPTER 1

The six young men sat in the back of the church on the last pew. Andre "Dre" Williamson III snickered at something his cousin Marcus said, just as his mom started walking toward them. Dre, along with his cousins and friends, all sat up as straight as they could and began focusing on the sermon Dre's father was preaching.

Gloria Williamson gave each of the boys a stern look, and they all knew what that look meant. Gloria, along with her husband Andre "Senior" Williamson Jr., raised their two biological twins, Dre and Drea along with their nephews Eric and Marcus. Gloria's sister Patricia was shot and killed by their father, in front of the two boys, before turning the gun on himself.

It took years of prayer and therapy to get the boys to sleep through the night without waking up screaming. Gloria loved her baby sister more than anything, and Karen looked up to her big sister. Losing her was one of the hardest things Gloria had ever endured, but she loved the fact that she still had a part of her sister with her through the boys.

Marc was the spitting image of his mother right down to his dimpled cheeks, and Eric had her shy, reserved personality. Senior and Gloria loved them and raised them as if they were their very own. Jayson, Rico, and Tony all grew up in the same neighborhood with the Williamsons, who were like second parents to them. They were at the house so much that it almost felt like they lived there.

Many of Dre's childhood memories involved his family, friends, and church. His father had taken over as pastor when his grandfather died, and everyone naturally assumed that Dre would take over when his father retired. Dre loved God, but he didn't think he was cut out to be a pastor.

Dre turned his attention back to the pulpit as his father continued speaking, "Life is all about choices. We *serve a God of redemption, but we must not forget that our*

choices have consequences," he said, looking directly at

his son. "God will not force us to obey him. He gives us

the option of free will to choose our paths. Choose ye this

day whom you will serve."

Senior began the benediction as the choir stood and

started singing John P. Kee's I Do Worship before he

dismissed the congregation. As Dre and the guys headed

out to the parking lot, Dre was so busy talking to Jayson

that he accidentally bumped into his girlfriend, Grayce,

and stepped on her foot. "Ouch!" Grayce said rubbing her

foot.

"I'm sorry babe, I didn't see you," Dre apologized

as he hugged her. "That's okay Dre; I didn't need that toe

anyway." They both smiled and exited the church. "So

what time are you coming over?" she asked as Dre walked

her to her car. "I'll be over after I eat dinner and change

clothes. You wanna come over?" Dre asked. "No thank

you, I told my mom I'd help her with dinner, so that's perfect. You need to let me cook for you one Sunday after church," Grayce smiled. "Ummm yeah about that," Dre joked. "Dre, you know I can throw down," Grayce laughed. "Yeah, sure I know...I believe you," Dre laughed.

"Dre, hurry up man I'm hungry," Marcus screamed from the passenger seat of Dre's car. "Babe let me go before this boy gets on my nerves. I'll call you when I'm on my way," Dre said as he hugged Grayce. She watched Dre walk away as did several of the other girls and a few women in the parking lot.

Grayce knew that Dre loved her and would never cheat on her, so she never had a reason to feel jealous or insecure. He treated her like a queen. As he entered the car, he looked up at her loving and mouthed I love you. She smiled as her heart melted.

CHAPTER 2

"Hello earth to Dre," Jayson said, trying to get his best friend's attention. Dre snapped out of his daydream. "Sorry man, for some reason I started thinking about Grayce. She's been on my mind a lot lately." Marcus shook his head. "Cuz I love you, but you are the dumbest dude in the world for letting her get away." "I know," Dre said quietly. "If I could go back and do things over she would be my wife right now."

Jayson cut an eye at Dre. "Did I just hear you use the *W* word? I never in a million years thought I would ever hear the bachelor extraordinaire, Andre Williamson III say that word. Dre laughed as he playfully shoved his best friend. "I know, but I'm serious. Not one woman that I have ever dated compares to her." "I know what you mean," Jayson smiled. "I wouldn't trade Jess for all the women in the world."

"Y'all are crazy," Marc said as they exited the pool hall. "I'm going to be single for as long as I can. She is gonna have to drag me down the altar screaming in hand and ankle cuffs," Marc laughed. "Jay, I still can't believe that you are finally a married man after all these years," Marc said. "It's about time," Dre laughed. My godsons would've been in college and they would still shackin."

"I adore Jess, but I didn't want to marry her without having my career on track. How many people do we know right now who divorced because of financial issues?" "My mother never worked, she stayed home and took care of me while my dad worked. I want to be that same kind of provider for my family. Besides, she's pregnant again, and both of our mommas would kill me if we had another baby without being married."

"What?!?" Marc choked on his bottle of water. "Man, this is what, number five?" "Yes," Jayson said proudly, with a huge smile on his face. "Man, Jess so fertile

I bet she gets pregnant every time she walks by you." The guys laughed as Jayson smacked Marc upside the head. "I'm finally getting my girl though," Jayson grinned. "I can't wait," Dre said. "I love my godsons, but it's going to feel good having a little girl to spoil." "I'm happy for you," Marc smiled. As they walked to Dre's truck, none of them noticed the two guys who'd been following them since they exited the club.

Dre unlocked the truck with his remote key when he felt the cold steel against his head. Before Marc had a chance to react, he felt a gun in his back. "This is Marcus Jackson, the new quarterback for the Washington Kings," he heard one of them say. The other gunman started to laugh. "We hit the jackpot with this one."

Jayson turned to look at the gunman. "Look, you don't have to do this. Every action in this world, be it good or bad, has a consequence. You can walk away right now from this. You can have whatever you want just put the gun down and let's talk. Whatever you're going through isn't worth this."

"I don't need you to preach to me. This ain't no afterschool special. I don't need your permission. Turn around and stop looking at me," the gunman ordered. Jayson turned to face the truck and began praying as thoughts of his wife and children entered his head. Just as the guys started rifling through their pockets, several other patrons exited the club with one of the bouncers and startled them.

The gunmen frantically began shooting as they ran off. Just as Marc bent down, he felt a piercing pain in his back and then nothing from his waist down. He immediately realized that he couldn't feel his legs. He laid on the ground screaming Dre's name but, in the chaos, he couldn't hear anything.

He looked over to Jayson as he tried to pull himself up. When he reached Jayson all he could do was scream as

Jayson lay there on the ground with his eyes wide open and

blood flowing from his head and mouth. He knew that his

friend was gone. Marc let out a gut-wrenching scream

before everything went black.

CHAPTER 3

Drea was sound asleep when something jarred her awake. She couldn't put her finger on it, but something was wrong with Dre. She immediately picked up her phone to call her twin brother. Her calls kept going directly to his voicemail. Her brother's phone never went to voicemail when she called. Drea jumped out of bed and frantically began searching for her clothing.

Her boyfriend Shawn turned over, looked at the bedside alarm clock and covered his head with the pillow. "Baby it's 2:00 in the morning, what are you doing?" "Something is wrong with my brother," Drea responded. Shawn sat up and yawned, "what do you mean, what happened?" "I can't explain it," Drea cried, "but ever since we were kids I could always tell when something was wrong with him and vice versa."

"Wow," he said sleepily. "So that twin thing is really true huh? Well, I'm coming with you," he said rubbing his eyes and reaching for his glasses. "I'm not letting you go out alone, and besides, you are way too upset to drive." "Thank you, Shawn," Drea said as she hugged him. "It's going to be okay baby. Let me use the bathroom and get dressed so we can go check on your brother okay?"

As Shawn headed into the bathroom, Drea sat on the edge of her bed, covering her head with her hands. She had never in her life, felt so helpless. Almost immediately she heard her mother's voice in her head. *When you don't know what else to do, pray.* Shawn exited the bathroom just as Drea knelt and began to pray. Shawn rolled his eyes and quietly backed into the bathroom.

Shawn was not spiritual or religious. Drea loved him and believed that she would be able to change Shawn's viewpoint, but lately, she's been hearing her mother's voice about being unequally yoked. Drea did her very best to hide Shawn's marriage from her parents. She knew that they both would be disappointed if they knew that she was involved with someone's husband. Dre, Marc, and Eric only knew because they all went to school together. They were not happy about it, but they loved Drea and promised to keep her secret from their parents, but Drea knew that her parents knew that something was off.

Drea and Shawn had been together for over three years, and they had only met him a few times briefly. Drea hated the fact that she allowed herself to fall in love with a married man. Drea never thought that she would end up in a situation like this before. Every time Drea tried to leave, Shawn found a way to lure her back with promises of divorcing his wife. Drea knew deep down inside that he would never leave his wife, no matter how miserable he claimed to be, but she couldn't find the strength to walk away from him.

Shawn softly closed the door and sat on the side of the tub while he waited for Drea to finish praying. *"Lord I don't know what's going on with my brother, but I need you now. Please place your protective spirit over my brother wherever he may be right now Lord. Watch over him and keep him safe from every peril of the enemy in Jesus name I pray, Amen."*

Shawn exited the bathroom slowly after hearing Drea finish her prayer. "You ready?" he asked awkwardly. "Yes," Drea said, too preoccupied to notice the shift in his attitude. Drea knew that Shawn had an issue with her relationship with God, but she didn't care.

As much as she loved him, Drea wasn't going to forsake God for him or anyone else. Shawn didn't understand how Drea could call herself a Christian when every Christian that he knew seemed to be judgmental and hypocritical.

Shawn gave up trying to get Drea to understand his point of view, but it still infuriated him. He also hated the fact that Drea kept trying to get him to leave his wife.

Shawn loved Drea as much as he could love any woman, but he would never leave his wife for her.

Lately, he could sense that she was getting tired of waiting, but he was not willing to let either of them go. He and Drea had a great relationship and rarely ever argued and whenever they did it was always about him leaving his wife or her going to church on Sunday mornings instead of sleeping in with him.

Shawn had promised to marry Drea several times. He even went as far as buying her a four-carat ring and proposing to her, but she continuously turned him down. Drea let him know from the moment they entered the relationship that God was first in her life, and she would not be his permanent mistress.

Shawn thought that if he treated Drea like a queen, she'd be satisfied and eventually stopped pressuring him, but that wasn't working anymore. The memories made Shawn angry all over again. He yanked on his sweatpants, tee shirt and shoes and they were out the door five minutes

later.

CHAPTER 4

"So where should we go first?" Shawn asked as he started the car and put on his seatbelt. "Let's check his house first," Drea said. As they pull up to Dre's house, they saw two police officers knocking on the door. "Oh God," Drea cried, "I knew something was wrong." "Calm down baby let's just talk to them first before we assume anything."

Shawn had known Dre from high school. They were not friends but were cordial to one another for Drea's sake. Dre hated the fact that his sister was dating a married man. He was angry with Shawn for even attempting to date his sister knowing that he was married. As much as he wanted to intervene, Drea was a grown woman, and he had to respect her decisions even if he did not agree with them or understand them.

Drea and Shawn slowly exited the car as the officers walked toward her. The first officer approached

Drea, "excuse me ma'am; my name is Det. Andrew Curtis, do you live here?" Drea could not find the words to speak and just shook her head no. Her heart was beating so loud that she could barely hear the officer.

Shawn spoke for her. "Her brother Andre lives here." The second detective had a look of shock on his face as he placed his hand on Drea's shoulder. Drea slowly looked up into the eyes of her first boyfriend. "Tony?" Drea questioned, confused.

Detective Curtis looked back and forth between the two, "Drea I'm sorry I didn't even recognize you for a moment." "Tony what's going on?" she cried. "Where is Dre?" "Drea sweetie listen to me okay, Dre is alive but he, Marc and Jayson were shot tonight."

Drea dropped to her knees. She could not believe her ears. "What? How?" Tony knelt next to her. "Drea, we need to get to the hospital. We can go over the details later, okay?" Drea nodded her head. "I was able to reach Eric and

Jess. I tried reaching your parents, but there was no answer when we stopped by, and I didn't want to leave a message like this on their voicemail. Do you have another number where I can reach them?" Tony was oblivious to the rage in Shawn's eyes as he watched Tony comfort his girlfriend?

"I can call them. Mommy and Daddy went away for the weekend with Grayce's parents." "Okay," Tony said, finally noticing Shawn. Tony assumed from the look the Shawn gave him, that this was her boyfriend. "Are you guys okay to drive or would you like to ride with us?" Tony asked. "We'll drive," Shawn said with an attitude.

"Okay," Tony said, "You can follow us over. He's at Kingdom Hospital Center." Shawn could see that there was a history between the two of them and he did not like the way the officer looked at Drea.

As Shawn followed the officers, Drea called her parents. Her father, answered the phone on the first ring, sounding as if he'd been wide awake. "Hey baby girl what's wrong?" he asked as soon as he picked up the phone. Drea began to cry. "Baby girl what's going on?" "Dre, Marc, and Jayson were shot tonight," Drea began rambling.

"I don't know what happened, but they were all shot. We're following Tony to the hospital now. He didn't give me any details, but he says that Dre is alive." "Okay baby, what hospital?" Senior asked. "Kingdom Hospital Center," Drea said wiping the tears from her eyes. "Okay baby girl, we'll see you there shortly."

"Don't worry, God's got this, and Kingdom is the best trauma center in the area. Dre is going to be just fine. Trust God baby girl." Gloria Williamson had been listening to her husband on the phone and was already praying when her husband hung up the phone. Senior joined his wife as they prayed for them before heading to the hospital.

Shawn and Drea were almost at the hospital when Shawn asked, "So how do you know the cop?" "He was my first boyfriend," Drea responded nervously chewing on her bottom lip thinking about her brother. Shawn felt like he had been punched in the stomach.

He knew there was something between them. "So that is *the* Tony?" he asked. "Yes," Drea responded impatiently. "Shawn, I don't have time for this right now. My brother is in the hospital." "Time for what?" Shawn asked angrily, "I simply asked you a question, Drea."

Before Shawn could continue, Drea's cell phone started ringing. Drea didn't recognize the number. "Hello?" Drea answered cautiously. "Hey Drea, it's Eric." Drea could hear the thickness of his voice and knew that he had been crying.

"Eric, I am so sorry I meant to call you, but things have been crazy. Shawn and I just arrived at the hospital, so I don't know anything yet. Are you holding up okay?" "Not really," Eric answered. "I'm in the car now on my way to the airport so I should be there within a couple of hours.

Please call me if there are any updates," Eric said. "Okay, I will see you soon. Be safe. I love you." "I love you too sis," Eric sadly said as he hung up the phone.

Eric still couldn't believe this was happening. He closed his eyes and prayed. *"God please save my brother. I cannot go through this again. I'll trade my life for his, just please let my brother live."* Eric still remembered the night his father shot his mother. He held his head as he tried to block out the memories of that horrible night.

"I'll park and come and find you," Shawn said. "Okay," Drea said as she opened the car door. She turned to Shawn before exiting the car, "Baby I'm sorry. This entire situation has me on edge. I'm so worried about Dre, but I didn't mean to take it out on you, and I'm sorry for snapping at you." "I understand," Shawn said as he rubbed her hand. "Go to Dre; I'll be right in after I park."

Drea exited the car and rushed over to Tony who escorted her to the emergency entrance. Shawn still had that sickening feeling in his stomach that things would never be the same again as he watched Tony touch the small of her back and guide her into the Emergency Room entrance.

Tony knew just about everyone in the emergency department, and they immediately escorted them to Dre's room in the intensive care unit. Drea choked back tears as she watched Dre through the large glass window where he was hooked up to several machines while his nurse checked his vitals.

"This is his sister," Tony said by way of explanation to the nurse as she exited the room. The nurse nodded her head and gently rubbed Drea's arm. "I will let the doctor on-call know that you're here," she said smiling warmly. Drea nodded her head, and she finally let go of the tears she'd been holding inside.

She softly touched the glass, silently praying that Dre could feel her presence there. "Tony what happened?"

she asked as she turned around. Tony shook his head and took a deep breath. "I was able to talk to a few witnesses briefly when we arrived on the scene, and according to them and the video surveillance, Dre, Marc, and Jay had just exited the pool hall. They were walking to the Dre's truck when two guys crept up behind them and attempted to rob them."

"How are Marc and Jayson? She asked. Drea saw the look on Tony's face, "What is it, Tony?" "Well, Marc was in stable condition when we left to notify your family although the docs think he may be paralyzed." "My God, no Tony. This cannot be happening; it has to be a dream". Tony gently took Drea's hand. "I wish this was a dream. Drea, I hate that I am the one who has to tell you this, but Jayson didn't make it." Drea lost what little self-control that she had been holding together. She fell into Tony's arms crying.

She couldn't believe that Jayson was gone. She had just attended Jayson and Jess' wedding, not even two months ago. "This is not fair," Drea cried. "I know," Tony said holding back his tears. "I went to see Jess before I came here. She is holding up as well as can be expected. I stayed with her until her parents arrived.

"Drea, I give you my word that we are going to do everything we can to find these guys, I promise you that Drea." Drea knew that Tony would do everything in his power to catch the guys that changed the course of their lives forever.

CHAPTER 5

An hour later, the nurse finally allowed Drea into
Dre's room. Drea was sitting next to him while Shawn
stood glaring at Tony when the doctor arrived. Shawn did
not like the fact that after finally finding a parking spot at
the end of the lot, he still had to wait to go to Drea since he
wasn't family.

Shawn didn't want to sound selfish, but the least
they could've done was let them know he was parking the
car. It was almost an hour before Drea finally thought to
call him and see where he was. After Shawn got lost twice,
he finally found someone to direct him to Dre's room
where Tony and Drea were hugging.

He understood that Drea was upset, but he also
didn't trust Tony. He saw the way that Tony looked at her
when he first saw her back at Dre's house. There was
something about it that did not sit well with Shawn, and he
was determined to keep him away from Drea.

"Doctor this is Mr. Williamson's sister," the nurse said as she smiled softly at Drea. "Hello, ma'am. I am Dr. Wills. I don't mean to be so terse, but the E.R. is swamped this morning. Your brother suffered a gunshot wound to his abdomen. The bullet pierced his right lung and unfortunately your brother loss a lot of blood which caused him to lose consciousness."

"I know all this equipment can be a bit frightening, but I assure you that it looks much worse than it actually is. During surgery, we were able to remove the bullet and repair your brother's lung which is excellent. We are very confident that he will be breathing completely on his own shortly."

"The ventilator is just a precautionary measure as are the endotracheal and chest tubes. We also have your brother on antibiotics to prevent lung and wound infections and of course pain medication to ensure that he's comfortable. Your brother is young and healthy, so I don't foresee any complications."

"Once he's off the ventilator, we will mobilize him from the bed to a chair to help prevent pneumonia and avoid any clotting. After that, we'll start him on respiratory therapy which will help his lung heal, and then we'll start him walking and put him on a strength building regimen. If there are no complications, we can release your brother in a week or so, but he'll have to rest for at least a month or two before returning to work."

"I know that was a lot to take in all at once," the doctor smiled, "so please let me know if you'd like me to go over anything again." "Oh my gosh," Drea cried hugging the doctor, thank you so much." Drea never felt so relieved in her life. "It's my pleasure," he replied. "Would you happen to have any information regarding my cousin, Marcus Jackson?" "I just finished up with Mr. Jackson, let me grab his chart."

Drea hugged Shawn as the doctor left to retrieve

Marc's chart. "I'll give you two a few minutes alone,"

Tony said. "I'm glad Dre is going to be okay, and please let

me know if you need anything at all." Drea walked over

and hugged Tony. "Thank you so much for everything. I'm

so glad that you are here." "Me too," Tony smiled as he

walked out of the room.

Shawn looked at Drea as if she had lost her mind.

Was she really flirting with this guy right in front of him?

Before he could respond, the doctor returned. "Okay, Mr.

Jackson's case is a bit more complex. I brought in the

neurosurgeon who actually performed the surgery." "Hello,

I am Dr. Lewis," the doctor said while showing Drea an x-

ray that he pulled up on the monitor.

"So, as you can see, the bullet lodged between Mr.

Jackson's T11 and T12 vertebrae, cutting into his spinal

cord and unfortunately leaving him paralyzed from the

waist down. We just completed surgery to control the

bleeding and salvage as much spinal function as we could. There is direct damage to the spinal cord along with significant secondary damage from the fractured vertebrae in the area resulting in a hematoma which we were able to remove."

"It was a tedious process, but we were able to remove the bullet. Recovery is extremely variable from person to person. I usually don't say this, but I am optimistically confident that with rehabilitation he will make a complete recovery. We will give him a few days to recover before we start rehabilitation." "So soon?" Drea asked. "Oh absolutely," Dr. Lewis replied, "you want to get started as soon as possible before the muscles start to become complacent."

"I expect him to remain here in ICU for approximately 3-4 days and if all goes well, we should be able to move him to a regular room and get started on a basic rehabilitation regimen. If he does well there, we'll get him over to the rehabilitation unit for a few weeks, and within the month he should be home." "Thank you so much, doctor. That is excellent news." "No problem at all," he smiled. "If you need anything else at all please have the nurse page me." "I will," Drea smiled relieved.

Tony returned to the room shortly after the doctors left with coffee and water for both Drea and Shawn. "Thank you so much, Tony," Drea said as she accepted the drink carrier. Tony had been off duty for hours, but he didn't want to leave Drea until her family arrived.

He could tell that Shawn didn't like him, but he was not going to allow that to deter him. "No problem at all," Tony smiled. "I'm going to step down the hall for a moment. I'll be right back." "Okay and thank you again," Drea smiled. Drea turned to Shawn as Tony left and handed him a cup of coffee.

"I don't want that," Shawn said, pushing Drea's hand aside, splashing the hot beverage on her hand and the floor. "Shawn, what is wrong with you?" "What do you mean, what's wrong with me? You're the one sitting here flirting with your little boyfriend right in front of me."

"Shawn, you are seriously losing your mind. I've lost one of my closest friends, not to mention, my brother and cousin could've died tonight, and you think I'm flirting with someone. Shawn please just leave, I am not in the mood to deal with you right now."

"Deal with me, you are the one all up in this guy's face Drea." "Shawn you really need to leave before I call security. I cannot believe you are behaving like this right now of all times in the world after everything I put up with from you. Please just leave Shawn." "I'm not going anywhere, I brought you here, and I'll take you home."

Drea rubbed her temples, trying to stop an impending migraine she felt coming. "I don't care what you do Shawn just please stay away from me right now." Tony couldn't help but overhear the heated argument as he returned from the nurses' station. He shook his head thinking about everything that Drea was dealing with right now. This was the last thing that Drea needed. Shawn glared at Drea as she walked over to Dre's bedside.

Tony decided to wait a few minutes before reentering the room to allow Drea and Shawn a few moments to collect themselves. He looked up from his phone as the elevator doors opened. Tony smiled when Senior and Gloria stepped off the elevator. "Hi Ma and Dad," Tony said as he walked over to them and hugged them both.

"Tony it's so good to see you," Gloria said. "It's good seeing you both too," he smiled "sadly, I just wish it were under different circumstances, but we can discuss that later, let me show you to Dre's room." Tony knocked before he opened the door as he stepped aside to let them enter the room first.

Drea ran toward her parents. "I'll be out here if you need me," Tony said. "Nonsense," Senior said as he pulled Tony into the room. "You are family." Senior and Gloria were two of the most beautiful people he'd ever known, and he hated that they were going through this. He could see the pain in their eyes as they looked at their son lying motionless in bed except for the breathing tube that was inserted.

"I can't believe this is happening," Drea cried as she hugged her mom tightly. "I'm so sorry that I don't have much information for you right now," Tony said apologetically to Senior and Gloria. "I promise you that this one is personal, and every available officer is out looking for the guys who did this."

"Actually, I need to get back to see if there have been any updates." Tony walked over and looked down at Dre blinking back tears and began praying for Dre. Senior and Gloria looked at each other and smiled as they clasped hands with Drea and place their hands-on Tony's shoulder as he prayed.

"Amen," they all said in agreement when Tony finished praying. "Wow," Senior said smiling as he hugged Tony tightly. Shawn felt like his blood was literally boiling. He refused to sit through this any longer. "I need to get home and get some rest, I'm sure he can give you a ride home," Shawn said gesturing toward Tony before hastily exiting the room without waiting for Drea to respond.

Senior and Gloria both looked at one another as Drea stared at the door in anger and embarrassment. This was the last and final straw. Drea was used to Shawn's moodiness but to exhibit that behavior in front of her parents during a time like this was unacceptable. Tony could see the heat rising to Drea's cheeks, and he had not missed the look between Senior and Gloria.

"Well, I'd better get going. If there is anything at all that you need, please do not hesitate to call me day or night," he said handing them all his business card. "Do you know what happened?" Gloria asked Tony sighed deeply. "Well as you can imagine the investigation is still very early, but the motive appears to be robbery. It doesn't appear that they were targeted for any specific purpose other than that. It was just horrible timing." "Do you know when we may be able to visit with Marc?" Senior asked. "I'm honestly not sure dad," Tony responded. "I know that he hasn't been out of surgery very long, so they may want everyone to wait for a bit. He's in the unit next door."

"Has anyone spoken with Jessica?" Gloria asked. "Yes, ma'am. I notified her myself. Her parents are with her right now. Jayson's mom should be arriving any moment now," he said looking at his watch. I had one of my officers pick her up." "My God, my God," Gloria said shaking her head.

"I'm so sorry that you all have to endure this," Tony said, "but I promise you that we will catch them. Our team is reviewing the footage from the security cameras as we speak to help us ID these guys. I will let you know as soon as I know anything."

Tony had always loved Drea's parents. They were more like parents to him than his biological parents had been. Tony hugged them both tightly. "It's so good to see you, I will be in touch soon," Tony said. "Everything is going to work out just fine Tony," Senior said.

"God has a way of getting our attention. I don't think he is particularly fond of the subtle methods," he smiled as he patted Tony on the shoulder. Tony slightly hesitated before hugging Drea. "Please call me if you need anything," he whispered softly in her ear. "Thank you so much for everything Tony," Drea smiled. "Anything for you," Tony smiled.

"It is good to see all of you." With the last part of the statement, Tony's eyes lingered on Drea. "I will be back later today to let you know what's going on with the case, but right now please try to get some rest. Oh, by the way, I know you're probably not hungry right now, but I ordered room service, and they will be bringing you all something up shortly." "Thank you so much, Tony. You have turned into a remarkable young man. I am so very proud of you," Gloria smiled. "Thank you so much ma," Tony blushed. "That means the world to me."

CHAPTER 6

Shawn sat in his car in the hospital parking lot talking to his sister on the phone. "…So now that her little boyfriend is back in the picture, she wants to start acting brand new." "Shawn, you sound crazy," his sister said. "You are mad at her when you really should be trying to comfort her. Drea's brother could've died, and you are letting your jealousy get the best of you." "You just don't know," Shawn said. "You didn't see them together."

"Shawn there is no way you are going to make me believe that Drea was drooling over some guy when her brother and cousin were almost killed. You are really losing it, and if you don't get it under control, you are going to lose her. You already said she's still pressuring you to leave Angie. Don't give her another reason to want to leave."

"I guess you're right," Shawn agreed. "I'll call you later." "Okay, well just make sure you calm down before you talk to her and put yourself in her shoes. What if it was me lying in that bed? Would you really be thinking about your ex?" Shawn shook his head. "You're right, thanks sis." Shawn sighed as he hung up the phone and thought about everything that had happened. It has been a very emotional day all around.

Shawn started to call Drea but thought it would probably be better if he sent her a text. *"Baby, I am so sorry for my behavior in front of your family. I don't know what came over me. I was an idiot. I love you. Please forgive me. I'm still in the parking lot. I'll be here when you're ready. Take all the time you need."*

Drea looked down at her phone as it vibrated. As soon as she saw that it was a message from Shawn she immediately deleted the entire thread and blocked his number. He had embarrassed her for the last time. Her relationship with Shawn was officially over.

She thought about what her father said, and she felt like God was trying to get her attention. Her relationship with God and her family were everything to her and Shawn had an issue with both.

Drea dreaded the conversation that she knew she would have to have with him, but for now, all she wanted was to be surrounded by her family. She hoped that once Shawn realized that she wasn't going to respond to his text messages or phone calls he'd get the hint and stop contacting her. At least that's what she *hoped*.

Shawn waited impatiently for almost an hour with absolutely no response from Drea. He'd even called her several times and went back into the hospital only to be informed that only immediate family would be allowed to see Dre. Shawn tried to keep his cool as he explained to the receptionist for the third time that he had just been in his room but had stepped out for a moment.

The nurse refused to budge. Shawn was just about to curse her out when the officer who had been with Tony stepped up and asked Shawn to lower his voice and have a seat or leave the hospital. Shawn was much bigger than the young officer and thought his size would intimidate him, but it didn't.

He left the hospital mumbling under his breath. If this is the game that Drea wanted to play, Shawn would be more than happy to oblige her. Shawn hated Drea's parents. He and Drea had been together for three years, and her parents never treated him the way that they were treating her ex-boyfriend.

They are always just cordial enough not to be rude, but he knew that they didn't like him, and the feeling was more than mutual. He was fuming during the entire ride home as he drove more than 90 mph.

CHAPTER 7

It had been a long night, but Tony decided to head back to the station. He was determined to catch the guys who hurt his friends. His mind drifted back to Jessica. She and Jayson had been together since elementary school. He couldn't imagine what she must be going through.

As Tony walked toward the lobby, he saw his partner sitting in the emergency room. "I'm sorry," Tony apologized. "I just assumed that you'd left without me." "No problem Tony, I didn't want to leave you here." "Are your friends okay?" Curtis asked as they walked to the car. "Well, they are as okay as they can be. Where would you like me to drop you off?"

"I'm going to head back to the station for a while," Tony said as he pulled off. The young rookie admired Tony a lot. "I'd like to go back with you if you don't mind. I'm just as anxious as you are to get these guys off the street." Tony was so proud of the young recruit. Even though

Curtis hadn't been on the job very long, he and Tony got along right from the start. Tony had mentored a lot of young recruits, and Curtis was by far his favorite.

A lot of new recruits came in thinking they knew more than the veterans, but Curtis followed directions to a tee and was a fast learner. "Are you sure Curtis?" "Yes sir, I've never been more certain of anything." "Seeing the look on the Jessica McCall's face this evening when you told her about her husband was one of the hardest things I have ever had to witness."

"I know Curtis, but they are a family of strong faith, and the Lord will see them through this. I also don't ever want you to forget that look on her face or the way you felt. We risk our lives every day to try to prevent things like this from happening. Once you forget why you came here, you may as well leave. This job isn't a race to a gold shield." "I understand sir," Curtis responded quietly.

"Can I ask you a personal question?" Curtis asked. "Always," Tony answered, stopping at the red light. "You are a man of God, right?" the rookie asked. "Yes, I am," Tony answered proudly. "Okay, well why do bad things happen to good people?"

"Well, bad by whose standards?" Tony asked. "First you have to recognize that our bodies are just physical suits. Think of your body just like that; a suit. That's all it is essentially, it's a covering. When people die, their souls live on. They still live on. Their suit just gets damaged. So, as you said, it seems like bad things happen to good people just as they start to get their life on track, right?" Curtis nodded his head.

"Curtis, God is omnipresent, he is everywhere. He knew all this would happen; the same way he knew you and I would be having this conversation right now. I know people don't want to believe it, but heaven and hell are real. They are as tangible as this car. Hell was never meant for mankind, it was meant for Satan and his crew, but when we choose evil, it opens us up to allow the enemy to trick us."

"Think about this, in Genesis, Satan is referred to as a snake, later in the Bible, they refer to him as a beast. Things only grow when we feed them. He fed off our fearfulness and our faithlessness. He already knows his destiny, and he's just like a crab in a barrel. You ever notice how when you see live crabs-every time one tries to get out, another crab pulls him back."

"That's how the enemy works. He knows his fate, but he doesn't want to go alone. He wants to pull as many people down with him as he can. So, ask yourself this, what if the quote-unquote *bad things* happen to prevent those same people from going to hell? What if God graces them with enough time to get their life right and takes them before they can fall into another trap of the enemy, so they can spend eternity with Him in Heaven?"

"Curtis smiled, wow I never looked at it like that. That makes me feel so much better. My cousin died last year, and I was so hurt because we grew up like brothers. He had finally given up the street life and found a job and even started going to church with my auntie when he was shot and killed. I was so angry with God. I mean he had just gotten his life on track and then he was gone."

"I can't speak on the reason why God does things the way that he does. It just helps me feel better to think that my loved ones are in eternity waiting for me. I know that God loves us more than we could begin to imagine and will do everything He can to spare our lives, but He also gives us free will. He will not force us to do anything."

"Would you mind if I went to church with you someday?" Curtis asked. "I'd love that, and my church is real chill, there is no dress code or special seating sections." "Good because I don't even own a suit," Curtis laughed. "Wait until I tell my mom I'm going to church," he laughed. "I am actually the first person in my family that I

know of to attend church more than just Easter and

Christmas," Tony laughed as they arrived at the station.

CHAPTER 8

Jessica still couldn't believe that the love of her life and father of her children was gone. This entire situation felt surreal. "Mom what am I going to do without Jayson?" she cried as she lay her head on her mother's shoulder. "Jayson has been in my life since I was eight-years-old." "I know baby," her mother cried as she tried her best to console her only daughter. "I don't know how to live without him."

"Baby listen, I cannot imagine how you must feel right now, I truly can't, but I can promise you that God will give you the strength to get through this. Jess you are going to have to lean on the Lord like never before, but He will strengthen and guide you. I have loved Jayson since he was a little boy and I grew to love him even more as my son-in-law, but God loved him more than any of us ever could." "He will see us through this." Jessica hugged her mom tightly as she gently rubbed her swollen belly, looking around the king-size bed at her sleeping children.

Her eldest son, 17-year-old Jayson Jr (LJ) had been a rock throughout this entire process. He was there when Tony informed her of Jayson's murder. She hadn't even noticed that he was there until she felt him hug her as she collapsed after hearing the horrific news.

He was so much like his father. Jayson always told him that whenever he was away LJ had to be the man of the house and he took that responsibility seriously. He was such a gentleman just like his father. Jayson has always taught the boys to open doors for her and every other woman they encountered. They are all perfect little gentlemen, and LJ idolized his father.

He always helped with his three younger brothers without having to be asked to do so and was so excited that he was finally going to have a little sister. Jess closed her eyes as she thought about Jayson not being here for the birth of their daughter. He prayed for his little princess.

Jayson could not contain his excitement when the doctor told them they were having a girl. Jayson had already started buying all types of pink clothes. Jess was going to miss that the most. He wasn't just a fantastic husband, he was a great father and her best friend. She looked around the bed at her sons with such determination.

Jess would make sure that they never forget just how special their father was and she would do her best to raise them to be honorable men just like him. She decided to let the little ones continue sleeping. She wanted to give them a restful night before she had to tell them the news that would change their young lives forever.

Senior and Gloria were sleeping in the waiting area when the doctor arrived to let them know they could visit Marc. "I take it these are your parents?" he asked, smiling at Drea. "Your brother is doing much better than we anticipated. We may actually remove his breathing tube later today." "Thank you, Jesus," Drea whispered, trying not to wake her exhausted parents.

"Before you head over to see Mr. Jackson let me just make you aware that we have notified him that he's paralyzed from the waist down. He took the news as well as can be expected, but I just wanted you to know." Drea thanked the doctor as she walked next door to check on Marc. She thought it would be better for her to see him first in case she needed to prepare her parents.

Drea slowly walked into the room and looked over at Marc. His head was turned toward the window when Drea walked in. She tiptoed in the room, thinking that he was asleep until she saw him bite his lower lip.

"Marc its Drea, do you want me to come back?" Marc shook his head and looked at her. "Is Dre okay?" Marc asked hoarsely. "Yes, the doctors think he will be just fine, he still hasn't regained consciousness yet, but he's stable," she said. Marc breathed a deep sigh of relief.

"Did you hear about Jayson?" he asked as the tears fell from his eyes. Drea's own tears began to fall as she quietly nodded yes. "Tony said her parents were with her and Jayson's mom came in from Delaware late last night. I'm going to call her a little later today. How are you handling everything?"

Marc looked over at his cousin who had always been more like a sister to him and his brother, "Drea I watched Jay take his last breath. "This isn't right, none of it. He didn't deserve to die like that," Marc cried. Drea leaned down and hugged her cousin.

"I know Marc, none of you deserve any of this, but we are going to get through this together. I love you Marc, and I'm going to be right here for you and Dre." "You will always be my big baby brother." Marc smiled as he wiped his tears, "I love you too sis." "Let peanut head know I'm okay and tell him he'd better keep fighting," Marc said while holding back more tears that threatened to fall. Drea smiled.

"I will definitely do that." "Have you heard from Eric?" Marc asked. "Oh, I'm sorry; yes, I talked to him earlier. He's on a flight back now and should be here any moment." "Good," Marc said. "How did he sound?" Eric had always been very emotional. "He seemed to be holding up okay," Drea said. "I'm sure that he will be better once he sees you." "I understand," Marc said.

Marc was only three-years-old when his father shot and killed their mother before taking his own life, but Eric was seven-years-old at the time and remembered every detail vividly. He still suffered from nightmares to this very day.

As Drea and Marc were talking, there was a knock on the door. "Come in," Marc answered, smiling when he saw that it was two of his closest teammates. "I'll let you talk to your friends, sweetie. I'm right next door if you need anything." "Oh, mommy and daddy are here. They are asleep right now. You know they will be over as soon as they wake up and they have the big bible and a giant bottle of oil with them so get ready." "Right now, I need all the prayers and oil I can get, so I'm looking forward to it."

Drea smiled as she hugged his friends before leaving the room. "Wassup bro?" his teammate and best friend, Cortez asked. "I am so glad to see that you're okay." "You know I was ready to go off when the coach called me. We had to bribe the nurses with pictures, autographs, and promises of tickets just to get in here to see you," Cortez laughed.

"Why are you so quiet over there Chris?" Marc asked. Chris just shook his head, trying his best not to cry. "I'm good," Chris responded not making eye contact. "Are you doing okay?" Chris asked. "I'm doing the best I can," Marc answered. "This all still feels like a dream."

"I mean yesterday I was walking, today they're telling me I might not ever walk again. I'm just in shock man. One minute I feel like I'm going to beat this, the next minute I'm crying like a baby. I think I'm crying more for Jayson and Dre than myself." Cortez nodded his head in agreement. "You will beat this bro. The devil is a liar. You are gonna come back better than ever. We're standing in the gap for you man, believe that."

The door opened slowly, and Eric walked into the room. His eyes were bloodshot red, and Marc could tell that he had been crying. "Alright, y'all let me talk to my brother." "Okay man, I will be back to see you a little later," Cortez said. "Call me if you need anything at all." "Alright man, thanks for coming," Marc said. Chris walked over and briefly hugged Marc.

Marc hugged him tightly before letting him go. Chris was not only the rookie of the team, but he was also the youngest player on the team. He looked up to Marc and

Cortez, and they did everything they could to guide him in the right direction.

Chris idolized Marc and was struggling with seeing him like this. Marc was always the one who worked out longer and pushed himself harder than anyone else on the team. The thought of him never being able to walk again was more than Chris could handle.

When Marc let him go, he saw the tears in Chris' eyes. Marc never realized just how much the young rookie had looked up to him until that moment. "I'm good Chris, I am still breathing so I'm good." "I know," Chris said as he hurried out of the room. "Keep your head up Eric and let us know if there is anything that we can do," Cortez said before exiting the room.

Eric could not seem to find the strength to look his little brother in the eye or speak just yet. Although Eric was the older of the two, he'd always felt more like the baby. It upset Marc to see his big brother hurting. "Come on and sit-down man." Eric finally looked at his baby brother and walked over to Marc's bed. "You okay E?" Marc asked. Eric shook his head no as he leaned over and let out a helpless scream of frustration.

Marc could no longer hold in his own pain as the tears flowed down his face. Marc put his hand on his brother's head as he closed his eyes. Senior along with the floor security heard the scream and ran next door to see what was going on. As he opened the door, Senior saw the encounter between the two brothers and closed the door to give them some time alone.

As Senior returned to Dre's room, he noticed one of his new parishioners reviewing Dre's chart with a few other doctors. "Good morning Sir," Pastor Rick Lawrence said, "I had no idea that Dre and Marc were here until I saw Ma," referring to Gloria. "I briefly read the names on the board but still didn't connect the two."

"Yes, I can honestly say this was the last thing that we ever expected," Senior said. "My God," Rick said shaking his head in disbelief. "Well I am going to be their doctor, and I've been blessed enough to have some of the best fellows in the world working with me, he said gesturing to the group of blushing young doctors behind him. Senior and Gloria smiled and nodded politely at the young group standing behind Rick.

"If I can have you all excuse us for a few minutes so we can examine him, I should be able to tell you more shortly." "It's going to take about an hour, so if you'd like to grab a cup of coffee or take a walk this is a perfect time," Dr. Lawrence suggested. "Thank you so much," Drea said hugging the young doctor on the way out of the room.

Rick Lawrence was the best trauma surgeon in the Washington, DC Metro Area. He did his residency at John Hopkins Medical Center before working at several renowned trauma hospitals all over the country. Rick finally chose to come to Kingdom Medical Center. He loved the fact that this hospital operated on godly principles and believed as much in spiritual medicine as they did in prescriptions and pills. He knew right off with no hesitation that this was the place where he wanted to begin his career.

Gloria hugged her husband of 30 years as they left the room. She prayed that the Lord would send the right doctors for Dre and Marc and God not only did that, but He also sent them a doctor who was a man of God from their very own ministry. Just as they started to walk to the waiting room to get coffee, Eric exited Marc's hospital room to get ice. "Uncle Senior," Eric called out as he rushed to his uncle's side.

They all embraced Eric as he began to weep. "Unc why? Why them Unc?" "Son I wish I had an answer that made sense, but I don't. All I can say is that the devil is busy and we gotta stay prayed up now more than ever." Eric nodded his head in agreement. "I was gonna check on your brother earlier, but I didn't want to disturb you two. Is he still awake?" Senior asked. "Yes sir, I was just going to get him some ice," Eric responded. "He's been asking about Dre."

As they all entered Marc's room, he smiled his famous dimpled smile as his aunt and uncle came over and hugged him. "How is Dre?" he asked. "Is he awake yet?" "Dre is going to be fine son. The doctor is in with him now," Gloria said. "You think they will let me see him?" Marc asked. "I'm not sure. Let's check with the doctor when he gets done."

"Unc this is crazy. I feel like this is all some crazy dream, and I'm gonna wake up and tell Dre and Jayson." Marc sighed deeply as the tears started to fall. "It's not a dream though is it?" he asked pleadingly looking at Senior. "No, it's not son," Senior said solemnly, "but with God's grace we will get through this." "Come on let's pray," Gloria said as Eric returned to the room.

when Drea left to stretch her legs. As she exited the room, she saw a woman talking to one of the nurses who looked very familiar, but Drea couldn't quite place her until she heard her voice as she thanked the nurse. "Grayce?" Drea called out as the woman turned around. Grayce hurried over to Drea and hugged her. "My God Drea, I was praying that this was some huge mixup. This did not feel real until I saw you," Grayce said as she tried to blink back the tears threatening to fall.

"How is Dre?" "Well, he is still unconscious, but he's in stable condition. They removed his breathing tube this morning, and he is breathing on his own now. The doctors are confident that he will be fine though so right now we're just waiting." "Come on," Drea said as she started to lead Grayce to Dre's room.

"Drea wait a second," Grayce said. "I need a minute. I feel like my heart is about to beat out of my chest. I never in a billion years thought I'd be visiting Dre in the hospital because he'd been shot." Drea nodded her head. "I understand, it's still surreal to me too. Come on, let's go grab some tea before we go in," Drea suggested. "I'd like that. I need to get myself together before I see him."

CHAPTER 10

A short while later, Drea and Grayce entered the room just as Gloria finished sponge bathing Dre. Grayce put her hand over her mouth and would've fallen had Drea not caught her. Grayce could no longer control the tears flowing down her face. Gloria and Senior rushed to her side. "It's okay baby," Gloria said as she held Grayce while she cried. Gloria had always loved Grayce. She had hoped that she would be her daughter-in-law and even after Grayce and Dre broke up, she'd never given up that hope.

After a few moments, Grayce gathered her emotions. "I'm sorry mom, I...I just. "It's okay baby," Gloria said. "I understand." Gloria stepped back and looked at Grayce. "Look at my baby. You are absolutely stunning," Gloria said as she gushed over Grayce. "Yes, she is," Senior said as Grayce blushed. She smiled as she turned to hug Senior.

Grayce left home two weeks after her high school graduation and had not seen Senior and Gloria since. "Is it okay if I go over?" Grayce asked nervously. "Absolutely," Gloria said. "We'll give you some time alone with him," Gloria said as she ushered Drea and Senior out of the room. Grayce slowly walked over to the bed.

She still couldn't believe that this was her Dre lying in this bed. She sat down in the chair next to his bed and softly held his hand. Dre had changed in the almost 15 years since she'd last seen him. He looked taller than she remembered, and she couldn't help but smile as she thought about the handsome man that lay before her.

He looked so different from the skinny young man she fell in love with before she knew what love was. She held his hand in hers as she closed her eyes and silently began to pray. She opened her eyes and rubbed Dre's hand against her cheek. "Dre, its Grayce I'm not sure if you can hear me or not but please come back to us We all love you and need you here with us. Please fight."

A while later, the family returned to the room with Eric. "Hey Grayce," Eric said hugging her tightly. "I've missed you so much." Eric had always liked Grayce. He thought Dre made the biggest mistake of his life when he broke up with her and told him so several times.

"It's so good to see you Eric," Grayce said, hugging him tightly. "I just wish it were under different circumstances," Eric said. "Me too," Grayce said, looking back at Dre. "Marc is next door and asked me to come and get you," Eric smiled. "Oh my gosh, I meant to ask about Marc. I'll be right back," she said to Gloria.

"How's he doing?" Grayce asked as she and Eric left Dre's room. "Well, the docs are saying he may never walk again so as you can imagine that was a devasting blow to him. He has his ups and downs, but overall he's doing well."

Eric walked ahead of Grayce as she shyly stepped around him. "Hey Lil Bit," Marc said with a huge smile on his face. "Stop playing shy and come over here and give me a hug." Seeing Marc in such great spirits made Grayce feel a lot better. "I got your Lil Bit Marcus Nathaniel." "Hey hey hey…. why you gotta be using my government name?" Marc laughed. Eric was so happy to see his brother smiling and laughing.

Grayce leaned down and hugged Marc tightly. "I've missed you guys so much." "It's so good to see you Grayce, we've missed you too. You look good girl, the army did you some good," Marc responded. "Army?" Grayce asked looking at him like he was crazy. "I am a Marine," she said firmly. Marc laughed, "Oh yeah I forgot, you're a big bad Marine." "And don't you forget it," Grayce laughed, softly hitting his arm.

"You didn't do so bad yourself. "I see your body finally caught up with your big head," Grayce teased. "Aww, that's messed up Grayce, how are you gonna kick a man when he's down?" Marc laughed. "That's alright though, the ladies love my big head." Grayce rolled her eyes. "I forgot how much he talks, Eric do you have any tape to cover his mouth?" Eric laughed, Marc and Grayce always fought like they were brother and sister, but everyone knew that it came from a place of love.

"Seriously though, how are you doing with this?" Grayce asked, gesturing to the hospital room as she sat down next to him? "It's been tough, really tough but I'm okay." I'm not going to pretend like it's easy, but I can't think of this as the end because if I do, it will kill me. I'm not going to let this beat me. I'm Marcus Jackson, and I am going to walk again." "I know you will," she smiled. "I'm just still in shock." "Wait, how'd you get here so fast?" Marc asked. "I thought you were still in Afghanistan." "I left the Marines last year," Grayce said, blinking back tears. "Why didn't you come to visit or call or something?" Marc asked.

"I saw Jess, Jayson, and the boys a few times when I came back to visit my parents in Richmond," Grayce said as she stuttered Jayson's name. "My parents were with Senior and Ma when Drea called, so they called me. I've been living in Richmond for the last eight months. "I can't believe you didn't call or anything," Marc shook his head clearly hurt. "I'm sorry Marc," Grayce apologized.

"You know I love you all, but a lot has happened since I left home. I begged my parents and Jess not to say anything, but I'm home because I was wounded during my last tour." Grayce paused and swallowed the lump in her throat. Two of my men were killed. I was lucky to make it out alive with my one good leg," she said, lifting her pants to reveal the titanium prosthetic leg. Marc and Eric were in disbelief.

"Grayce, I am so sorry," Marc said fighting back his tears. "Grayce, we had no idea," Eric began as his voice cracked. "You guys can stop feeling sorry for me right now. I am fine. I'm alive, so I'm blessed". Marc nodded. "You're right Lil Bit. I..I didn't know." "I know Marc. I didn't want you guys to know because I didn't want to see that look on your face right now. This has been a difficult journey, but I'm here."

"Two of my men didn't make it, so I refuse to feel sorry for myself." Marc smiled. "You just encouraged me so much. I can make it through this." "Yes, you can," Grayce said hugging him tightly. "I also know that I should've called, but honestly it's still hard for me seeing Dre and reminders of Dre," she cried. "Marc, I still love him, I never stopped loving him." "I know," Marc smiled, "He is gonna be fine, Lil Bit," Eric smiled. "Dre is the strongest dude I know. He's gonna pull through just fine," Marc agreed.

"It's crazy because as we were walking to the truck that night we were talking about you. He was daydreaming about you and said you'd been on his mind a lot lately. He still loves you." Grayce smiled, "I'd love to believe that, but for now I can't focus on that. I just hate seeing him like that." Marc nodded, "They won't let me see him yet. "I guess they think it's gonna upset me or something." "That makes sense," Grayce agreed as she rubbed his hand.

"It's my fault Lil Bit," Marc cried. "It was my suggestion to go play pool. They didn't even want to go, but I suggested it because I wanted to see this waitress that works there, and now my friend is gone because of me. It's my fault." "Marc you didn't put the gun in those guys hands or conspire with them to do this. It's their fault, not yours and no one blames you; not Ma and dad, not Jess, not anyone. This could've happened anywhere to anyone of us. Do you hear me?" Marc nodded his head. "Now the question is, did you get her number?" Grayce smiled trying to lighten the mood. Marc smiled showing his famous dimples. "You know I did." "Boy you are a mess," she laughed. Marc laughed with her.

"So, are you going to stay or are you leaving again?" Marc asked, suddenly serious. Grayce sighed deeply. "Honestly, I'm not sure." "We missed you so much. I even tried calling you several times, and your phone went straight to voicemail then suddenly it was not in service." Grayce started to tear up.

"Aww Marc I know, and I missed you guys too," she said reaching out for Eric's hand and pulling him close to them. "It was just so hard." "Once Dre and I broke up I needed a change, and I didn't think it would be right for me to keep in touch with everyone except him." "I understand," Marc said quietly.

"So, where are you staying right now?" "I am going to get a room later." "My parents are at Senior and Ma's house at the moment." "Apparently you guys have a lot of family coming in, so they are helping to get them settled while Senior and Ma are here." "Eric give her the key to my house. I'm not letting you stay in a hotel." "Marc, I am fine, really. I'm still getting accustomed to being back in town, so I am taking it all in little by little. It's strange because it feels like Déjà vu." "I'm not taking no for an answer Grayce, you are not staying in a hotel."

"Hotel, who is staying in a hotel?" Senior asked as he entered the room. "Grayce," Marc blurted out like a little kid. "You most certainly are not," Senior said. "We have more than enough room. Actually, you can sleep in Dre's old room." Grayce was facing Marc, so Senior didn't notice the look of panic on her face, but it was not lost on Marc at all. "Dad, seriously I don't want to impose," she pleaded. "It's no imposition at all, and it's settled. You are staying with us." "Yes sir," Grayce smiled weakly.

"Well, I need to call Jess. Big Head, I will come by a little later. Eric, please call me if you need anything at all," Grayce said hugging him as she walked out of the room. As soon as the door closed behind her Grayce sighed deeply. She wasn't ready to be back in Dre's house let alone in his bedroom.

"Excuse me miss, haven't I seen you somewhere before?" the deep voice behind her echoed. Grayce turned around and smiled. "Oh my gosh, Tony I have not seen you in forever. How are you?" Grayce asked hugging him tightly. "I'm doing okay. It's so good to see you." "You too…wait, you're a police officer now?" Grayce asked.

"Yes ma'am," Tony smiled, "Detective actually." "Oh, excuse me, Detective Weems." Grayce laughed. It felt so good to laugh. "How are you holding up?" Tony asked. "Tony, to be honest, I am running on adrenaline right now. "I haven't really had time to process everything." "Tell me about it," Tony sighed. "Have you talked to Jess yet?" Tony asked. "I spoke to her earlier, but I have not seen her yet. I was just about to call her to see if now would be okay for me to drop by." "That sounds like a great idea" Tony smiled. "I will let you get to it then."

"How long will you be in town?" Tony asked. "I wish I knew," Grayce responded, "I wish I knew." "Well for what it's worth, I hope you stay," Tony said hugging her tightly. "It's crazy how it took this to bring us all back together," Tony said shaking his head.

"For some reason, I feel like all of this has happened for a reason. I can't explain it, but I feel like something amazing is going to come out of this." Tony smiled at Grayce. He had been thinking the same thing since everything happened.

CHAPTER 11

Grayce was sitting in the waiting room nook with tears streaming down her face as she hung up the phone. Grayce hurt so much for her best friend. Hearing the pain in Jess' voice was more than Grayce could bear. The thought of her godsons growing up without their father broke her heart. Their father was gone, and their godfather was lying in a hospital unconscious.

Grayce knelt and began to pray, not caring who was watching or listening,

Father, I come before you on behalf of my family and friends. I ask that you bless them and give them comfort during this difficult time. Lord, I know that in every action there is a purpose, even when we don't understand that purpose. So, I ask that you calm our anxious minds and help us to trust you as we've never trusted you before. In Jesus' name, Amen. "Amen," one of the gentlemen in the room smiled. Grayce smiled at him as she exited the room.

Senior and Gloria suggested that they all leave to go home and rest and return Sunday after church. It had been a very long day, and they all needed to rest. Grayce wanted to visit Jess before it got too late, so Drea gave her spare key to Grayce. "Drea I don't know about this," Grayce admitted as she pulled Drea aside. "I know but you know they will not take no for an answer and they will never let you stay in a hotel, besides your parents are staying with them too." "I know," Grayce said giving in. "Give me your number so I can text you when I'm on my way back," Grayce said.

CHAPTER 12

Grayce felt exhausted by the time she left the hospital, but she had to see her best friend and her godsons. It was a little after 7pm when Grayce arrived on Jess' street. There was not a single space available in the usually empty cul-de-sac.

Grayce found a spot in front of a home two streets over. As she stepped out of her car, a young woman exited the house with two small children. Grayce smiled. "I hope you don't mind me parking in front of your house. My friends' street is packed." "Not at all," the young mother smiled. "You wouldn't happen to be friends with Jayson and Jessica, would you?" "I am," Grayce smiled sadly.

"I am sorry for your loss," the young woman responded. "My name is Tina. Jayson and Jessica have always been good to my children and me. We were on our way over too. Do you mind if we walk over with you?" she asked. "I would love the company," Grayce smiled, "It's nice to meet you, Tina; I'm Grayce." "Nice to meet you too, and thank you so much for allowing us to walk over with you. I always get so nervous during these times."

"I don't want to say or do the wrong thing, and you never know if they want company or would prefer to be alone." "I understand," Grayce said. "How long have you known them?" Tina asked. "Jess has been my best friend for 30 years," Grayce smiled.

"I met her on my very first day of school in kindergarten," Grayce smiled as she thought back to the day that she met Jess. They were inseparable from day one. When Grayce wasn't at home, she was at Jess' house, and she loved Jess' mom just like her very own mom. Grayce still couldn't believe this was happening.

"Wow," Tina said, "We've only known them about three years. We moved to the neighborhood right after my husband left and Jayson and Jessica have been amazing. Jayson included the boys in a lot of activities with his boys and treated them as his very own. "He even took them to a King's game and allowed them to meet Marcus Jackson."

Grayce smiled. Marc has always loved children. "Jayson and LJ shoveled my snow in the winter, raked my leaves in the fall and cut my grass every summer, and they wouldn't even allow me to pay them," Tina said choking back tears.

"That sounds just like Jayson," Grayce said, wiping tears away from her face, thinking about her friend. "I am going to miss him so much," Tina said. "The boys were devastated when I told them. They made cards for Jess and the boys."

Grace smiled and kneeled down to talk to the boys. "That is so sweet of you both and red is her favorite color." The boys beamed. As they approached the house both women became quiet; each lost in their own thoughts, and they seemed to walk a little slower. It felt like as long as they didn't reach Jess and Jayson's home, there was still a small bit of normalcy, but Grayce knew in her heart that things were anything but normal.

CHAPTER 13

The house was packed. Grayce and Tina made their way through the packed crowd and spotted Jess sitting on the sofa with her mom. Grayce couldn't help but notice how tired Jess looked. Jess locked eyes with them and attempted to stand, but they told her no and made their way over to her.

Tina was the first to reach her. Jess' mom and aunt stood to allow them to sit next to Jess. Tina hugged Jess tightly as Grayce hugged Jess' mom Annmarie. "I heard you were back in town," Annmarie smiled. "You have grown into a beautiful woman." "Thank you so much, Mrs. Waters," Grayce blushed.

Jess stood and hugged her best friend for the longest time. "Thank you so much for coming," she cried. "Where else would I be?" Grayce asked wiping away her tears. "How are Dre and Marc? Are Ma and Dad okay? Jess asked. "Well Dre hasn't regained consciousness yet, but he's doing better. He's breathing on his own, so that's a great sign.

The doctors are saying that Marc is paralyzed, but the devil is a liar." "My God," Jess said shaking her head. "Ma and Dad are in great spirits though, you know them." Jess nodded her head. Senior and Gloria have the faith of Job. "Marc is in good spirits considering, although he's blaming himself." "What? Why?" Jess asked. "Well it was his suggestion to go to the pool hall, so he feels responsible." "That's crazy," Jess said. "I agree, but you know Marc."

"I think I'll go see him tomorrow after church," Jess said. "That's a great idea, I know he would love that," Grayce smiled. "How are you holding up sweetie?" Grayce asked." "I'm leaning on God girl, that's about all I can do right now. Sometimes I am good, and other times I'm breaking down, but I'm doing my best to be strong for the boys and this little princess here," she said rubbing her belly. "Good," Grayce said. "Can I speak to you in the bedroom for a moment?" Grayce asked. "Sure," Jess said quickly.

When they reached the bedroom and closed the door, Jess hugged her best friend. "Thank you so much, Grayce. I am so grateful for the outpouring of love and support, but it's definitely taking a toll on me." "I know, I could see it all in your face," Grayce said. "Where are my godsons?" Grayce asked.

Before Jess could respond, LJ entered the room with his brothers in tow. "Hi Aunt Grayce," LJ smiled hugging her tightly. The little ones ran to Grayce. They didn't get to see her often but when they did it was always a treat. "What you bring me?" Elijah asked with his gap-toothed smile. "Elijah," Jess reprimanded. "You know better than that. You don't go around asking people what they brought you."

"Wellll," Grayce smiled as she pulled the bag from behind her back. She bought them the latest X Box gaming system with all the accessories including four controllers and games in which they could all play at once. "Wow," LJ smiled. "Thank you Godmommy," the boys yell. "Ma do you want me to set this up for them now?" LJ asked. "Yes baby, thank you," she said. "Okay, come on y'all."

Grayce shook her head and smiled. "Jess, LJ is huge, when did he get so tall?" "I know girl," Jess smiled. "It seems like he shot up overnight. He is the spitting image of Jayson." "How are they?" Grayce asked. "I don't think the little ones really get it yet. LJ has been quiet. Every now and then I'll catch him laying on Jayson's side of the bed crying, but as soon as he sees me, he pretends that he wasn't and changes the subject."

"You know he takes being the man of the house so seriously. I talked to him last night and let him know that it's okay for him to cry or be sad." "Aww Jess I am so sorry you are going through all of this," Grayce said. "I am just so glad to have you here with me," Jess said. "God's timing, I tell you," Jess sighed.

"Marc and I were talking about that earlier." "Did you get to see Dre?" Jess asked. Grayce couldn't help but blush and smile. "Yes, I did," she said quietly. "What is that smile about?" Jess asked teasingly. "Jess it's like as soon as I saw him, I felt like a little girl all over again. I did not think it was possible for him to get any finer...whewww." Jess laughed.

"Yes, I must admit that they have all aged very well." "Well, I better let you get back to your guests. Ma and dad insisted that I stay with them and I don't want to be too late." "Okay, thank you so much for stopping by." "Of course, If you'd like, I can come back with you tomorrow." "Okay; hopefully, things will be a lot quieter by then," Jess sighed. "Let's pray," Grayce smiled. "I'll text you when I get in."

"Call me later if you want to talk," Jess said. "I will," Grayce responded, hugging her best friend again. "May I?" Grayce asked gesturing to her stomach. "Of course, after all this is your goddaughter." "Girl you know I can't wait," Grayce beamed. "I have some things in the car for her." "I will bring them in tomorrow."

"Try to get some rest." "I will," Jess smiled sadly. "I think I am going to take a nap." "I am exhausted." "Jess, please take care of yourself. Have you eaten today?" Grayce asked. "Of course," Jess laughed. "Ann-Marie has been pushing plates at me all day." "She looks amazing," Grayce said. "Yeah girl she dropped almost forty pounds, and you can't tell her or daddy nothing."

"How is your dad?" Grayce asked as they walked back to the door. "I didn't see him." "He's okay but you know how much he loved Jayson, he's taking it really hard." "Girl you know I am praying for you all." "Call me if you need anything at all, I don't care what time it is." "I will boo, I love you." "I love you more," Grayce said

fighting back her tears.

CHAPTER 14

Grayce arrived at the Williamson home shortly after 10:00pm. She'd planned to arrive sooner, but traffic was horrible. She was hoping that everyone hadn't gone to bed yet. Grayce didn't want to disrupt the house. Before she could pull the key out of her purse, the door opened. Her father smiled and opened his arms to her.

She had forgotten how much she missed her parents. Grayce hugged him tightly. "I hope you weren't waiting up for me," Grayce said. "It's only 10:00, what do you think I am, an old fogey or something" he teased. "Not my daddy," she smiled, hugging him again. "I just know it's been an exhausting day." "Yes, it has," he said, rubbing her arm. "How's Jessica?" "Surprisingly, she is doing much better than I expected. The boys are also doing well."

"Good, we're all going to head over there tomorrow after church before we head back to the hospital." Grayce smiled. "Actually, she will be going to the hospital tomorrow to see everyone." "Well okay then," he laughed.

"Great minds think alike," he winked. "That they do dad."

"Where's Ma?" "Your momma and Gloria are on

the phone with her prayer warriors. They will probably be a

while, so I am going to read for a little while longer before

I hit the hay. Senior put you in Dre's old room up the stairs

and to the right." "I thought I heard my name," Senior said

entering the room. "How are you holding up baby?" Senior

asked. "I'm doing fine, I should be asking you that."

"Babygirl, I'm fine. I'm just waiting to see what God is

doing behind the scenes. This is not happening for nothing.

God will get some glory out of this. I feel it." "I do believe

that," Grayce smiled.

"Well, I am going to sneak me another slice of cake

before Gloria gets off the phone," Senior laughed. "There

are fresh towels and washcloths in the bathroom and if you

are hungry help yourself to anything in the kitchen."

"Okay, thank you so much, but I am exhausted," Grayce said.

"I'm just going to shower and go to bed," she said, hugging her father and Senior one last time before heading up the stairs. Grayce felt so guilty, little did they know she knew precisely where Dre's room was. Unknown to Senior and Gloria, Grayce has been in Dre's room more times than she could recall.

As Grayce entered the room, all the memories came flooding back to her at once. She quietly walked around the room looking at all of Dre's things. His parents had not changed one thing. The picture of them together on their prom night remained on his dresser. Grayce smiled, thinking back to the time when they were so young and in love.

Little did they know that one week later everything would change. Grayce put the picture back as the tears began welling up in her eyes. She sat on the edge of the bed, praying for the man that she still loved. She did not know what she would do if something happened to Dre.

Her worst fear had always been receiving a call from Jess that Dre was getting married or had a baby on the way. Dre getting shot was the furthest thing from her mind because he wasn't that type of guy. She continued to pray that they would get through this.

CHAPTER 15

Grayce woke up in the familiar room and hugged the pillow tightly half expecting it to smell like Dre. Grayce turned over as she reminisced about the last time she was in this room. She and Dre had just returned from the movies and were in his bedroom watching television.

Dre has been a flirt since they day she met him and Grayce overlooked it because she loved him, and she knew without a doubt that he loved her and would never cheat on her. Their only issue was that Grayce was a virgin and planned on remaining so until their wedding night and Dre wasn't happy about that decision.

The day Dre told her that he didn't think he could remain faithful to her while she went off to the Marines and he went to college. Grayce sat there, momentarily stunned, before running out of his bedroom and his life. She cried for days and days but refused to tell anyone except Jessica why they really broke up.

Grayce closed her eyes as the emotions flooded back to her. She was lost in the past when she heard a faint knock at the door. "Come in," she said as her voice cracked with emotion. Gloria slowly opened the door. "Hi baby, did you sleep okay?" "Not really," Grayce said softly. "I guess being here brought back too many memories." Gloria laughed.

"Grayce I may be a well-seasoned woman, but I remember the struggles of teenage love. I'm so proud of you for staying true to yourself and your beliefs. I know it wasn't easy." Grayce felt a huge weight lift off her shoulders. "Ma, how did you know?" Gloria laughed. "I see more than most people think I do, and I know my son like the back of my hand."

"Sometimes I wonder if I made a mistake. I still love Dre so much," Grayce cried. "When I saw him yesterday it was like I was a teenager all over again. I hoped that I would be over him," she cried on Gloria's shoulder.

Gloria lifted her face and looked Grayce in her eyes. "Don't ever let the enemy make you regret obedience. This may be a little too much information, but I was a virgin when Senior and I met. He's a handsome man and I thought several times about giving in to him." Grayce put her face in her hands as she laughed. "Ma, please spare me the details." Gloria laughed with her as she continued.

"I'm serious, he tried telling me, well we are getting married anyway, so it doesn't matter if we do it now or later. I said okay if it doesn't matter, let's wait. He was disappointed, but I never gave in, and God blessed our union because of our obedience. God will bless you too whether it's with Dre or some other worthy man."

"Your virginity is a most precious gift you can give a man, more valuable than any material item you will ever own. Cherish it." Grayce smiled as she hugged Gloria. "I will, thank you Ma." "Good now breakfast will be ready

shortly so come on down whenever you're ready." "Okay

and thank you so much. I really needed to hear that."

CHAPTER 16

Drea realized that she'd overslept and jumped out of bed. She was so busy rushing around getting ready that she didn't hear Shawn enter her apartment. She screamed when she turned around to see Shawn standing in the doorway of the bedroom staring at her. "Shawn what are you doing here and why are you just standing there?" "What do you mean what am I doing here and where are you going this time of morning?"

"I'm going to church," Drea smiled. "Church? Shawn exclaimed, "Are you serious?" "Yes Shawn, I am very serious," Drea said. "With everything that's going on right now, I feel a need to be closer to God than ever before." Drea sat on the edge of the bed. "Can we talk Shawn?" "We're talking now," Shawn responded angrily.

"You know what, I am not going to let the devil steal my joy this morning. Shawn, I cannot continue doing this. You never had any intention of leaving your wife, but

I don't blame you. I blame myself. I was wrong on so many levels, and that's something that I am going to have to deal with God about, but we are done."

Shawn could no longer contain his anger and sit quietly. "Oh, so we're done now that your little first love is back in the picture, right?" "Shawn this has absolutely nothing to do with him. This is all about you and me. You know what, no it's not. It's about my relationship with God. Shawn, you are married, and at the end of the day, deep down inside I've always known that you are never going to leave your wife."

"Why would you when you have both of us at your disposal whenever you want. This is not right, and I can't keep living like this. I wasn't raised like this. My parents would be so hurt if they knew I was dating a married man. I am not proud of this. I hate the fact that I love you but love or not, I will not continue to do this any longer.

"So that's what this is about?" Shawn asked standing over her. "Your family? It's always about your family. I'm so sick and tired of hearing about your family. You always put them before me anyway. "Put them before you?" Drea asked. "Shawn in case I wasn't clear, there was never an issue of putting my parents before you. The only person that comes before my family is God."

"I love you, and you know that, but my family is my family. I don't even know why we're having this conversation. I'm done," Drea said. "I don't need this, and I won't continue to live like this. I'm not perfect by a long shot, but I know that God is not pleased with this. I want a man who loves God more than he loves me and we both know that you are not that man. I will always care for you, but it's over; for good this time. Please have your things out of my home when I return."

"Baby you know you don't mean that. We've been together too long. Look I know I've been trippin', but you know that I love you." "I love you too Shawn, and if love were our only issue, we'd be together forever, but it's not. I knew we were doomed to fail the moment you told me that you didn't believe in God. I made the mistake that most women make by thinking that I could change you. I can't change you, and I am tired of you trying to change me."

"I've never judged you for being an unbeliever, but you constantly felt the need to mock me. I need a man who not only shares my beliefs but grows with me in them. I pray to God that you find whatever it is that you're looking for Shawn and I wish you the absolute best."

"So, after all these years, this is how you want to do things? It's fine if you want to run back to your little boyfriend but don't use my marriage as an excuse. You were not worried about me being married when you were sleeping with me," Shawn exploded. "Shawn I'm not using anything as an excuse. For once, I'm thinking clearly. Shawn, I deserve better." "You know what Drea, you are right, so do I," he said as he walked out of the room and slammed the door.

Drea sat on the side of the bed in shock. As much as she knew this needed to happen it still hurt. Drea and Shawn had been together for years, and she truly loved him. Drea shook her head as she began talking to God.

"Father I thank you for interceding on my behalf. As much as it hurts to watch Shawn walk away, I know that there is something greater in store for my life. I am so tired of running. Lord I hear you and I surrender. I give you my heart, my mind, and my soul. Have your way Lord," she prayed.

Drea finished dressing before heading out the door. Drea could feel a shift in her spirit that she has not felt in a long time. As she walked to her car, she was happier than she had been in a long time. Shawn sat in his car fuming. He was just about to go back and apologize when he watched Drea exit the building with a huge smile on her face.

"I cannot believe this," he said. "Here I am stressing about us breaking up, and she's smiling like she doesn't have a care in the world. If that's the way Drea wants to play this fine. I got something for her and her little boyfriend," he fumed, pulling off screeching his tires in the process. Drea looked up startled as Shawn drove by screaming obscenities at her. Drea just shook her head. "Everything happens for a reason," she sighed as she turned on her favorite gospel station and sang along.

CHAPTER 17

After church, everyone decided to pick up take-out from Marc's favorite BBQ restaurant and have dinner at the hospital. When they walked into the intensive care unit, Grayce's parents were already in the waiting area with Jess, Rico, and Kim.

"Oh my gosh Rico I have not seen you in ages," she said finally getting around to him after hugging her parents and Jess. "Hey Lil Bit," he smiled. "It's good to see you again." "You too," Grayce smiled. "This is my wife Kim," he said introducing Grayce to his pregnant companion.

"It's so nice to meet you finally," Grayce said as she hugged Kim. "I'm sorry, I'm a hugger." "Me too," Kim said. "We will get along just fine," Grayce laughed. Rico shook his head. "So, you are the infamous Grayce, it's nice to put an actual face with the name," Kim said. "I have heard so much about you that I feel like I know you." "I hope they were good things, you never know with these guys," Grayce joked.

"They were all wonderful," Kim smiled. "So, are you staying?" Rico asked. "I'm seriously thinking about it. It feels so good to be back among family. I've missed you all so much," she said looking around at her family and extended family. "We've missed you too," Drea said as she hugged Grayce.

"How's our guy doing today?" Grayce asked as she slowly walked over to the window looking in Dre's room. "He's doing great according to the doctor," her mom said. "When we arrived, the doctors told us that he'd been showing subtle signs of improvement throughout the night and they're confident that he'll regain consciousness sometime within the next 24-48 hours."

Drea and Grayce hugged tightly while their parents began to praise God. Grayce suddenly became nervous. The reality of seeing Dre both excited and frightened her at the same time. She wasn't sure what he'd think of her. Jess told her that he hadn't seen anyone seriously since they'd broken up, but there was still a lot of hurt in her. As they entered the room, they notice that the hospital room had been altered to make space for Marc.

As they ate and fellowshipped, they reminisced about the past and the good times they'd shared. Jess laughed until she cried when they shared stories of how terrified Jayson was when they found out that she was pregnant with LJ. Grayce smiled at her best friend. At that moment Grayce knew that they were going to be okay and that she would never be able to leave them again. This is and would always be her home.

Dre and Marc had a steady stream of family and friends visiting throughout the day. Grayce and Jessica decided to give the family some time to spend with them alone. When they stepped out of the room, Jess hugged Grayce tightly. Grayce smiled at her friend. "I am so happy that you are here." "Me too," Jess smiled. "I needed this. I love my family, but I really needed to be around all of you today." "Did you get a chance to talk to Marc yet?" Grayce asked. "I did, and you know it's funny I held it together until I saw him break down crying."

"It's something about seeing a man cry that will truly break you every time." Grayce nodded in agreement. "Is he okay?" Grayce asked. Jess smiled. "I think he's going to be just fine." "Marc kept telling me how he owes the boys and me and that he wants to sign over everything that he owns to me." "I told him if he wants to repay me he needs to get right with God."

"I know where Jayson is right now and that is the one thing that truly comforts me. I want all of us up in heaven rejoicing together." "Girl I know that's right" Grayce smiled. "We are going to make it, by the grace of God we are going to make it," Jess said as they walked arm and arm into the cafeteria.

CHAPTER 18

Gloria was massaging Dre's legs when she felt his leg move. She looked up and his face and noticed that his eyes started fluttering. "He's waking up," she yelled as she pushed the button for the nurse and informed her that Dre was beginning to wake up. Everyone in the room stood and started praising God. Dr. Scott rushed into the room moments later with his interns.

Dre's mouth began to move, but nothing came out, the nurse slightly raised his bed while the doctor started to check his vitals. "Okay, I'm going to need everyone to exit the room while we examine Dre." "Okay everyone, today's been quite a day, I think we need to let Dre and Marc get some rest right now," Senior said, looking at his son with tears in his eyes. Everyone left with well wishes and blessings as Senior, Gloria, and Drea waited behind to talk to the doctor and hopefully Dre.

The doctor emerged from the room moments later. "Dre appears to be very weak, but I will let you see him, but I need you to make it brief. He needs to rest if he's going to progress well. His throat will probably be pretty sore for the next few days because of the breathing tube so the nurse will bring in some ice to help with the soreness shortly." "Thank you, son," Senior said hugging Rick.

"To God be all the glory," Rick said stepping aside to allow them to reenter the room. "Hi baby," Gloria said rubbing Dre's head. He continued to attempt to speak, but only two words come out of his mouth that was clear to everyone, Marc, and Jay. "I'm right here D," Marc said as Dre slowly turned his head to the sound of Marc's voice.

"Jay?" Dre asked. Dre could tell by the strained look on Marc's face that something was wrong. Dre closed his eyes as the tears fell down his face. "Look I will give you all a few moments alone with him," Rick said, "but please make it brief. Welcome back Dre," he said as he patted Dre's shoulder and signaled for the interns to leave the room.

Grayce and Jess were turning the corridor down the long hall when she saw everyone leaving Dre's room. Some were in tears, and she watched as the doctors exited shortly after. Grayce panicked and dropped her phone as she raced down the hall.

All she kept thinking was she could not lose Dre again. As she rushed into the room, she was shocked as she stared into the eyes of a very startled Dre. Grayce backed against the wall. "I'm sorry," she said as she started to hyperventilate. "I saw some of the people coming out crying, and I thought…" Grayce slide down the wall as she began to weep before completing her statement. Eric and Senior ran over to her to help Grayce over to the sofa.

Dre's heart was pounding out of his chest. For a moment he thought he was dreaming. This cannot be Grayce he thought to himself. Grayce was so upset that she felt like she couldn't breathe. "Come on baby, just breathe, he's fine," Senior said trying to calm her down as Jess entered the room and walked over to Grayce. "Jess," Dre said as tears fell down his eyes. Jess had been so concerned when she saw Grayce laying on the couch that she had not even noticed that Dre was now awake.

"Come on now, not you too," she said leaving Grayce with Drea and walking to Dre's bedside. "I'm so glad you're okay," she said using a tissue to wipe his tears. "Jess I"..Dre, stop. "I know, I know," she said fighting back her own tears, "but you know he wouldn't want any of us sitting around crying." Dre nodded his head and took a deep breath. "Is she okay?" he whispered. "Yes," Jess smiled. "Now that you are okay, she will be just fine."

You could hear a pin drop as Grayce and Dre stared at each other for what felt like an eternity. Dre had not seen Grayce since they broke up shortly after graduation and she looked even more beautiful than she did the last time he'd seen her. Grayce looked away as she blushed as if reading his mind.

Both Dre and Grayce were about to speak when she smiled. "You first," she said. "Are you okay?" he asked. "Yes, she smiled. "I'm sorry. I don't know what happened. I just overreacted a bit. I am so embarrassed. I know the entire floor thought I had lost my mind, running down the hall like a crazy woman. I'm surprised they didn't call security." Dre smiled. "I'm sure I would've done the exact same thing." He sighed deeply. "I didn't realize how much I missed you until just now." "I had a dream about you," he smiled. Grayce looked away; his smile got the best of her every time.

"Alright everyone, let's give Dre and Grayce some time alone," Gloria suggested as she walked over and hugged her son. "I love you so much, Dre." "I love you too," Dre whispered. His throat felt like it is on fire, but the ice chips the nurse gave him were helping. "Marc you make sure he behaves okay?" she said kissing her nephew on the cheek. "No problem ma. If he gets out of line, I'll hit him with this water bottle." "I wish you would," Dre smiled.

Senior was extremely happy to have both his boys back. He prayed over them all before they said their goodbyes and left the room. Marc put on his headphones and pushed the button to close the curtain to give Dre and Grayce some privacy.

With everyone gone, the reality now sunk in that Grayce was actually here with Dre. "I still love him," she thought to herself as she shook her head. Dre smiled, "What was that about?" he asked. "What?" she said shyly. He rolled his eyes. "That smile when you shook your head." "Nothing," she said softly, "I was just thinking about something." "You can come closer you know. I don't bite." "Grayce smiled as she walked over to Dre. "Can I ask least get a hug?" he asked.

Grayce leaned down and hugged Dre gently. The second she was in his arms she felt like she was home. "Thank you for coming," he said. "Of course, where else would I be, Dre?" "Grayce, I owe you an apology." "Dre, we don't need to do this right now." "Yes, we do," he said as he reached for her hand and continued.

"I was young and immature. I was listening to my friends talk about sex, and I felt like I was missing out on something. I know that I hurt you and I am so, so sorry. I spent the last 15 years chasing what I already had in you even back then, and I am so, so sorry that I hurt you. By this time, Grayce's tears were flowing. She had waited so long to hear those words. "I accept your apology, Dre," she said as hugged him again. Dre held her close to him, fearing that if he let her go she would disappear and he'd wake up and realize that this was just a dream.

When she finally pulled away from him, they stared at each other with tears in their eyes. Both were admiring the fact that time had been kind to them both. Even lying in a hospital bed after being shot and almost killed he made her knees weak. She sat down next to him and held his hand once again. "How are Jess and the boys handling everything?" Dre asked as his voice cracked. "They are doing remarkably well under the circumstances. It's going to be tough, but they will get through it, we all will."

As Marc lay in the bed listening to his iPhone, he couldn't help but think about the interaction between Dre and Grayce. After all these years it was like nothing had changed. He was so happy for them both. He loved them both deeply, and they deserved one another. Marc felt some type of way though. Here he lay paralyzed over something that he had no control over.

He tried his best to come to terms with never being able to walk again, but it was hard. Everything that he'd worked so hard for was now gone. He couldn't believe that his career was over. He was determined to fight. I know this is not God's plan for my life he kept telling himself. He planned to use his status to obtain assistance from the best rehabilitation team in the world. After seeing his cousin regain consciousness, he is prepared to do whatever he had to do to walk again.

CHAPTER 19

As the family sat in the lobby waiting for Grayce, Gloria hugged her husband tightly, thanking God for healing their sons. Everyone noticed the stolen glances between Dre and Grayce. Gloria had always prayed that Dre would end up with Grayce. She was such a sweet girl, and Gloria had no doubt that she'd take excellent care of her son. She could tell by those glances and blushes that they shared, they'd be back together soon enough.

She disliked the fact that Dre was such a flirt. He never brought any of the women he dated to her house, but she knew none the less. The same way that she knew that Shawn was married. Gloria decided to talk to her daughter when things settled down a bit. Drea deserved the absolute best and Shawn was not the best person for her daughter.

It was almost 10 pm when Dre began to yawn. "I'm sorry, I know you're exhausted, you need to get some rest."

"No don't leave, I'm okay," Dre said. "I lost track of time, and I need to get back to your parents' house. They have me staying in your room," Grayce smirked. "It's been a long day, but I'll be back first thing tomorrow." "Okay," Dre said quietly, feeling her absence already.

"Give me a hug, Big Head," Grayce said as she walked over to Marc's bed to hug him goodnight. "He still loves you," Marc whispered to her before letting her go. Grayce's eyes began to mist as she walked over and quickly hugged Dre again before exiting the room.

"What was that about?" Dre asked looking at Marc. "I told her that you still love her" Marc smiled. "Is it that obvious?" Dre asked. "Duh," Marc laughed. Dre laughed and shook his head. "I'm glad you're okay Marc. I don't know what I would've done if I lost you too." "I feel the same way. I just still can't believe Jay is gone. I'm sorry; I feel like all of this is my fault.

Everyone keeps telling me it's not, but I decided to go to the pool hall. If we had just gone to eat as you suggested, none of us would be in this situation." "Yes, we would've," Dre said, looking at his cousin.

"Marc, you and I both know that when it's your time, it's your time. If we went to dinner, it just would've been some dude trying to rob us outside the restaurant or a shooting in the restaurant or a car accident. I don't know, I just know that no matter where we were, Jay would still be gone.

As much as it hurts my heart to think about it, it was his time, and for the record, I'm a grown man, if I didn't want to go, we wouldn't have gone plain and simple. It wasn't about who wanted to do what. We all knew you wanted to go so you could talk the waitress and we just wanted to hang out. This could've happened anywhere, and one thing Pops always taught us was when it's your time, it's your time. This is not your fault. Did they catch the guys who did it yet?"

"No, but Tony is working the case." "Our Tony?" Dre asked. "Yep, he's a detective now." "What? I never would've Tony pegged for a cop as much trouble as he used to get into." "I know right," Marc laughed. "Man, you know what's crazy though. This whole situation brought the whole family back together." "That it has," Dre yawned again thinking about Grayce. "Get some sleep bro, you know it's going to be another full day tomorrow," Marc suggested.

Marc and Dre both drifted off to sleep almost immediately. For the first time in a long time, Dre fell asleep smiling with thoughts of Grayce in his head.

Dre and Marc were finishing up breakfast when there was a light knock on the door. Rico and Tony entered the room. "Well well well, look whos up," Tony teased. "Hey Tony, Marc and I were just talking about you last night." "I'm glad you are here to talk man," Tony said as he walked over and hugged Dre. "You and me both man."

"That makes three of us," Marc added. Tony walked over and hugged Marc. He shook his head as he looked between the two cousins. "Man, that night was the worst night of my life. I think I'm going on a routine call, and the next thing I know, I'm standing there watching my family fight for their lives. I have never felt so helpless in my life," Tony said.

"I'm just glad that God had other plans for both of you." "Amen," Rico said. "When we got the call in Hawaii, I felt like my heart stopped." "Oh yeah," Marc said, "It didn't even dawn on me that you cut your anniversary trip short." "Anniversary?" Tony asked. "Rico Suave actually got married." The guys laughed at Rico's childhood nickname "I know man but that's my baby, and we're expecting twins." "Aww man, that's a blessing. I am so happy to hear that," Tony said hugging his longtime friend.

"What's been up with you Tony?" Rico asked. "Well, I have been a police officer for about ten years, and I'm also a youth pastor." Marc almost choked on the juice he was drinking. "I guess God really can do ALL things."

Dre laughed. "Oh y'all got jokes huh?" Tony laughed.

"I mean you were the worst one out of all of us back in the day," Marc added. "That's true," Tony laughed. "Maybe that's why God wanted to use me though. Who better to lead a heathen to Christ than a former heathen?" "You ain't never lied there," Rico laughed. "I'm proud of you though." "Me too, man I am so proud of all of us," Dre said.

Marc looked at his legs and looked back at Tony. Tony walked over to Marc and placed his hand on Marc's legs. "Man, this is just a setup for the comeback of all comebacks. Last night I dreamt about you playing in the Superbowl, and all of us were right there cheering you on." Remember everything that I am telling you right now." "You will walk again, and you are going to be better than you were before." "I receive that," Marc smiled.

CHAPTER 20

As the guys were catching up, Dre and Marc's cousin Jerome entered the room. Jerome was the Martin Lawrence of the family, he was the guy who could find humor in any and every situation.

He was usually the life of the party, but he was also a bit of a hothead at times. He had been in and out of jail since he was 16-years-old. From the moment Jerome walked into the room, the guys could tell that he was upset. Jerome was one of those guys who became quiet when they were angry. Everyone could feel Jerome's anger from the moment that he walked into the room. "What's up Big Rome?" Marc asked.

"Come over here and sit down," Dre said, but Jerome remained standing near the door. "I found out who did this," he said. "What? How?" Marc asked. "You know the streets talk," Jerome said. Dre felt numb for a moment. He knew why Rome was there. They were brought up in an era where most people did not depend on the police for justice. Dre wanted justice for Jay's murder, but he knew that retaliating against the guys who killed him wasn't the right thing to do.

"Jerome, look I know you're hurting too but let the police handle this, Dre said. "They are not worth it."

"What?" Rome yelled. "Man y'all could've died. Jay is gone. His kids will never know their father because of these dudes, and you are talking about let it go? I can't let it go," he said bitterly.

Marc sighed. "Rome, you know me, and I'm not gonna lie when I think about never playing ball again, I wanna kill them both myself, but I agree with Dre on this one. This is not the answer. If you don't want to listen to us, think about Jay. Just before the guys started shooting, he was trying to talk some sense into one of them." Before Rome could respond, Tony walked over to him and hugged him.

"Big Rome I love you man, and I am not going to let these punks ruin your life. They have caused this family enough heartache, and there are too many black men dead and incarcerated over senseless violence. I won't let you become a statistic man. I promise you, we will get these guys. We all know that this is not right, and Jayson would not want this.

Before Tony could finish, his cell phone began ringing. "Text me the address, I'll be right there," Tony said into the phone. "Look I just received a tip about two possible suspects. Rome, I told you, God is in control of all of this. We don't need any more bloodshed. I'll talk to y'all a little later when I have more information," Tony said to Dre and Marc as he rushed out the door.

Dre was still in a lot of pain as he tried to position himself in a way that took the pressure off his wound. "You okay cuz?" he asked noticing that Rome was still quiet. "Yeah, I'm okay." "Man don't lie to me what's up?" Dre asked. "I know that Unc taught us that vengeance is God's and I know that's true, but a part of me wants payback. Every time I think about it I get angry. I mean Jay just got married, Marc just renewed his contract. I don't know it just makes me want to scream sometimes."

"I was always the one in trouble. I deserve this not y'all." Dre ignored his pain as he sat and looked his younger cousin directly in the eyes. "Rome no one deserves this, not even them. I'm not going to lie, I'm angry too, but that anger won't bring Jay back, and at the end of the day, I'm focusing on honoring him. These dudes are not worth it. "It's way too many people dying. Let God take care of them." "You're right D, I know you are; I just get so frustrated."

"Trust me I get it, but people like that get theirs, in the end, one way or another and like pops use to say touch, not my anointed says the Lord. They will answer to a higher power than any court system for what they did to

Jay. I know it doesn't seem like it, but they will." "I guess," Rome said as he gazed out the window.

The guys were eating lunch with their family, Grayce, her parents, Rico and Kim when Tony returned with a somber look on his face. "What is it?" Dre asked nervously. Tony cleared his throat. "We caught up with the guys, and a chase ensued. The car crashed, but we didn't know that one of the suspected shooter's son was in the car," Tony said as his voice cracked.

"The shooters died when the car burst into flames, but the little boy was thrown from the car. They just flew him in a few minutes ago." "My God," Senior said. "Come on let's pray for that baby. They all joined hands and prayed that the little boy would survive." Drea hugged Tony and held him tightly as he wept in her arms. "If I had known he had a child in the car I would not have chased him," Tony cried. "How did I miss that?" Drea pulled back from him and held his face in her hands. "Tony this isn't your fault."

"His father was selfish. His only job was to care for and protect his son, and he failed him on so many levels, Tony. You are a good man who was doing his job. How could you have known that there was a child in the car?" Tony nodded. Deep down inside he knew she was right but seeing that little body being ejected from the car devastated Tony.

During the remainder of the visit, they were all quiet. Everyone was lost in their own thoughts and praying for the little boy whose father had transformed the lives of every person in that room. Tony was just about to go check on him when Dr. Scott entered the room. "Hey guys, I'm sorry that I haven't had a chance to come to check on you. We were swamped in the ER." "It's okay Rick," Marc said.

"Hey Tony, I was wondering where you went," the doc said when he noticed him seated next to Drea. "Is he going to be okay doc?" Tony asked nervously. Rick started

laughing. "Let me tell you how good my God is. I've never

seen anything like it. He has some cuts, bruising, a few

broken ribs and a nasty rash but he's going to be fine.

When he was ejected from the car, he landed in an area

with a lot of brush and poison ivy. Trust me Brian is a

tough kid, he's been through a lot worse."

"Man, you just made my year," Tony smiled.

"Thank you, Lord," he prayed. "Has his mom arrived yet?"

Tony asked. "Brian's mom worked here. She passed away

six months ago. He's an only child; his father and elderly

great-grandmother were caring for him." Tony felt like he

was going to be sick to his stomach. He sat back down,

feeling like his knees were about to buckle. "And I took his

father away from him," he said quietly.

"Tony, let me tell you about his father," Rick said

bitterly. "Brian was here about two months ago. That little

boy still has bruising over 75% of his body that is not

associated with the accident. His father has been investigated more times than we can remember for child abuse. "Brian is quite a regular in here with everything from broken arms and jaws to fractured ribs. That father of his was also the prime suspect in the murder of Brian's mother. "I don't wish death on anyone, but I will tell you the truth, there are some people that I will not shed tears for, and he's one of them."

Tony nodded his head. "Would it be okay if I check in on him a little later?" Tony asked. "Sure," Rick smiled. "Just give them a couple of hours to get him settled." Drea rubs his back softly. "Thank you, son," Senior said as he hugged Rick. "Sure thing dad. It's packed in here today so if you don't need anything else I need to get back." "Of course," Senior said. "Yeah, we're fine. Thanks, Rick," Dre said.

"This has been some day Gloria said hugging Grayce's mom Patricia." Perhaps we'd better call it a day," her father James suggested. "Yeah that sounds like a good idea," Senior smiled. "Yeah, I'd like to go tell Jess myself," Tony said. "You mind if I ride with you?" Drea asked. "I have been meaning to go back to visit them, but things have been crazy." "We'll be back tomorrow," Senior said, hugging his sons.

"Grayce, would you mind staying for a few minutes?" Dre asked quietly. "Ummm actually I rode with your mom and dad." "No problem," Drea smiled, "you can just take my car if Tony doesn't mind dropping me off at mom and dad's," she said, reaching for her the keys. "Not at all," Tony smiled. Gloria smiled and winked at Grayce as she headed out the door.

"What was that about?" Dre asked when they were finally alone. "I was wondering the same thing," Grayce smiled. "How are you feeling?" she asked. "I'm okay a little sore but okay." "Good," she smiled as she sat down next to him. "So, what's up?" Grayce asked. "I've been thinking a lot the past few days," Dre began. "That's always a good thing" she teased. "There you go," he laughed. "I'm sorry please continue," Grayce smiled.

"It's just I feel like..I mean." He sighed out of frustration. "I want us to be friends again. I have missed you so much, and all of this has shown me that tomorrow is not promised. I need to have you back in my life." Grayce felt like she was on top of the world, but there was still a lot of hesitation.

"Dre, I didn't want to do this but since you wanted to have this conversation here goes. Dre, you hurt me to my core when you broke up with me. I thought that you were the man that I would marry and whose children I would carry, but you turned your back on me solely because I wouldn't sleep with you." Grayce didn't try to hide the tears that fell down her face.

"Since that time, I have not been able to love any other man. For years I regretted my decision. Wondering if

I had given in where we'd be right now." Grayce accepted the tissue that he handed her and noticed that his hand was trembling. As she looked at his face, she saw the pain in his eyes. "Dre, I really want us to be friends, but that will come with time because we've never really been friends."

"I understand," he said. "Can you please just promise me that you will at least try?" "Of course," she said as she gently held his hand. "Thank you," he said quietly. "Are you going back to Afghanistan?" he asks. "I've actually been back in the US for a while now." "Dre didn't attempt to hide his shock or the hurt expression on his face.

"So, if this had not happened would you be talking to me right now?" She looked at him and answered his question as honestly as she could. "Probably not." Dre closed his eyes. He wasn't sure how to respond. "Dre what would I have said to you? It's been years, and we both have very different lives now."

"Grayce, I still love you," he said looking her dead in the eyes. "I never stopped, and I never will. I was a coward, and I am sorry for that, but I feel like all of this is happening for a reason and I can't lose you again. I won't lose you again," he said. Grayce wiped the tears from her eyes.

"Look why don't we cross one bridge at a time." "Let's work on establishing a true friendship first." Dre smiled, "that works for me." "Good," Grayce sighed. "So, friend, any word on when you may be getting out of here?" "Rick said I should be able to leave Thursday or Friday," Dre smiled. "Wow that is great," Grayce smiled. "I can't wait," Dre said. "I am so ready to sleep in my own bed." Grayce smiled.

"What?" he asked. "I was just thinking about how weird it is that I'm actually sleeping in your bed at mom and dad's house," Grayce said shyly. "I think mom purposely did that." "How was it?" he asked. "It was a little odd at first, but it's also comforting." "There are so many

memories in that room, thankfully more good than bad."

Dre looked away from her as he nodded in agreement.

"Well I'd better go, I want to help Jess with the

boys before I head in." "Okay," Dre said, sad to see her go.

"Please give her my love." "I will," Grayce smiled. He

didn't want her to leave, but he didn't want to put too much

pressure on her. Dre wanted to take his time and court

Grayce the way she deserved to be courted. He was

determined to make her realize that he was serious. Dre

was on the mission of his life.

CHAPTER 21

Marc laid in his bed as the days flew by. He couldn't believe that it was almost a week since everything had happened. He and Dre were both quiet. Today was Jayson's funeral. They had both been so fortunate, they knew several classmates and associates that had been shot and killed, but it had never hit so close to home.

They had all grown up together since elementary school. Dre sat with Drea on the side of the bed while his parents helped the nurses get Marc dressed. The doctors advised him against attending the funeral, but Marc was adamant. Jayson was like a brother to him, and he was going to be there for his home-going celebration and help to support his family.

Eric arrived early that morning with Marc and Dre's suits and accessories. Jess requested that they all wear white. Grace was at the house with Jess helping her get the boys prepared to see their father for the final time. Grayce was doing everything that she could to remain strong, but she consistently found herself leaving the room to avoid crying in front of them. She knew that this is going to be hard enough for them and she didn't want to make it any worse.

Jess was so focused on ensuring that everyone else was okay, that she didn't have time to focus on herself. She was most concerned about LJ. He had been increasingly quieter the closer they got to the church. She knew that he was doing his best to be strong for her and be the man of the house, but she didn't want him placing that burden on himself.

She decided to take the children away for a week after the funeral. She thought that they all could use a break away from everything. The last week had been hell on earth for her so she could only imagine what it was like for her children.

The ride to the church was somber for Dre. He still couldn't come to grips with burying someone so close to him. Jayson was the one person who knew just how bad losing Grayce had hurt him. Dre pretended with everyone else, but Jay could get to the core of him. Dre thought back to the day that he had broken up with Grayce. Dre felt sick to his stomach. He knew that he had made a mistake, but his pride would not allow him to go after her. Dre pretended to be sick for the next few days just to avoid seeing her.

Grayce told Jess what happened, so Jayson was the only one who knew the truth. "What's wrong with you?" Jayson asked as he entered Dre's room. "I don't know I think it's a stomach bug," he lied. "Dre we've been friends for too long for you to lie to me. Grayce is at Jess' house right now. She told her what happened." Dre refused to let Jayson know just how bad breaking up with Grayce had hurt him.

"Man, I am a grown man, and she keeps wanting to act like we're in junior high school." "Man, please tell me you didn't really break up with this girl over sex," Jay said. "Jay, why are you coming at me like that? Jess is pregnant right now." "I know that," Jayson said, "but even if she had told me she wanted to wait I would've waited, not broken up with her."

"Jay she's going into the Marines, and I am going off to college. I cannot promise her that I will be faithful and the last thing in this world that I would ever want to do is hurt her. I love that girl more than anything. You think this is easy for me?" "I know it's not," Jay said, "which is why I don't understand why you did it, but you did hurt her. That girl loves you, and she's been crying her eyes out for days man. Dre, you're my brother, and I love you but trust me when I tell you; you are going to regret this." "I already do," Dre said quietly.

Dre snapped out of his daydream when he realized that they had arrived at the church. He took a deep breath before Rico helped him exit the car. The church was packed. Dre wasn't surprised by that at all. Jayson was a good man, and everyone who knew him loved him.

Dre and Marc were stopped every few steps by someone hugging them and telling them that they were praying for them. Although Dre grew up in church, after he moved out of his parents' home, he pretty much only went to church on Easter and Christmas to appease his parents. His missed the fellowship in the church. There is a connection between believers that just could not be explained.

When they finally reached the front of the church, Dre's heart felt like it was about to beat out of his chest. He could not bring himself to look at Jayson's face. Dre alternated between staring at the back of Jess' head and staring at LJ standing to her left with his arm around his mother. It broke Dre's heart. He could not imagine losing his father as a full-grown man. No child should have to lose their father, especially the way it happened.

When it was Dre's turn to walk up to the casket, he couldn't move his legs. He started to hyperventilate just when he felt a soft hand in his. Dre closed his eyes, immediately knowing that it's Grayce without looking at her. "Are you okay?" she asked. He nodded before opening his eyes. Dre gripped her hand firmly as they stepped up to the casket. Everything felt surreal. Dre couldn't believe that this was his best friend lying here.

The tears that he'd been holding back began to fall as he looked down at Jay. He almost forgot that Grayce was there until he felt her weight on him. Eric rolled Marc over to the casket as he tried to help Grayce keep Dre from falling over.

As they walked away from the casket, Dre pulled Grayce to sit with him. Throughout the service, Dre still couldn't believe that Jayson was gone. Jess asked him if he would deliver the Eulogy. Dre wasn't sure if he would be able to go through with it, but he could not say no. Dre stepped up to the pulpit with the assistance of Rico and Eric. As he started to speak his voice began to crack. Dre closed his eyes tightly before looking down at the paper in front of him. He prayed silently to himself and cleared his throat before he opened his eyes and began to speak.

"First off I would like to thank God for giving me the strength to do this. I know that were it not for Him I would not be able to stand here and do this right now, so I give Him all the honor. I would also ask that you all bear with me. I never in a million years thought I would ever be here."

"He shook his head as he bit down on his bottom lip. I thank you all also for your love and support for Jess & the kids and Mrs. McCall. When Jess called me and asked me if I would deliver the eulogy, I said yes without question, but when I hung up the phone, I suddenly became terrified. Jayson McCall is hands down one of the greatest men I have ever known so I wasn't sure how I would be able to express that in a way deserving of him, but I accepted the challenge anyway because I knew that if the situation were reversed, Jay would be standing here without question."

"Jayson Bartholomew McCall." Dre stopped for a moment and looked over at Eric as he and the other guys started to laugh. "I'm sorry Momma Mack but you have no idea how much Jay was teased about Bartholomew. I'm sorry LJ," he smiled looking down at the young man. The entire church erupted in laughter as Jess hugged her firstborn son named after his father.

Dre looked up toward heaven. "I'm sorry Jay, you know I had to do it." Dre cleared his throat once again. "I knew that Jayson McCall was a special person from the moment I met him on the playground at Harriett Tubman

Elementary School. I remember back in third grade, there were two guys about to fight on the playground and while the rest of us stood around waiting for the fight to start, eight-year-old Jayson, the new kid nonetheless, came over and started diffusing the situation."

"We all looked at him like he was crazy but sure enough, he was able to get them to squash it and walk away. I know that Marc still thanks God for that to this very day. Big Mike would have beat him senseless." The entire congregation erupted in laughter once again, looking at Marc remembering how scrawny he was in his youth as he shook his head.

"Jay was a peacekeeper and always had a heart of compassion. Even in the end," Dre choked, "he tried to help the man that ultimately took his life." Dre stopped as he clenched his fists and shook his head. "That's the type of guy that Jay was, and it hurts me that I have to stand here today."

"If we had more men like Jay, more fathers like him, this world would be such a different place. He could empathize with anyone about any situation, and the one thing that I really loved about him was the fact that he would minister to anyone anywhere. Jay was the type of guy who saw the positivity in any situation. I don't care what I was going through he always had a different way of looking at it."

"There were a few murmurs of amen in the crowd. I'm not going to lie as I stand here my heart is so heavy. I was always raised to trust God in ALL his ways, but God and I have been having some serious heart to hearts the last few days because I don't understand this one." Dre dropped his head as the tears flowed down his face. Rico handed him a tissue as he stood behind him and placed his hand on his shoulder for support. Dre sighed heavily.

"I'm sorry Jess." "I promised myself I would be strong for you." Jess smiled at Dre as the tears fell down her face. She knew how much they all loved Jayson and she was so grateful to God for their presence in her life. "Jay was more than my friend he continued. He was my brother, my best friend, my confidant and when I needed it, he would not hesitate to correct me."

"That's one of the things that I loved most about him. He could call you on your mess and instead of you getting angry at him; you'd walk away with not only a new direction but having even more respect for him than you did before."

"I remember a time when I was going through one of the roughest points in my life. Dre looked into Grayce's eyes. "Jay sympathetically told me that it was my fault and I needed to step up or step off. That's one of the things I will miss most. In an age where were have so many people willing to go along to get along, Jay always stood up for his convictions but never begrudged anyone for theirs."

"Jess not that you need me to tell you this, but Jay loved you in a way that you rarely see any more. You were and will remain the love of his life, and I give you my word that we will be here whenever you need us, and we will make sure that you, the boys and that little angel in your belly never want for anything. We also promise to work with you to make sure that they all know just how special their father was."

"In conclusion, Eric, Rico, Marc and I have decided to start The Jayson McCall Youth Foundation to help keep inner city young men on the right path and help give them direction. If you know anything at all about Jay, you know that he was passionate about uplifting the youth and motivating them to achieve greatness. I just ask that we all do continue to do everything that we can to ensure that Jay's memory lives on forever." Jess clasped her hands together, put her hand over her heart and mouthed I love you to Dre.

As Dre made his way off the pulpit with Eric and Rico's assistance, the boys ran over to hug him. Dre hugged the boys and then made his way to Jess. He hugged her as they cried together. As Dre took his seat next to Grayce, he held her hand tightly. Grayce had never seen Dre in so much pain, and it broke her heart. The dark shades hid his eyes but did not hide the tears that fell down his cheeks.

They all made their way to the casket for the final viewing of their brother. They held each other tightly as they saw their brother for the last time, at least on this earth.

As they walked back to their seats, none of the group could watch as the casket was closed except Jessica. She had stood by Jayson and supported him through everything in his life, and she would do the same for him in death. The remainder of the funeral went by in a blur for Dre even though it lasted almost 3 hours.

Jay was loved by every who had ever met him.
Person after person stood to give their remarks about Jay.
There were comments from everyone from their former pee
wee football coach to the Mayor of the city. Everyone
respected Jay more than he ever really knew.

Dre smiled to himself thinking how embarrassed
Jay would be by all of this. He hated to talk about himself.
As the final benediction was read everyone stood as they
prepared to exit the church and head to the cemetery.
Although Dre and Marc are unable to assist with being a
pallbearer, Dre leads the casket out while Eric pushed Marc
at the rear of the casket.

CHAPTER 22

As they all made their way to the cemetery for the burial, Dre closed his eyes tightly relieved that it's almost over. He kept telling himself that if he could just make it through this one last part, he would be okay. The car slowed as they entered the cemetery.

Suddenly Dre couldn't breathe. He took his seatbelt off and tried to remove his tie. Eric asked the driver to pull the car over to the side of the road. Grayce calmly took his face in her hands and turned him to face her.

"Dre sweetie I need you to calm down. Baby, I need you to look at me. That's right baby just look at me and take slow, deep breaths okay?" Dre calmed down instantly as he nodded and started breathing slowly. "That's it, baby." "It's okay." "I've got you." "We're good," Eric said to the driver once Dre settled down. Dre laid his head on Grayce's shoulder as they continued their journey.

They finally arrived at the location where Jayson's plot was prepared. Dre felt like his legs were made of lead, but he pressed on as he took small comfort in the fact that with every step he took, the worst was almost over.

That fact brought both relief and dread. He would be glad to have the ceremony over and done with but with the conclusion of the service comes a new reality, that Jay was really gone forever.

Marc looked forward during the entire internment. He was so angry that the media didn't even allow them to have privacy during this heartbreaking time. All everyone wanted was a photo of the now crippled NFL player. He tried his best to remain focused on the ceremony, but if he was honest with himself, he welcomed the small distraction. He didn't want to think about putting one of his best friends in the ground. He wanted to go back to that night before all their lives changed.

He still blamed himself. If only they had gone bowling as Jayson wanted or out to dinner as Dre wanted. Marc wiped away the tears that fell down his face as he looked at Jayson's children. He spoke with his lawyer and accountant yesterday and set up an account for Jess so that she'd never have to work again. He felt that it was the very least that he could do.

Grayce was shocked by the number of people that had come out to pay their respects to Jayson's family. A small part of her regretted leaving her friends and family behind. She had missed out on so much of their lives. She kept in touch with Jess and Jayson via phone calls, social media, and annual visits but it wasn't the same. She made her decision right then to stay in DC. There is no way that she'd ever be able to leave them again.

Eric couldn't take his eyes off Jess. He had never seen a stronger woman in all his life. He spent most of his time in school or studying so he never really hung out with them as much as Marc and Dre did, but they were close, and he loved them both.

Jess and Jayson had been together for as long as he could remember. Eric could only imagine the pain that she must be enduring. As he listened to the pastor speak, Eric thought about all the time he'd spent studying, wishing that he'd spent more time with his family and friends.

As Jess sat in the hard seat, she wondered what Jayson was doing right that second. She wondered if he were in Heaven looking down on them at this very moment. Jess knew that she had to remain strong for the children. The little ones didn't fully grasp the realization that their father was gone forever. They keep asking for him, and it broke Jess' heart every time that she had to tell them that daddy wasn't coming home.

LJ has been her rock throughout this entire process. Jayson was always so proud of the man that they raised. Jayson was LJ's best friend. They did everything together.

Jess remembered how scared she'd been when she found out she was pregnant. She'd known several girls who'd gotten pregnant by their boyfriends who loved them so much one week and were dumped a week later after the same boyfriend found out he was going to be a father.

In her heart, she knew that Jayson would never do something like that, but her head was well aware of that possibility. The day she told him, he was terrified and happy at the same time. His exact words to her were "the timing may not be right, but every baby is a blessing." Jess believed that in her heart and she knew that all of this was happening for a reason. She didn't understand it, but she was determined to stand on her faith more now than ever before.

Thankfully the internment didn't last very long. Jess asked her mom to take the kids back to the repass for her. She wanted to be alone with her husband one last time. The workers told Jess to take as much time as she needed. Jess wrote Jayson a letter to express exactly how she was feeling. As the crowd slowly began to disperse, Jess pulled the letter from her purse.

She took off her shoes and sat down on the ground next to her husband's casket. She laughed aloud. "Jay, I know these people here probably think that I am crazy, but I truly believe in my heart that you can hear me somehow. I had so much in my head that I didn't want to forget anything, so I decided to write down all my thoughts and feelings."

My Dearest Jay,

I miss you. Not like the normal you've been away on a business trip kind of miss you. This is the type of feeling that borders between terrifying fear and utter despair. My heart is shattered. As I laid in bed last night finishing this letter, I envisioned you laying in your heavenly bed thinking about the kids and me. Baby, please watch over LJ. He's so much like you. I see that more and more every day. Please help me to be the best mother that I can be for our children. By the way, I decided to name our princess Jayda. I thought you would like that.

The guys have all been holding up as best as they can, but they are hurting. I never truly realized how many people love you. My mind won't even allow me to focus on the future. I find myself only wanting to stay in the present. I can't think about the future because then that means I must imagine a life without you and right now I cannot fathom that.

I cannot picture our children going to off to prom and graduating and you not being there taking a million pictures. I can't imagine summer BBQ's, graduations and vacations. I can't even fathom the idea of our anniversary, your birthday or Father's Day. I know everyone says it, but I really wish I had known when you walked out that I'd never get to kiss you or feel your touch or tell you I love you again. I would've made sure to hold you just a little while longer-scratch that. I wouldn't have let you go. The kids and I would've selfishly and unapologetically kept you for ourselves. We miss you terribly.

Everyone keeps telling me that it will get easier day by day and eventually I will be able to think of you without feeling like my heart is being torn apart. I cannot wait until that time comes because right now all I see is the pain but through that pain, I will continue to praise God for the time we had and for the beautiful children that you've given me. Until we meet again on that glorious day, I will love you immeasurably and think of you daily. Rest well, my love.

Jess neatly refolded the letter, kissed it and laid it atop of Jay's casket and walked away.

CHAPTER 23

Dre sat at the table at the repass as Grayce, and his mom forced him to eat. They were two of the most important women in the world to him. Dre glanced at Marc as Senior rolled him back from the restroom. His puffy red eyes told him that Marc had been crying. Dre turned his head as he felt the emotions tug at his own heart. He also noticed his father's own red eyes. Dre knew this was hard on his parents. They loved Jayson deeply and treated him as if he were their very own. Even allowing him to vacation with them when they were younger.

Dre noticed how aged his father looked. He needed to spend more time with his parents. They were everything to him. He could not imagine losing them. His father turned and looked at him as if reading his mind. Senior smiled as if to reassure him that he was okay and would always be there. Dre smiled back at his father. He wanted to be there for Jay's kids the way his pop had been there for him. Dre could not remember one thing in his life that he ever hid

from his father including his breakup with Grayce. Senior

was one of his best friends.

Dre wasn't sure if it was the drugs or the emotions

of the day, but he felt an overwhelming desire to hug his

father. I'll be right back he whispered to Grayce as she

helped him stand. Senior was walking away from the table

when Dre walked up to him. "Hey son, are you doing

okay?" "Yeah Pop I'm fine, you got a minute?" Dre asked.

"Sure," Senior said concerned. He looked to his wife who

just hunched her shoulders in confusion.

As they exited the door, the fresh air was just what

Dre needed. "What's going on son?" Dre shook his head as

tears began to fall. "I love you Pop," he cried as he tightly

hugged his father. "I just don't feel like I tell you or Ma

that enough." Senior didn't realize he was crying until he

felt the wetness on Dre's jacket.

"Dre, me and your mother know how much you love us. Action always means more than words to us, but it feels good to hear it." Dre nodded. "I just felt like I needed to tell you that. I mean what if that was me?" Dre asked, gesturing toward the cemetery. "I would never want to leave this earth without my family knowing just how much they mean to me. I can't even remember the last time I told Jay I love him Pop. He was my best friend, and I can't ever remember telling him."

Jess happened upon the intimate moment. "I'm sorry," she said, startling them. "It's fine baby girl," Senior said wiping away his tears. Dre couldn't even bring himself to look at her. "Dre can you please look at me?" she softly asked. Dre reluctantly looked at her as more tears fell.

"Jayson knew you loved him. Every second of every day. He knew it when you got out of your bed at 3AM to pick him up from the airport when you had to be at work by 7AM. He knew it when you stood aside and shared your father with him when his father walked out of his life, and he knew it when he chose you to be the godfather of our children. He knew that you'd love them just as much as you love him. We all know how much you love and care for us." Dre hugged her tightly and took a deep breath.

"We will get through this Andre." He pulled away from her and laughed. "Oh, we back to Andre now." "Hey, you started it when you came for my baby. You know I had to come back," she teased. "You got it," Dre laughed hugging her again. "I love you Jess," he smiled. "I love you too Peanut Head now let's go feed your goddaughter."

CHAPTER 24

Dre, Eric, and Grayce followed the private ambulance as they headed back to the hospital to drop off Marc. They finally moved him to another ward of the hospital, and he was scheduled to start physical therapy tomorrow morning. Marc was so happy that they would be starting immediately. It would give him something to focus on and help him deal with his grief. It wouldn't take his pain away, but it will help him process it.

Marc was determined to work hard. He hated being in the hospital. Dre being there was the only thing keeping him sane. Now that he was leaving Marc was determined to do whatever he had to do to go home as soon as possible. Today made him realize that he needed to stop feeling sorry for himself.

"If Jess can endure this, definitely handle this situation," he said to himself. "I owe it to Jay to strive for something bigger than myself." Fortunately, Marc wouldn't have to worry about money. He received an 8-figure irrevocable signing bonus when he signed with the Kings. In addition to that Marc wasn't like a lot of athletes. He invested his money wisely and lived modestly.

With his frugal living, salary, and endorsements, he was the wealthiest athlete in the NFL. He had a modest but beautiful home and drove a simple SUV and his Lexus. He didn't spend his money on Bentley's and Ferrari's like a lot of his teammates. He didn't judge them, but that just wasn't his lifestyle.

Senior and Gloria taught them all that living the fast life was not the key to a successful life. They encouraged them to put God first, family second, and community last. He lived by that creed although he had not been to church in years. He still prayed every day and read his Bible faithfully. He gave to several charities on a regular basis in addition to the foundations that he created. Marc was a fighter, and he knew that it would take all his strength as he prepared for the fight of his life. He would not let Jayson

die in vain.

CHAPTER 25

Grayce and Dre got closer and closer as she helped
him during his recuperation. They both avoided discussing
the past. It was still extremely painful for Grayce and Dre
didn't want anything reminding her of how much he'd hurt
her. Walking away from her was the hardest thing that he'd
ever had to do and unbeknownst to her, it killed him to let
her go. Dre still loved her just as much as he did back then,
but he knew that he would have to take things very slow if
he did not want to push her away.

Grayce was still in love with Dre, but she refused to
let him know that. She was very uncertain about giving him
her heart again, but Dre could tell that Grayce still cared
even though she tried her hardest to hide it.

Her eyes gave her away every time. When Dre told
her that he still loved her in the hospital, she was
overjoyed. However, she had just gotten to a point where

she could think of him without crying. She wasn't sure she could handle walking away from him again.

After hours of tests and instructions, Dre was finally given his discharge papers. Dre could not wait to sleep in his own bed even though his parents begged him to stay with them. They eventually dropped the issue after he promised to allow his mom and Grayce to check on him daily. That was just fine with Dre if it meant he got to sleep in his own bed and as long as he was given an opportunity to spend time with Grayce.

Dre's truck had been towed away during the night of the shooting, so Grayce offered to drive him home and take the first shift after leaving his parents' house. As they entered the living room, Dre watched her as she walked ahead of him, thinking of how much she had grown from the teenaged girl he had seen last to this beautiful woman standing before him.

Grayce was one of the sweetest women that Dre had ever met. Grayce nervously looked around while trying to pretend that she didn't notice Dre watching her. "This is a beautiful home Dre," she said trying to control the flip-flops in her stomach. "Thank you," he smiled. "I just moved in 3 months ago, so I still have to put some finishing touches on it. "Please have a seat," he said. "Would you like something to drink?" "Andre Williamson if you don't sit yourself down. You are supposed to be taking it easy now sit." "I was just going in the kitchen," he said, feeling like a kid who had just been chastised by his mother.

"Dre, I have strict orders to make sure that you rest and that's what you're going to do. I'm sure I can find my way to the kitchen," she said as shook her head and walked toward the kitchen to get him some water to take his pain medication. Dre loved having her there to take care of him.

Grayce reentered the living room and handed Dre the bottle of water and two of his pills. "You need to lie down. It's been a long day." Dre looked at her with a solemn look. "I hate to ask, and I don't want to be an imposition, but I don't want to be alone right now. Will you please stay with me until I fall asleep?" "Of course," she said softly. "Do you have a throw?" He looked at her puzzled. She just smiled as she shook her head. "You are such a guy. Do you have with a blanket?" she asked.

"Oh yeah, you can grab a blanket and pillow off the bed upstairs. It's the bedroom up the stairs and straight ahead." "Okay," she said as she walked up the stairs slowly. There was something about being in his bedroom that made her a little uneasy. As she entered his bedroom, she noticed the same prom picture and her senior picture on his nightstand just like at his parents' home.

She smiled as she touched the frame remembering that day so vividly. Grayce grabbed the pillow and blanket and rushed back out. Grayce aided Dre in taking off his jacket, tie, and shoes before helping him to slowly lie down while she covered him with the blanket and made sure that he was comfortable.

"Would you like me to turn the television on?" she asked. She didn't really want to watch TV, but the silence was deafening, and neither of them were ready to talk just yet. "Sure," he said. "Let me show you how to work the remote control. It's a little complicated." Just like its owner, she thought to herself.

Grayce sat on one end of the large couch while Dre tried his best to stay awake. Grayce was watching an episode of Law & Order when she heard Dre's slight snoring. She looked over and smiled, pulling the blanket over him a little more.

As she watched him sleep she laid her head on the back of the sofa and sighed deeply. She knew within herself that she was already gone. Grayce shook her head as she smiled to herself and returned her attention to the television before falling asleep herself.

Dre slowly awakened as a delicious aroma filled the house. For a while, he was a bit confused because of the medication. He slowly sat up and tried to stand without putting any pressure on his side. Just as he was about to stand Grayce entered the room. "Dre what are you doing?" she asked as she rushed over to him.

"I need to use the bathroom," he said, still slightly disoriented. "Here let me help you," Grayce said. She braced herself while Dre tried to stand without putting too much pressure on her. She was so thankful that Dre had a bathroom on the main floor. He was very heavy. She gave him some privacy as she headed back to check on dinner while he was in the bathroom.

When she heard the bathroom door open, she rushed out to help him. "Something smells good," he said. "Thank you," she smiled. "I'm surprised that you were able to find something in there," Dre said. Grayce laughed. "Yeah right. I went to the grocery store while you were asleep." "I'm sorry," he smiled embarrassedly. "No worries, I love to shop." "Some things never change," Dre smiled as he shook his head. "You mind if I come in the kitchen with you?" he asked. "Not at all, as long as you promise to sit," Grayce said sternly. "Yes ma'am," Dre saluted. "Good soldier," she laughed pinching his cheeks.

"It smells amazing in here," he said. Dre didn't realize how hungry he was until he smelled the food. "You cleaned the kitchen too?" he asked as he looks around. "And the bathroom," he said thinking back to the new shower curtain and bath rugs. "Wow, how long was I asleep?" Dre asked. "You were out for about ten hours," she said.

"Thank you so much, Grayce. You didn't have to do any of this, but I greatly appreciate it." Grayce smiled as she walked over to him and touched his hand. "It was my pleasure, Dre. I didn't want you to have to worry about cleaning while you're recuperating." That simple gesture meant the world to Dre. He had entertained several women in his homes over the years and none of them ever even attempted to make up a bed let alone clean his entire house.

He loved Grayce more and more with every second that passed. They finally sat down to the delicious meal Grayce prepared. After Grayce blessed the food, Dre immediately dug in and started devouring his food. "This is delicious," Dre said. He wolfed down the rockfish stuffed with shrimp and crab, risotto and spinach. "Dre, please slow down," she laughed. "There is plenty more."

"I can't help it," he said when he finally came up for air. "This is amazing. I'd pay for food like this in a restaurant." "I'm glad you like it," Grayce smiled. "Cooking is one of my favorite passions." "Good because eating is one of mine," he laughed.

They made small talk during dinner "You are so silly," she said as she cleared the table, laughing at one of Dre's jokes. She had forgotten about his sense of humor.

"This was nice Grayce, thank you so much for everything."

"It was nice," she smiled. "I wasn't sure how I would feel being around you again, but I'm surprisingly comfortable."

"Anyway, I picked up a few other items while I was at the grocery store. I really miss cooking so on the days I am here I'd love to cook for you if you don't mind."

"Woman, are you trying to fatten me up?" Dre laughed.

"You are still silly," she laughed. "Do you have room left for dessert?" she asked. "Dessert too??? Oh, see you spoiling me now," Dre beamed.

"Good," she said excitedly. "I tried this new recipe for a chocolate strawberry pie. Please give me your honest opinion." Dre rubbed his hands together as she sliced the pie, put a dollop of her homemade whipped cream on top and brought their plates to the table. "Babe, this looks delicious," he said before devouring the delicious dessert.

Grayce enjoyed the pie, but she was a little caught off guard by Dre calling her babe. It felt so...right. As hard as she was trying not to allow herself to get caught up, the more she felt herself falling for him. "Penny for your thoughts," Dre said noticing that she seemed distracted. "I guess I'm just a little tired," she fibbed.

"Yeah it has been a long day," Dre said looking at his watch. "Wow I can't believe it's midnight," he said. "I didn't realize I had slept so long." "Grayce would you mind staying the night?" he asked nervously. "I don't want you on the road at this late, and I know you're just as exhausted as I am."

"Dre, I'm not sure that's a good idea," she said. "Grayce please, you can sleep in the other room, I just know I won't be able to rest thinking of you driving around this late." "Okay," she said, finally giving in. "If you're sure it's no trouble." "Not at all," Dre smiled. "I'd love it." "Okay, well I guess we'd better get you to bed."

She closed her eyes and began to blush, realizing how that sounded. Dre couldn't help but laugh. "I know what you meant," Dre said. "Stop laughing at me," Grayce said as she started laughing with him. "Actually, I am not very tired," he said. "I'll just watch a movie until I fall asleep on the couch." "Okay, where should I sleep?" Grayce asked.

She noticed the look on Dre's face. "Would you mind taking my bedroom upstairs?" he stuttered. "Not at all," Grayce said. "Please yell for me if you need anything." "I will," Dre said. "There are tee shirts and sweats in the closet." "I never took my suitcase out of the car, so I'll be fine." Dre was hoping Grayce didn't take his hesitation the wrong way.

Dre never allowed any of his overnight guests in his bedroom. That was his sacred area. Grayce wasn't some one-night stand and the thought of her sleeping in the same room, the same bed that he'd shared with other women sickened him. He also felt guilty about her cleaning his house. Especially the guest room where he usually entertained his female guests. This was turning out to be

one interesting week Dre thought to himself.

CHAPTER 26

Grayce had never slept so comfortably in her life. For a moment she didn't remember where she was, then it hit her that she was in Dre's house. Grayce turned to her side, thinking about Dre's reaction when she asked him where she should sleep. Grayce knew why he didn't want her in the room downstairs.

While cleaning the room, she noticed several empty condom boxes in the wastebasket. She assumed that was Dre's bedroom. Grayce still felt repulsed by just the thought of him touching another woman but they were not together, and she had not expected him to be a monk. As she turned and looked up at the ceiling to stop the tears that threaten to fall, Grayce finally pulled herself out of bed, showered and got dressed. Grayce decided to fix Dre breakfast before heading to his parent's house. She needed a bit of distance from him.

As she entered the living room, she noticed Dre sitting on the couch. "Are you okay?" she asked concerned. He shook his head no as tears fell from his eyes. "Are you in pain?" He again shook his head no, swallowing the lump in his throat. "I had a dream that Jay was alive," he said quietly. "It felt so real Grayce, and then I woke up and realized that he…" Grayce held him as he wept. She knew then that no matter how much it hurt, she would never be able to walk away from him again.

CHAPTER 27

The doorbell rang as Grayce finished preparing lunch for Dre. "Hey mom," she said as she opened the door for Gloria. "How's my baby?" Gloria whispered as she hugged Grayce and looked at Dre sleeping on the couch.

"He had a pretty rough morning," Grayce said, also whispering an effort not to wake him. "What happened?" Gloria asked. Grayce ushered her into the kitchen so they could talk freely. Grayce sighed. "He had a dream that Jayson was still alive." "When I came downstairs he was crying."

Gloria shook her head. "Dre and Jayson were like two peas in a pod. "I know this isn't easy on him." Grayce nodded her head in agreement. Gloria rubbed Grayce's shoulder. "How have you been doing baby?" "I've been okay," Grayce said quietly.

"It was strange being here last night, but I made it through okay. Dre and I had a nice dinner. I had forgotten about his crazy sense of humor. "That boy is still as silly as ever," Gloria agreed, laughing with Grayce. "That's how he got away with so much coming up," she smiled. "How long did it take you to clean this mess?" she asked. "How did you know it was me?" Grayce asked. "Because you and I are so much alike," Gloria said hugging her. "It didn't take as long as I thought it would. It also was nice to have something to do. I've been feeling helpless lately.

"Baby trust me, your presence here means so much more than you know. God times everything for His divine purpose. He knows what He's doing, just trust him and follow his path." Grayce nodded her head as she laid her head on Gloria's shoulder and let the tears flow down her face.

CHAPTER 28

Marc's first session of physical therapy wasn't at all what he had expected. He had trained hard since he was a child playing ball and it never felt like work to him because he loved it. He was so pumped about his plans to get back on his feet and walk again. This first session disappointed him greatly.

"Hey bro how did it go today?" Eric asked as the nurse rolled him back into the room. "It was okay," Marc said expressionlessly. "He did great," the male nurse said. "It's going to take him a while to get used to the process, but he went far above what we expected." "That's great Marc, you are going to be up and out in no time." "I guess," Marc said.

The nurse had seen this time and time again. People come into physical therapy thinking it was a fast and easy process but it's a lot of hard work. "I will give you two some privacy," the nurse said. "It was nice to meet you man and thanks again for the autograph." "I'll be praying for you." "Thanks," Marc said as he closed his eyes and tried not to focus on how much he felt like a failure.

"Man, what are you looking so down for, did you hear what he said?" Eric asked. "Yeah, I heard him," Marc said. "But it doesn't feel like I accomplished anything." "This is a process baby bro. You can't focus on what's not happening. Pay attention to everything that is happening and focus on the end result."

"I am so sorry, but I have a meeting that I can't miss. I will be back for dinner. I'll call you to see what you want." "Okay big bro, good luck today." Eric looked at Marc, surprised that he remembered that today was the day of his big company merger. "Did you think that I forgot?" Marc laughed. "I mean you do have bigger things on your mind." "I'm proud of you E, I really am. Who would've thought my big brother would be the youngest CEO of a fortune 500 company.

We've come a long way," Marc smiled. "Yes, we have baby bro and thanks again for your help. I wouldn't be where I am if it wasn't for you," Eric said. Marc felt himself starting to tear up. "Go 'head with all that mushy stuff man," Marc laughed. "Okay well, I need to run so I can overlook everything one last time before the meeting." "Okay E, call me once it's done." "You know I will," he smiled before heading out the door.

CHAPTER 29

Jessica had just put the boys down for their nap when her phone started ringing. "Hey girl," she whispered as she quietly tiptoed out of the room. "I can call you back if this is a bad time," Grayce said. "No, you're fine, I just put Aaron and Amir down for their nap." "How are god mommies babies?" Grayce asked. "Girl they are good. I took them to the park earlier, and they wore me out."

"Aww that sounds nice," Grayce said. "How are LJ and Jackson doing?" "They are doing okay overall. Jackson has been glued to LJ's side, and Eric came over yesterday and took them to Dave and Buster's." "That was so sweet of him," Grayce said. "I know, I love my babies, but I needed that break." "I'm sure," Grayce agreed. "How have you been?" Grayce asked as she sat down on the sofa.

"Honestly Grayce, I still haven't had time to process everything fully. I think the proof will be in the pudding when mom and dad leave." "Well you know I am right here if you need me," Grayce said. "I know sweetie, and I love you for that. So how have YOU been?" Jess asked.

"That's a somewhat complicated question to answer" Grayce answered. "I'm at Dre's house right now." "What?!" Jess exclaimed. She was so relieved to focus on something other than herself. "I know. Mom and I are taking turns taking care of him, and I'm on the first shift." How is that going?" Jess asked. "It's surreal. Being in his home. Thinking about all the other women that were here before me." "Baby don't think about that, that's the past. Just focus on the here and now," Jess advised. "I know, but it's a little difficult to do that when I'm finding condom boxes in the trash." "Ouch, I'm sorry babe," Jess empathized.

"Do you think you will ever be able to look past all of that?" Jess asked. "Jess I love him so much, even after all of these years. It's like time has not diminished anything. The other day in the hospital, he asked about us working on being friends, and I want more than anything in this world, but I am so scared Jess. I just don't understand how this man can have me so hung up on him after all of these years, but I have been praying on it."

"Girl that's all you can do, just give it to God."

"Well, I need to go check on him and see if he needs anything, please call me if you need anything, Jess."

"Aww, she's checking on her Pookie." "Girl stop it," Grayce blushed. "I do love catering to him though. This has been so much fun, but as you and I both know, there are major ramifications that come along with playing house."

"Girl trust me, I know all about that. I have a whole starting lineup here as a testament to that," Jess laughed. "Okay baby, get some rest while the little ones are napping and kiss my babies for me." "I will Little Dre," Jess teased. "Bye girl," Grayce said hanging up the phone smiling at the nickname they used to call her in school.

Dre didn't mean to eavesdrop, but it's not like he was very mobile at the moment. He could tell that Grayce was talking to Jessica. Hearing her say that she still loved him was like music to his ears. Grayce walked into the room to check on Dre when he stood. "Hey sleepyhead," she said. "Hey yourself," he smiled. "I was just coming to talk to you." "Are you okay?" Grayce asked. "Yes, I'm fine. "Ummm…Grayce, I couldn't help but overhear your conversation with Jess." Grayce was so embarrassed. "Dre I…" "No baby let me stop you for a moment."

"Grayce I allowed my hormones and immaturity to get the best of me back then. There was not one day that we were apart that I did not think of you, your smile, everything. It killed me to be away from you. I'm embarrassed to admit it now, but I used those women to get over you, and it didn't work. I knew that you deserved better than me. Even when I was young and dumb, but I was smart enough to realize that I would not hurt you more than I already did by cheating on you. That would've destroyed me. You meant everything to me, and I wanted the best for you. The best was not me at that time. I was a coward, Grayce."

Grayce began to cry as she stared into his eyes. Grayce finally found her voice. "What about now Dre?" "Now, I am a man, not a little boy. I will never, ever take you for granted again. I know I said I'd give you time, but I don't want to waste another second of my life being without you Grayce. You are everything to me. I'm so sorry that it took all of this to open my eyes." Grayce continued to cry as she laid her head on his chest.

CHAPTER 30

The doctor on call was checking Marc's vitals when Rico walked in. "Hey man, I thought. Oh, I'm sorry," Rico said realizing that he'd interrupted the nurse. "No worries," the young nurse smiled. "We're just about done." "What's up, Rico?" Marc asked with a huge smile. "Hey man, I'm good." "How are you doing?" "I'm getting better every day," Marc said.

"You must be, I was happy to hear that they moved you. That must mean things are progressing well." "Doc said that things are going very well. I can't really tell, but I'm going to have faith and take her at her word," Marc smiled. "He's doing very well," the beautiful young doctor smiled as she entered the room while Marc grinned like a Chester cat.

Rico did not miss the little connection between them. "I heard you did well today Mr. Jackson" she smiled. "I need you to remember that this is a marathon, not a sprint. The last thing you want is to overdo it and set your recovery process back." "I'll keep that in mind doc," Marc smiled. "I'm sorry Doc, this is one of my best friends, Rico. Rico this is Dr. Drew."

"Nice to meet you, Rico." "Nice to meet you too, Dr. Drew," Rico said standing to shake her hand before she turned her attention back to Marc. "Great job today and make sure you get some rest, I'll see you tomorrow."

"Where's Kim?" Marc asked as the doctor exited the room. Rico smiled to himself, noticing that Marc was still blushing. "She is out with her sister doing some shopping for the babies, she sends her love. I still can't believe I'm going to be a father man. I just want to be a better example to my children than my father was to me and my brother," Rico said shaking his head.

I am so excited though; if you had told me two years ago that I would be a father I would've thought you were crazy, now I am counting down the days." "I am so happy for you Rico," Marc smiled. "You and Kim are going to be great parents." "I hope so, I'm afraid of raising a daughter. I know how I was before I met Kim and the last thing I need is some guy treating my daughter the way I treated women back then."

Marc laughed, knowing that Rico was dead serious. He was the definition of a player until he met Kim. When he met her, it was curtains for every other woman in his life. "But enough about me man, what's up with you?" Rico asked. "Today started out bad, but it's getting better every second," Marc smiled.

"I had my first session of locomotor training today. I didn't feel like it went well but thinking back, I think I was more embarrassed than anything else because I am not used to being so helpless." "I can understand that but like she said take your time man. By the way, what's up with Dr. Dimples?" Rico teased. "What are you talking about?" Marc blushed.

"Come on Marc I saw the way y'all looked at each other. You don't have to front for me." Marc couldn't help but laugh. Rico always knew when he was lying. "She is my doctor man, she's not thinking about me." "Yeah okay," Rico laughed. Marc was attracted to his doctor and hope that maybe that maybe there was a spark between them, but a part of him thought he is crazy for even entertaining that idea. What educated, attractive woman would want a cripple? He shook the thoughts from his head as he changed the subject once again.

CHAPTER 31

Eric was on cloud nine as he exited the restaurant with dinner for he and Marc. He just signed the deal of a lifetime. He and his family would never have to worry about money for as long as they lived. Eric was so preoccupied that he hadn't noticed the proximity to the car parked next to him as he opened his driver's side door and hit the passenger door.

"This day just keeps getting better," the young woman said as she exited her car. Eric turned around embarrassed. "I am so sorry. I was distracted," Eric apologized. "I see," she said slightly annoyed. Eric started to apologize when he noticed the tears falling from her face.

He immediately turned to her. "I'm sorry, are you hurt?" he asked concerned. She shook her head no. "I'm fine," she finally answered. "It's just been a very long day." Eric felt horrible. "I should've been paying more attention.

Are you sure you're okay?" he asked. "Yes," she smiled.
"You hit the car, not me. Thank you for your concern
though."

Eric retrieved his briefcase from the car and pulled
out his checkbook. She tried to stop him when he asked for
her name. "I can't take your money, besides with all the
other dents in my car yours just blend right in with the
others," she smiled. Eric looked at the beat-up car and felt
even worse.

"I know I don't have to, but it's the least I can do,"
he said. "Here is a check for 2,500.00, that should be
enough to cover your damages as well as a little something
for your inconvenience." "Sir you don't have to do this."
"Please call me Eric."

"Thank you so much," she cried hugging Eric.
"Thank you, Jesus," she said. "I hate to ask but will I be
able to cash this now?" she asked apologetically.
"Absolutely," he smiled. "I can do better than that, I bank

at the PNC across the street. I can run over and just get the cash out that way they won't charge you a fee." "That would be great," she sighed.

"Excellent, by the what is your name?" "I'm sorry, my name is Michelle Williams." "Nice to meet you Michelle, you can follow me over if you'd like." "Okay," she said sighing deeply. Michelle let the tears flow as she sat in her car and looked back at her sleeping children.

She'd been praying all day that God would provide for her and her children. She was laid off earlier today, only to have her neighbor call and tell her that there had been a fire in their apartment building and the entire building was condemned. Michelle planned to use her last to purchase dinner for her children before heading home to see where the Red Cross would send them.

"Thank you, Jesus," Michelle cried. As Eric got back in his car, all he can think about were her beautiful eyes as he dialed Marc's cell. "Where are you man, I'm starving?" Marc said answering the phone without even saying hello. "I know bro, and I'm sorry, but I am going to be a little longer than I anticipated. I just dented someone's car, so I need to deal with that. I will be there as soon as I can." Is everyone okay?" Marc asked concerned. "Yes, we are fine, and there is no major damage." "Well don't rush, take care of that and be safe." "I will and sorry, I'll be there as soon as I can." "No rush," Marc said. "Rico is here, I'll ask him to grab me something so take your time."

Eric thought about the young lady with the beautiful eyes. She was one of the prettiest women he'd ever seen. Eric was sure to drive slowly, he didn't want to lose her in the rush hour traffic. "I'll be right back," Eric said as he walked up to her car, noticing the two children in the back seat for the first time.

The bank manager exited his office as soon as he saw Eric. "Hello Mr. Jackson, how are you today?" "I'm well Matt and yourself?" "I'm great, just ready for the weekend." "Me too," Eric said smiling. "I'd like to make a withdrawal," Eric said looking back at the car. "Is everything okay Mr. Jackson?" Matt asked. "Oh yeah Matt, I'm fine. I accidentally dented the young lady's car and rather than go through insurance I'd rather pay out of pocket."

Matt looked out the window at the beautiful woman playing with the young children. "Okay, I can help you with that," Matt smiled. "How much would you like to withdraw?" "$5,000," Eric said. Matt did a double take. "Wow, how big is the dent?" "I get the impression that she is going through some things right now, so I just want to help her out a little," Eric said. "Okay, but be careful," Matt warned.

At that moment Tony walked into the bank. "Hey E, I thought that was your car out front. How are you?" "I'm good Tony, how are you?" "Things are good on my end. I'm on my way to see your brother. What's going on?"

Tony asked as he noticed Eric's focus on the car and the young lady outside.

"I had a minor fender bender and decided to pay the young woman out of pocket." "Are you both sure you don't want to go through the insurance company?" Tony asked. "No, it's fine. I'd rather just handle it myself." Eric knew what Tony was thinking. In the past, Eric had been played for a fool more times than he wanted to remember.

"Tony, I promise, its fine. I got this okay?" "Okay," Tony said reluctantly. "Well, I'm on my way to see Marc, so I'll catch you later." "I was picking up dinner for us when this happened. Would you mind taking his food to him?" "No problem at all," Tony said as they walked back to his car.

"Tony this is Michelle, Michelle this is one of my oldest friends, Tony." "Nice to meet you," Michelle smiled. "You too," Tony smiled. He saw why Eric wasn't in a rush to leave. Eric was a nice guy, but he had always been a sucker for love and Michelle was beautiful.

"Well unless you two need anything from me, I'll let you get everything settled," Tony said. "Yes, we're good and tell Marc I'll be there later." "Okay," Tony smiled. "Oh, text me Marc's room number." "Okay," Eric said before turning his attention back to the Michelle. "Michelle again I'm sorry that I wasn't paying attention. It's been a very long week." "No, I am sorry if I was rude, it's been a long week for me also, and I am just a little stressed."

"I'm sure," Eric said looking at the two little ones in the back seat. "I apologize for you adding to your stress," he smiled shyly. "Actually, God used you to answer a prayer. In addition to being laid off, I found out that there was a fire in our apartment building so needless to say, we could use this money now more than ever. But enough about me, I'm sorry for keeping you from your visit."

"It's not a problem, I'm grateful for the distraction."

"My brother shot but thank God he's alive and getting better every day." That's when it clicked. "Oh, my gosh, Marcus Jackson from the Kings is your brother?" "Yep, that's my baby brother," Eric smiled proudly. "I thought you looked familiar and it didn't register until just now. I am so sorry to hear that, but I am glad that he's okay. I've been praying for him. My son is a huge fan." "Thank you," Eric said. "I was picking up his dinner when I dented your car."

"I am sorry," Michelle apologized. "Here I am holding you up while you were trying to feed your brother. Please forgive me," she said with a shy smile. "No need to apologize," Eric said hunching his shoulders. "I am the one who hit you." "Well, I don't want to hold you any longer. I'm sure your brother is wondering where you are by now." "I called him on the way here, and Tony is taking him his food, so he's okay for the moment.

Maybe one day we can arrange for your son to meet him. He loves children." Michelle was shocked. "Are you kidding me? He would love that." "Great," Eric smiled. "Mommy I'm hungry," Eric heard as he looked over at the little girl in the back seat. "Okay, sweetie, we'll get you guys something right now." "Okay," the little girl said as she sat back in the seat waving at Eric.

"If you don't mind, I'd like to take you all to dinner. There's a cute restaurant nearby that I think they'd love." "You don't have to do that," Michelle said. "You've been more than generous." "No really, it's not a bother, and I'd really think they'd enjoy it."

"Um...I.. sure, I guess." "Great," Eric said excitedly. "You can follow me over. It's about 15 minutes from here." "Sounds good," Michelle smiled. This day is getting better by the minute Eric smiled as he picked up the phone to call his brother to let him know that he'd be later than expected.

CHAPTER 32

Things between Dre and Grayce were going great. They spent just about every day together, and Dre was excited because he was able to move around a little more every day and the doctor had given him the green light to go back to work the following week on a part-time basis until he was up to returning full-time.

Dre wasn't much of a cook, but he loved to grill. He invited Grace over for dinner and a movie. It was such a beautiful evening that they decided to eat outside.

"You have a beautiful home Dre," Grayce said enjoying the view from the patio. "Thank you, I designed everything myself," he responded proudly. "I majored in economics and minored in architecture." "I heard," she smiled. "Hmm so you've been keeping tabs on me I see," he teased. "I wouldn't go that far," Grayce smiled. "I'm really proud of the man you have become Dre."

Dre smiled so hard he thought his cheeks would burst. "Thank you, coming from you that means everything to me." "I mean it, you've accomplished all of the goals we talked about in high school." "Not all of them," Dre said looking directly at Grayce. "The steaks smell great," Grayce responded, changing the subject. She wasn't sure how to react to Dre's comment.

Dre returned to the grill, thinking about how much money he spent customizing his home, but he rarely took time to enjoy it. "Want to go on a tour after dinner?" Dre asked. "I'd love to," Grace smiled. Dre was taking the steaks off the grill when the doorbell rang.

"That must be ma checking on me again," he laughed, shaking his head. "Would you mind getting that for me?" Dre asked. "Sure," Grayce said getting up to answer the door. Grayce opened the door expecting to see Gloria and was more than a little surprised when she was what she assumed was one of Dre's "friends" standing

there.

The woman was just as surprised to see Grayce. The

woman rolled her eyes once she composed herself. "Where

is Dre?" she asked rudely. "Just one moment," Grayce said,

but before she could turn to let Dre know that someone was

at the door for him, the woman pushed past Grayce.

"Dre, Dre, where are you?" she began yelling. Dre

thought he was hearing things until he saw Ashley walking

through his home. Dre slammed the steaks down on the

table. "What are you doing here?" Dre demanded. "What?

What do you mean what am doing here?" "I came to check

on you and who is this?" Ashley asked angrily gesturing at

Grayce.

"*This* is my woman," Dre said taking Grayce's

hand, and you need to leave our home. "Your woman?" she

scoffed. "She wasn't your woman when you were sleeping

with me." Dre tried his best to keep his temper in check.

This was the last thing that he needed while he was trying to get closer to Grayce.

Dre looked at Grayce apologetically. She looked hurt and shocked as he squeezed her hand reassuringly. "Dre, I think I should leave," Grayce said quietly. "No, she is going to leave." Dre took a breath before addressing Ashley. "Ashley, first off, you and I both know what it was. You were never my woman, and I thought you knew better than to ever come to my home uninvited. I'm going to ask you one more time nicely before I lose my temper. Get out of my house and don't you ever come back."

Ashley looked like she wants to cry, but instead, she preceded to call Dre everything except a child of God before walking out and slamming his door. Dre and Grayce were quiet for what felt like a lifetime before Grayce looked at Dre and jokingly asked, "friend of yours?" Dre couldn't help but laugh as he felt a huge relief.

"I am sorry Grayce, Ashley has never shown up here unannounced. I am not sure what that was about."

"Dre, I know you were not innocent. I just hope this does not become a pattern," Grayce said with a serious expression. Dre grabbed her hand and looked her deeply in her eyes. "Grayce I give you my word right now that I will never, ever allow anything like this to happen ever again." Grayce smiled. "I know now come on and let's eat. I am starving, and those steaks smell amazing." Dre watched as she walked off toward the patio.

"Thank you, God," he said, grateful that God had given him a second chance to correct the biggest mistake of his life. "Thank you, Lord. I promise that I will not mess this up."

CHAPTER 33

Marcus was on the phone with Senior when his doctor walked into his room. "Dad, my doctor just walked in, I will call you a little later." "You didn't need to hang up the phone," Dr. Drew smiled. "I just wanted to check in on you before I head home for the evening. Do you need anything?" the doctor asked smiling at Marc. "Yes, I need a Five Guys burger and an order of fries," he laughed.

Dr. Imani Drew laughed. "Well I really wish I could get you that right now, but I am pretty sure Five Guys is closed. What are you still doing up anyway?" she asked. "I couldn't sleep," Marc said. "You've had a pretty long day yourself," he remarked as she tried to stifle her yawn.

"Yes, I was covering for a colleague, but at least I get the day off tomorrow. I feel like I have not been home in weeks." "I can imagine," Marc said genuinely disappointed that he wouldn't get to see her tomorrow. Little did he know, Imani felt the exact same way.

She tried her best to try to halt her attraction toward Marc, but she was powerless. There was something between them, but due to ethical and emotional implications, she would never even think about the possibility of any relationship with him other than doctor and patient.

Imani had been engaged to one of the doctors on staff for the last two years until he decided that marriage was not for him. She was heartbroken when he broke up with her over the phone. It didn't help that one week later he was dating one of the younger nurses. Imani tried her hardest to play it off, but everyone knew that she was devastated. She would never allow herself to be hurt like that again.

"Well Mr. Jackson, I will see you soon, and if you need anything at all, please have the nurse page me."

"Okay I will, have a good night and enjoy your day off," Marc smiled as the doctor exited the room. Marc sighed deeply as the door closed smiling to himself as he closed

his eyes and attempted to sleep, thinking of Dr. Drew.

CHAPTER 34

Dre noticed that Grayce has become very distant since the incident with Ashley. He was determined to do whatever he had to do to regain her trust. Dre decided to call her and invite her out on a real date. The phone rang four times, and Dre was just about to hang up when Grayce finally answered. "Hi," Grayce said softly.

"Hi, how have you been?" Dre asked, realizing how much he'd missed hearing her voice. She smiled into the phone. Grayce could not stay mad at him no matter how hard she tried. "I've been okay," she said, "and you?"

"Not so good," he said honestly. "I miss you so much. I was calling to see if you have plans for the weekend. If not, I'd like to take you out." Grayce hesitated a little. "Dre, I don't think that's…" Dre stopped her.

"Grayce, I know that Ashley showing up here put you in a really uncomfortable position and I am so very sorry for that. I just want an opportunity to prove to you that I am serious about us. I promise you that everything will be fine." "Dre, you don't owe me any explanations, you're a grown man, and you have a life." "Grayce please just think about it okay?". "Okay, I will" Grayce sighed.

Against Grayce's better judgment, she accepted Dre's invitation. He arrived at Jess' house at 7:00 on the dot with two beautiful bouquets of flowers for Grayce and Jess. He was in the middle of a wrestling match with the boys when he heard someone clear their throat. Dre looked up to the most beautiful sight he'd ever seen. "Aunt Grayce you look beautiful," LJ said as he elbowed his godfather.

"Aww thank you sweetie," Grayce said kissing him on his cheek. "Hey LJ, stop trying to steal my woman." "Your woman huh?" Grayce laughed. "Yes, my woman," Dre said boldly looking her in her eyes as he handed her the flowers.

"Okay boys give Auntie Grayce and Uncle Dre a hug and go wash your hands for dinner," Jess said. Dre hugged all the boys before turning his attention to Jess.

"And these are for you Jess," Dre said as he hugged her. "How have you been?" "I'm doing okay Dre, but I'm pretty sure your doctor would advise against you wrestling on the floor with a bunch of rambunctious boys." "I'm fine," he said sheepishly. "You still have to be careful Dre," Grayce said. "I will," he said, knowing that he would not win this battle.

"You two have fun, I need to go feed my men," Jess said. "Okay, I'll text you when I'm on my way home," Grayce said hugging her best friend. "Call me if you need me."

Grayce suddenly became nervous once she was in the car. "Thank you so much for coming," he said as he started the car. "I was hoping and praying that you wouldn't change your mind." "I almost did," Grayce

laughed. "I'm sure," he smiled.

"You look beautiful Grayce." "Thank you," Grayce

said shyly. "You're looking rather dapper yourself Mr.

Williamson." "Thank you," he smiled. "I made reservations

at this new seafood restaurant at the Harbor that Rico told

me about." "How is he doing?" Grayce asked, "I haven't

seen much of him since the hospital, but he's doing okay."

"He's been working two jobs so that Kim can stay

home." "He's such a good man, you all are. Jess and I were

talking about that earlier. So many women complain about

there being no good men, and they surround us. "Thank

you," Dre blushed.

"I want to take you out to first and foremost to

thank you for taking time to nurse me back to health, cook

for me, clean for me and just be there for me. I seriously

cannot thank you enough for all that you've done." "Dre, I

care about you. I always have, and I always will. No matter

what happens between us, I will always be there whenever you need me." "You have me feeling like I'm 12 again," Dre confessed. "Stop it," Grayce blushed. "I'm serious," he laughed. Little did Grayce know, Dre was already planning to do whatever he had to do to make her his wife.

CHAPTER 35

"That was one of the best meals I have ever had," Grayce says after dinner. "I agree," Dre smiled. "I think this will be our new spot." Grayce smiled. "I'd like that." "Me too," Dre said reaching for her hand across the table. "Grayce I love you, and nothing will ever change that. I just want to prove to you that I am a different man. I can't explain it, but that night changed me forever. I'm not the man that I used to be. I am embarrassed by the things I used to do. I don't want you to ever think of me negatively. Please give me an opportunity to show you the man that I truly am. I want to make you proud of me."

"Dre, I love you too, and I am very proud of you and your accomplishments." Before either of them knew what was happening, Dre leaned across the table and softly kissed Grayce. "Grayce I have never, ever stopped loving you. I am not going to lie to you; I am not a virgin, and I have been less than a gentleman in my past but never even allowed other women to enter my bedroom because I felt like that was disrespectful to you.

Leaving you was one of the hardest things that I've ever had to do in my life. I can make excuses, but I won't. I was young, selfish and stupid. Will you please forgive me?" "Dre, I love you too, and of course I forgive you. Loving you has never been an issue for me, but the last thing in the world I want is to be hurt again.

There are still some things you don't know about me, Dre. "Nothing matters except having you back in my life Grayce." Grayce took a deep breath. "Dre during my last mission, I was injured badly." Dre tensed at the thought of Grayce being hurt. "What happened?" he asked, moving closer to her. "Two of my men were killed and I.. I lost my right leg, Dre." Grayce closed her eyes to keep her tears from falling. She was terrified of seeing the look on Dre's face when he realized that his "perfect Grayce" wasn't so perfect after all.

Dre felt like he had been hit by a mack truck. "I'm so sorry baby," he said. "I had no idea. Are you okay? Why didn't you call?" "The only ones that knew were my parents, Jess and Jayson. I begged them not to tell anyone. This has been a difficult road for me, but I'm still standing.

Dre felt horrible. All he kept thinking was had he done the right thing, Grayce would never have been hurt. Grayce saw the look on Dre's face and immediately regretted telling him. "Dre, this is why I didn't want to tell anyone. I don't need or want pity," she cried. "Grayce it's not pity that you see in my face, it's regret."

"I regret not being there to help you through this. I regret all the years that we lost, and most importantly I regret that I wasn't man enough to love you like you needed to be loved. "Well, God times things according to His plans, not ours. I don't spend time asking why me, I focus on the fact that I am still alive, so that means he is not done with me yet." "That's my girl," Dre smiled.

"Well not so fast," Grayce continued. "I *am* still a virgin, and I will not have sex before marriage. "Can you handle being in a relationship with me again, without having sex?" Grayce asked. Dre smiled. "Grayce I feel like God gave me a second chance to correct my mistakes. I love you, and your virginity is a gift that I will gladly wait the rest of my life for if necessary. I love you Graycie." "I love you too," Grayce said softly.

Dre felt like the luckiest man in the world. "Soooo does this mean that we are officially a couple again?" he asked. "I guess it does," Grayce smiled. Dre grabbed her up by her waist and spun her around. "Baby, I am so happy right now." Dre hugged her tightly as tears fell down her face.

CHAPTER 36

The guys went together to pick Marc up from the rehabilitation center. Marc was all packed and ready when they enter the room. "What took y'all so long?" he asked. "I've been up since 6:00 this morning". Rico laughed. "I see somebody is anxious to get out of here." "Come on let's go grab something to eat, I know you're tired of this hospital food," Eric said.

"Actually, believe it or not, the food is pretty good. There must be somebody's big momma in the kitchen putting it down" he laughed. "I'm a little tired though. Let's just pick something up and eat at home." "Sounds like a plan," Dre said. They were just about to step into the elevator when the doors open and there stood Dr. Drew.

"So, you were just going to leave without saying goodbye," she teased. "No..no, not at all," Marc stuttered. "The nurse said you were in a meeting that was scheduled to last all day." "Sure," she smiled. "Did he give you all of your instructions and inform you that you will need to come back once a week?" "Yes, I'm all set," Marc smiled. "Great, I guess I better not hold you up. I'll see you next week and here is my card in case you have any questions or concerns." "Thank you," Marc said returning her smile.

As soon as Rico pressed the button for the lobby and the doors closed they all started teasing Marc. Imani could still hear them and couldn't help but laugh. Marc turned to CJ, the orderly who had been assisting him during his stay. "Do you know anything about her CJ?" he asked.

"Well, she was dating one of the doctors here. That dude must be crazy. He broke up with her two days before the wedding and the next week he was dating one of the nurses. "Wow, that is crazy," Marc said. "Yep, I heard they were engaged for a couple of years too." Marc shook his head and smiled. Maybe God was saving her for me he thought to himself before brushing the thought off as wishful thinking.

CHAPTER 37

The guys finally arrived home after stopping at Five Guys. After they finished eating, the conversation turned to Grayce. "So, Dre I notice you and Grayce getting cozy last night when we left," Rico teased. Dre blushed slightly. "What???" Rico laughed. "She got my boy blushing, let me call Tony Perkins. This is a Fox 5 breaking news story". Dre laughed. "No seriously man it's like we never broke up. I love that girl so much," he blushed.

"It's about time," Marc said. "The last thing we need is another Uncle Joe up in the club trying to be a player." Dre laughed, thinking about his mom's 50-year-old brother who still went to the club every week. "I can't lose her again."

"She makes me feel like we're back in high school again. Did you know that she lost her leg while she was overseas?" "Yeah, she told me at the hospital," Marc said quietly. Dre shook his head. "I can't believe that I came so close to losing her forever and didn't even know it. I don't know what I would've done if she didn't come home," Dre said, fighting back his tears.

"She also told me that she's still a virgin and has no plans of having sex before marriage. I cannot believe that she is still a virgin," Dre smiled. "I didn't think there was such a thing as a virgin over the age of 16 anymore," Rico laughed. "I love that though. Trust me Dre, I know from experience it's going to be hard, but it's worth it. "I never told y'all, but I didn't have sex with Kim until we were married." "No wonder she got pregnant so quick," Marc laughed.

"Whatever," Rico laughed. "Like I was saying, when we met she had just rededicated her life to God, and she would not give in. The difference is that Grayce is a virgin, Kim wasn't. I would love to be able to say I was the only man my wife had ever been with." Dre smiled, "I know."

"If I weren't so young and dumb we would probably be married with a couple of kids right now."

"True," Rico said, "but don't focus on what went wrong in the past. Focus on doing the right thing now. I felt the same way when I met Kim. She had heard so much about my past that she almost didn't give me a chance, but I thank God every day that she did. That woman has been the greatest blessing in my life."

CHAPTER 38

Marc enjoyed being home, but he had to admit that he missed seeing Dr. Drew every day. They'd exchanged a few friendly text messages, but that had been the extent of their conversation. Marc was going crazy sitting at home thinking about her, so he decided to get out of the house.

Since he'd been home, he hired a personal driver to transport him around so that he would not have to depend on his family and friends so much. Marc loved his independence. That was the hardest thing about this entire situation. Marc hated burdening others which is why he also hired a cook and personal nurse to attend to him daily.

Eric had been wanting Marc to come to meet his new girlfriend for weeks, so Marc called Eric and decided to have dinner with him, his new girlfriend and her children. Marc was a bit skeptical especially with her having children.

Eric was known to be a little soft when it came to women, and several women have deceived him in the past, but Marc wanted to give her the benefit of the doubt. He also wanted to make sure that his brother would not get hurt again.

When Marc arrived, he noticed a brand-new Mercedes in the driveway. He smiled to himself, look at my big brother doing it up. As Marc exited the vehicle with the assistance of his driver, Eric ran out to meet him. Marc had never seen his brother happier.

"Marc I am so glad you made it," Eric said smiling from ear to ear. "Me too, I like the new ride," Marc commented as they passed by the new car. "Thanks," Eric says, "I decided to treat myself to something nice."

"It's about time, you work hard, and you should enjoy the fruits of your labor. So where is the mystery woman?" Marc asked when they entered the house. "She's in the kitchen cooking dinner. She's a little nervous about meeting you, so be nice okay?"

Marc looked at his big brother, "when have I not been nice?" he asked. Eric looked a little embarrassed. "I know I have been a bad judge of character in the past, but she is different."

Marc could see the concern in his brother's eyes. "Look E, I trust your judgment, and if you say she is a good woman, I have to believe that." "Thanks," Eric said, relieved that his brother trusted him.

"So how have you been?" Eric asked. "I can't complain. It still takes some getting used to, but things are progressing well." "Man, it smells good in here," Marc said. "What is she cooking?" Eric smiled proudly. "She is originally from New Orleans, so she is fixing a bunch of her family favorites." "I think I love her already," Marc laughed. His stomach growled loudly making them both laugh.

CHAPTER 39

Marc and Michelle got along great, and he loved her children, Kiara and Kevin. They were very polite and mannerly. Marc felt a slight longing. He'd always wanted kids, and now he wasn't sure if that would ever be possible. The kids also loved Marc. They asked him questions about football all night.

Marc thought they would jump out of their seats when he told them that he'd take them to a game with him. During dinner, Marc noticed the looks and touches between Eric and Michelle. He was so happy that his big brother was in love. "So, Michelle tell me about yourself," Marc said after she returned from cleaning the kitchen and putting the kids to bed.

"Well, I am originally from New Orleans. We relocated to this area after Katrina. Unfortunately, I lost my mom and brother during the storm," Michelle said fighting back her tears. "My God Michelle, I am so sorry I didn't mean to bring up bad memories," Marc apologized. "You know, the pain never truly goes away, but every day it just gets easier. I'm sure you both can relate, Eric told me about your parents," she says rubbing Eric's hand.

Marc and Eric both nodded, each lost in their own thoughts. Michelle sighed. "I met their father a few weeks after I moved to town and at the time I thought he was a blessing. Things were great until his estranged wife, who I knew nothing about, called and decided that she wanted him back."

"She found out about the children and told him she didn't want him to have anything to do with them, so he offered to pay me to allow him to sign over his rights. I told him to sign over his rights and keep his money. I know that probably wasn't the smartest thing to do but at the time I just wanted to be rid of him. I don't understand how someone can create a life and completely abandon them."

"Since he left, or I should say since he threw us out, it's just been us until I met Eric. I didn't honestly know love until I met Eric," she said smiling at him. "I still cannot believe that it's only been a few weeks, I feel like I've known him all my life. The day we met I had just been laid off at work, and my apartment building burned to the ground, but even amid all of that, God still got the glory."

"Who would've thought that a dented car door would lead to this?" she laughed. Eric blushed and looked at Marc. "She was the woman whose car I dented," Eric explained. "Gotcha," Marc smiled, shaking his head.

Marc yawned, "I'm sorry I am still not sleeping well. Thank you so much for dinner Michelle, everything was delicious," Marc said stifling another yawn. "It was a pleasure meeting you too," Michelle said bending down to hug him and handing him the leftovers that she had packed for him.

"Thank you so much," Marc smiled. "Yeah E, you need to keep her," Marc laughed as Eric walked him to the car. "You really like her?" Eric asked. "I do, she seems nice, and her kids are adorable. I see what you see in her. Something about her reminds me of momma."

Eric nodded his head. "Thanks for coming over Marc. It's good seeing you up and about. Marc smiled, "it feels good to be up and about. I am going to watch the guys practice on Thursday, talk to Michelle and see if it would be okay for her and the kids to come along. Better yet, why don't we all go, make it a family outing and I can take you all to dinner after?"

"That sounds like a plan," Eric said excitedly. "I could use some time off." "Perfect, see you Thursday big bro, I love you." "I love you too Marc," Eric said as he watched his little brother roll up into the van by himself. Marc was so much stronger than Eric ever knew. There was no doubt in his mind that his brother would beat this. Eric turned and walked back into the house happier than he had

ever been in his life.

CHAPTER 40

Jess was enjoying the getaway with the boys. She decided to take them somewhere that wouldn't have any sad memories, so she took them to an indoor water park that had just opened. The boys were having a blast. She usually never got in the water, but she wanted to come out of her comfort zone for the boys' sake.

They were all having a great time, even LJ who was usually too cool for stuff like waterparks. Marc called earlier to invite them to a Kings practice game at the end of the week, so that thrilled them even more. Ever since the funeral, the rush of people in and out of the house had significantly diminished.

They were finally able to get back to their regular routine. It never really occurred to Jess how many things would change now that she was a widow. Jess shook her head. She still couldn't believe that she was a widow at 35. It just didn't seem right.

When she thought of widows, she thought of her grandmother and her great aunt. All the little things that she took for granted were now emphasized. Like the fact that Jayson always took the boys to get their haircuts. She would now have to do that.

Jess was sitting on the edge of the pool watching her boys pull her mom into the water when her cell phone started vibrating. Jess smiled when she saw Grayce's picture on the screen as she answered the phone, "Hey girl." "Hey Jess, what are you up to?" Grayce asked.

Girl, I am watching LJ try to teach my mom and the boys how to play ring toss." "That pic you sent me of them is too cute," Grayce smiled into the phone. "I thought you'd like it," Jess smiled. "It looks like they are getting bigger by the day," Grayce said.

"I know girl; I can't believe LJ will be 18 this year." "Girl me either," Grayce smiled. "He is so handsome." "I know," Jess said rolling her eyes. "I have seen a few of these little girls walking by trying to get his attention.

"Who does that remind you of?" Grayce laughed.

"I know. Jayson always had a flock of women around him, they all did." "Yep but he chose you," Grayce smiled. "That he did," Jess smiled into the phone. "God, I miss him so much" she sighed blinking back the tears. "How am I going to get through this?" Grayce wiped away her own tears as they began to fall.

"You will make it with God and with us by your side." Jess nodded her head. "You're right." "I love you girl," Jess smiled as she wiped away her tears. "I love you too." Jess sighed. "Okay, I need to change the subject, what's up with you?" "Well Dre and I are back together, and I'm torn between being happier than I've ever been and being terrified," Grayce said nervously.

"That is great news, why are you afraid?" Jess asked. "Jess, it was a huge difference when we both were still virgins. He didn't truly know what he was missing.

"Now that he's had more women than I care to know about, who's to say that he can restrain himself?" "Don't start thinking like that Grayce." "He may have dated other women, but they obviously didn't mean very much to him because we never met any of them and he was with us all the time."

"Girl trust me the what-ifs will eat you alive if you let them. I did that with Jayson, especially during my pregnancies. Knowing that he was at work around all of those attractive skinny women," she laughed. "I hated it, but I had to trust and believe that he loved and honored me." "Dre loves you. "I have never seen him look at anyone the way that he looks at you. I'm so happy for you both. It feels so good to have some good news."

"How are you holding up?" Grayce asked. Jess sighed. "I have my good and bad moments, but overall I am doing okay. How is Dre?" Jess asked. "Dre is Dre," Grayce smiled. "We should all get together for brunch this weekend. "I would love that, Grayce I am so glad that you are back in town. I've missed you so much."

"I missed you too Jess; I feel like I've missed out on so much. Before I know it, LJ will be going off to college and getting married." "Girl please don't remind me," Jess laughed. "I'm just glad to be back with my family," Grayce said. "Good because we are never letting you go again," Jess laughed.

CHAPTER 41

Tony still felt guilty about the crash. In his heart, he knew that he'd done nothing wrong, but his heart broke for Brian. In less than a year, he'd lost both of his parents. Tony visited him every day and made time to have dinner with him every evening. He hated the thought of any child suffering.

This little boy reminded him so much of his little brother Andrew. Tony walked into the room, and Brian's eyes lit up. He had gotten accustomed to seeing Tony every day. His grandmother who uses a wheelchair didn't get to visit him, but Tony made sure that Brian talked to her every day by phone and Tony also visited her daily to run errands for her and make sure that she was okay.

Tony couldn't control the joy he felt whenever he saw the young boy. He was such a sweet and happy little boy, and he did not deserve the abuse that he had suffered at the hands of his father. Tony was committed to doing

everything he could to change the boy's life.

CHAPTER 42

Marc was so excited about going to therapy. He would finally get a chance to see Dr. Drew again. Marc woke up early and took his time getting dressed. He wanted to look nice for her.

As soon as he entered the rehabilitation center, his eyes immediately found Dr. Drew. His heart started to beat a little faster as she smiled at him and started walking toward him.

Marc had the biggest crush on her, but in the back of his mind, he felt that she would never be interested in him. Who would want to date a cripple? He couldn't protect her or take care of her.

Marc rolled away before she reached him leaving her puzzled and slightly hurt. The session allowed Marc to get out a lot of his anger and frustration. Dr. Drew asked him to take it easy several times, but he just ignored her warnings and continued his strenuous workout.

Although it hurt her feelings, Imani didn't take it personally. She'd worked with several athletes during her career, and she had been on the receiving end of their anger more times than she could count. She had never felt any attraction to any other patient the way she did with Marc. There was something about him, and it hurts her to see him in so much pain.

Marc wore himself out to the point where he couldn't move. When he looked around, he and Dr. Drew were the only ones left in the room. "That was some workout," she smiled. Marc didn't know how to respond, so he just remained quiet.

Imani sighed softly. "I think you'd better do a few minutes of massage therapy. If not, you are going to be in a lot of pain tomorrow." Marc just nodded his head solemnly. He knew that God could heal him and even though he believed He would, the reality of the situation was starting to get the best of him.

"Things won't always be like this, I promise," she said as she walked away to call the massage therapist. That's easy for you to say, Marc thought to himself.

Marc had to admit that the massage therapy made him feel much better. He had just finished dressing when Imani returned to the room. "You look a lot better," she smiled. Marc couldn't help but smile back.

He cleared his throat. "I am so sorry about before. Some days I'm good and then other days, not so much." Dr. Drew sat down in the chair next to him. "That is to be expected, Mr. Jackson. This is going to be one of the hardest things that you have ever endure physically, but I truly believe in my heart that you will walk again and while you are conquering this mountain, God is showing you your true strength."

"In this line of work, I have encountered many people in your situation, but you have a bit of an advantage over them." "Really?" Mark asked. "What's that?" "You know the true power of God," she winked. "I saw you reading your bible and praying with your family. His strength will get you through this. I promise you that." Marc smiled. "So, you're a Christian?" he asked.

"I am," she proclaimed boldly. "I knew there was something different about you," Marc smiled. "Well, we've kept you long enough Mr. Jackson. "Do you have a ride home?" "I do," he said as she walked him out of the rehabilitation center.

Marc was just about to ask her to have dinner with him with this Idris Elba looking guy walked up and hugged her. "Oh my gosh when did you get here?" Imani asked jumping into his arms. "Well thank you, Dr. Drew. Have a good evening," Marc said rushing off.

Was that Marcus Jackson?" her baby brother asked as Marc rolled away before either of them could say anything else. "Yes, he's my new patient." "That is perfect, you think you can get me an autograph?" her brother

Manny asked. "He's had a really long day" she sighed. "I'll talk to him next week." Imani was a little taken aback by Marcus' abrupt departure.

"You're early," she smiled as they walked back into the hospital arm in arm. "I wanted to surprise you," Manny said hugging his big sister tightly. "I've missed you so much." "I've missed you too," she said, thinking about Marcus and praying that God granted him the strength that he'd need to get through this.

CHAPTER 43

Tony arrived at the hospital for his daily lunch with Brian when Pam, one of the nurses, stopped him to inform him that Brian's grandmother had passed away and someone from CPS would be picking him up once he was released.

"Does he know yet?" Tony asked "Yes, we just told him," Pam said as she shook her head. "My heart breaks for that little boy." Tony fought back his own tears as he nodded in agreement. "He's lost everyone close to him. It's just not fair."

Tony suddenly came up with a plan. "Pam, I know this is going to sound crazy but is there any way that you can keep him here for one more day? I want to see if I can get temporary guardianship over him." Pam beamed. "Tony you are just the sweetest man. We already informed them that he wouldn't be able to leave until tomorrow when we are done evaluating him, so please work fast". "I'm on it," Tony said, and he rushed in to talk to Brian.

Brian was laying in his bed with the saddest look on his face. "Hey little man," Tony said, rubbing his head. "I heard about your grandmother. Brian, I am sorry." "She's in heaven with my mommy now," he said quietly. Tony noticed that he did not mention his father. "I have to go to a foster home now," Brian said as the tears fell down his cherubic face.

"Actually, that's what I want to talk to you about. I want you to come live with me, would that be okay with you?" Tony asked. Brian sprang up from the bed. "For real Tony?" he asked. "Yep, for real," Tony smiled. "I can't make any promises, but I am going to work hard to make it happen okay?" "Okay, Tony." Nurse Pam walked in and smiled at the two of them. They need each other more than either of them truly realized. "Mrs. Pam, I might go live with Tony," Brian said excitedly. "I heard but for now I want you to eat all your food okay?" "Okay Mrs. Pam," he smiled as he started devouring his lunch.

"Okay little man I need to go talk to some people, I will be back by dinnertime okay?" "Okay Tony, I love you." Tony swallowed the lump in his throat. "I love you too little man," he choked as he rushed out of the hospital, blinking back the tears that threatened to fall.

Tony sat in the car as the memories of his little brother's death come flooding back to him. He cried as he thought about how the situation had affected his mother. She had virtually shut down because she blamed herself for her youngest son's death.

Theresa had been out drinking with friends the night before and returned home in the middle of the night. She was so drunk that she had not even closed the front door when she came in and passed out on the sofa. Unbeknownst to her, her two-year-old son Andrew woke up that morning and walked right out the door and into the street and was hit

and killed by a speeding car.

That moment changed his mother forever, she went

from drinking to doing drugs as a means of finding a way

to deal with her pain. She never stayed high enough to

shield herself from the pain that she felt. Tony had not seen

his mother in years, but he prayed every single day that she

was okay and that God watched over her and protected her.

CHAPTER 44

Dre was on his way to work when his phone started ringing. He didn't recognize the number, and everything in him told him to ignore the call, but he decided to answer anyway. "Hi Dre, it's Ashley," the soft voice said. Before he could say anything or hang up, she rushed to speak. "Dre I am so sorry, I know you asked me not to contact you, but I just wanted to let you know that my mom passed away this morning." "I'm really sorry to hear that Ashley."

As angry as he was with her for the incident at his home, the loss of a parent wasn't something that he'd wish on anyone. "Is there anything I can do?" Dre asked. "Actually yes, I am at the W hotel right now. Would you please meet me for coffee? I just really need someone to talk to right now."

Dre didn't think it was a good idea, but he did remember her mentioning once before that it was just she and her mom. "Sure," Dre said, against his better judgment.

"I will be there at noon." "Thank you, Dre, I really appreciate it." "Sure," he said. Dre decided to call Grayce to tell her of his conversation with Ashley and his plan to meet with her for coffee, but her phone kept going directly to her voicemail. True to his word, Dre met Ashley for coffee. As he expected, she was distraught over the loss of her mom. It brought back thoughts of Jayson and Dre did his best to gain control over his own emotions.

Grayce had just wrapped up a meeting with a friend at a restaurant across the street from the W hotel. As she and her friend began flagging down a taxi, she looked across the street and noticed Dre. She smiled as she tried to get his attention. Moments later, Ashley walked over to Dre and gave him a long hug.

Grayce could not believe her eyes, she felt sick to her stomach. Dre looked over to hand his key to the valet when he locked eyes with Grayce. He knew immediately from the look on her face that she thought something was going on between him and Ashley. Dre yelled her name just as her taxi pulled up. Dre tried to run across the street, but before he could reach her in time, Grayce jumped in the cab and asked the driver to pull off.

Dre ran to jump in his car to follow her when he realized that the valet had not returned with his car yet. "Are you okay?" her friend asked. Grayce closed her eyes, "No, no I'm not," she said, wiping away the tears that fell from her eyes.

Dre frantically tried calling Grayce but just kept receiving her voicemail. Ashley had been watching the entire scene and walked away feeling horrible. As much as she wanted Dre for herself, she cared about him and hated to see him hurt because of her. She was just about to go talk to him when he picked up the valet sign and threw it.

Ashley thought it would be best if she gave him time to calm down as she walked back into the hotel. This cannot be happening Dre thought as bystanders looked at

him like he'd lost his mind.

CHAPTER 45

Marc needed to get his mind off Dr. Drew. He didn't want to think about her. He jumped at the opportunity to get away when Cortez invited him to spend the day at the beach with the team. As they drove to the beach house in the Outer Banks, Marc was so glad that he decided to come.

It was beautiful and just what he needed. "So, you like it?" Cortez asked. "Man, what's not to like? This is beautiful. Thanks for inviting me. I really needed to get away," Marc said as he followed Cortez onto the deck before the others arrived. "So how have you been?" Cortez asked. Marc sighed as he shook his head.

"It depends on what day you ask me," Marc laughed bitterly. "I'm just basically living and doing my best to push through." "Marc, I am not going to sit here and pretend like I know how you feel because I don't, but I promise you that I will have your back. You are my brother, and I love you." "I love you too man," Marc said.

"How is rehab coming along?" Cortez asked making Marc groan. "Man, I don't even want to think about rehab. That's part of the reason why I needed to get away." "What's going on?" Cortez asked concerned. "I have the biggest crush on my doctor. She is beautiful and smart, and whenever I am around her I just feel like…I don't know." Cortez smiled. "So, what's the problem?"

"Man look at me Tez. She is a doctor. What is she going to want with a cripple?" "Marc, you have to stop talking like that. You have a lot to offer any woman." "The last time I was at rehab, I got the feeling that she liked me too and just when I was about to ask her out some guy walked up hugging and kissing on her. I knew right then that I would never be good enough for her; at least in the condition that I am in right now."

"Even if she offered to be with me I would refuse because I wouldn't want her settling." Cortez shook his head. "Marc, I have always been honest with you, and I am not going to change now. That's your ego talking. I know this can't be easy for you, but this is your current situation. You can sit around moping and throwing pity parties for yourself, or you can work as hard as you can to change it."

"You said yourself that the doc said it may or may not be permanent. That right there is a chance bro. I want you back out there on that field with me. Now are you going to sit here singing woe is me or are we going to make that happen?" Cortez asked. Marc shook his head.

"We are going to make it happen," Marc smiled. "Alright then, that's my boy talking. We can spend some time chilling and working out." "Sounds good," Marc said excitedly. "Thanks, Tez. This is the first time in a while that I have been excited about anything." "Me too," he said.

"Now let's go check out this beach." "Man, you know this wheelchair is not going to make it in the sand," Marc said.

Cortez smiled. "That's why I had my man trick out this beach chair. You have to see this thing man it looks like the Batmobile or something." As they made their way to the other end of the deck, sure enough, there was a wheelchair more than capable of tackling the sand.

"Man, this is nice," Marc said excitedly. Marc couldn't wait to try it out. Before Cortez could help him swap chairs, he was already maneuvering himself onto the new chair. Marc started it up and almost fell off. The new chair had also been tweaked with a new motor. It was a mix of a motorcycle and wheelchair in one. Marc was in love. "Bro I love this, thank you so much." "I thought you would," Cortez smiled.

CHAPTER 46

Drea couldn't believe that her relationship with Shawn was over. More importantly, she couldn't understand the way that Shawn was behaving. In the last few days, her car had been keyed, and her tires had been slashed.

She couldn't prove it, but she knew for sure that Shawn was behind it all. Drea had been thinking about buying a new car for some time. She decided that with her relationship ending it was the perfect time for a fresh start. Drea felt so good as she drove off the lot with her brand-new BMW.

She had to be honest with herself and admit that as much as she loved Shawn, she had not been happy for a very long time. She would never be content with someone who didn't believe in God. Her parents would be so disappointed if they knew that she was dating a married man although for some reason she suspected that they knew the truth.

Drea pulled into her designated parking space and exited the car as her neighbor headed to her car. "Hey Angie," Drea said startling her. "Hey girl, I didn't even know that was you. I love the new car." "Thank you so much. It was time for a change."

"I see, why you didn't tell me that you and Shawn were moving?" Angie asked. Drea looked at her inquisitively. "I'm not moving," Drea said knowing that something was wrong. Angie sensed it too.

"I'm sorry Drea; I saw Shawn with a moving truck earlier today. He was loading up the furniture and some boxes, and when I asked him about it, he told me that you guys were moving," Angie said closing her car door. Drea closed her eyes as her head began to throb. "Drea, what's wrong?" Angie asked concerned.

"I broke up with Shawn a few days ago, and he had been harassing me ever since. I can't prove it, but I know he slashed my tires and keyed my car which is one of the reasons why I purchased a new car. He refused to return my keys. I actually scheduled an appointment to have the locks changed tomorrow." "Drea, I'm sorry, I would've called you had I known. I feel horrible.

"Maybe we're overreacting for nothing," Angie said. "Let's go check to see what he took." Drea tried to put on a good face as she smiled and walked with Angie to her unit, but she already knew in her heart that Shawn had taken everything.

Sure, enough as soon as she opened the door, she saw that Shawn has taken everything including the appliances. He even ripped the cabinets off the wall and broke the light fixtures. Tears began to fall from her eyes as Angie hugged her. "I am sorry, girl. Let's call the police."

Drea thought about Tony. "Actually, I have a friend who's

a detective, I'll give him a call."

CHAPTER 47

Marc felt terrible about his last interaction with Imani and wanted to make it up to her. He ordered a beautiful bouquet of flowers to be sent to her. As Marc nervously entered the center, hoping that Dr. Drew had accepted his peace offering. As soon as he rounded the corner, he literally ran into Dr. Drew, causing her to fall on top of him.

It took Marc a second to process what happened before he began apologizing profusely. "Dr. Drew, I am sorry. Are you alright? Did I hurt you?" he asked concerned. Imani Drew laughed. "No, I am fine. My ego may be a little bruised, but I am physically fine. I'm known as a bit of a klutz," she explained. "Did I hurt you?" she asked looking him up and down.

"Dr. Drew I have had 300-pound men knock me unconscious. I think I can handle little ole you falling on me," he laughed shaking his head. "Little ole me huh?" I assure you I am much stronger than I look." "Sure," Marc laughed. Dr. Drew was suddenly serious. "Thank you so much for the beautiful flowers, they made my day."

"I'm glad," Marc smiled. "We have a little time before your appointment. I was going to take a walk; would you like to join me?" she asked. Marc tried his best to play it cool, but he had not been this happy in a very long time. They walked together in silence for a short while before she spoke. "I love your new chair," she smiled. "Me too," Marc smiled. "Let's sit here," she said leading him to a gazebo tucked away in the beautiful garden.

"This is my most favorite spot in the hospital." "I can see why," Marc said. "This is beautiful but don't tell anybody that I said that. I would lose my man-card," Marc laughed. Imani smiled, "You have my word. I will never tell anyone that big bad Marcus Jackson likes the pretty flowers," she laughed.

Marc couldn't help but laugh with her. "Dr. Drew I would like to apologize for my behavior at my last appointment. This situation has been...I don't even have a word to describe it. One minute I feel like I can conquer the world and the next I feel like curling up in a ball crying like a baby."

Marc looked away from her realizing that he'd never shown a vulnerable side of himself to any woman. He was suddenly very uncomfortable until she reached over and touched his hand. "Marcus listen first off you have nothing to apologize for. Your life changed dramatically in the blink of an eye because someone decided that he wanted to take the easy way out instead of getting a job. I truly cannot imagine how you feel. It hurts me to my heart when I see the men, women, and children that come in here due to senseless violence and the ones that make it to this point are the lucky ones."

"I don't say this very often, and I would probably get in a lot of trouble if anyone heard me say this, but I believe that you will walk again. With God and hard work, I know it can happen. I've seen it happen." Marc smiled. I spent a few days with a couple of my teammates at the beach, and it was just what I needed. I'm going to start training with them." "That is fantastic," Imani exclaimed, "but please make sure you don't overdo it." "I won't I promise." "Good," she smiled.

"I wanted to talk to you to let you know that I will be leaving Kingdom in two weeks." Marc was shocked. He didn't know what to say and remained quiet, so she just continued. "I love this hospital, but lately I've been feeling the need for a change, so a colleague and I are opening a new sports rehabilitation facility."

"Wow, congratulations, that's great!" "So, when this does new sports rehab center open?" "Next month but I want to take some time off because it's going to be a while before I get to do that again. I'm a little nervous about branching out on my own but I prayed long and hard, and I believe that this is my purpose."

"I'm excited for you this is a big step, but I have faith that you are going to surpass your own expectations. You are an amazing doctor." "Thank you so much," she smiled. "It means a lot coming from you. Before I forget, may I please have your autograph for my baby brother, Immanuel...Manny? I didn't get an opportunity to introduce you guys the last week when you were here," she said.

Marc burst out laughing. Imani looked at him questioningly. "I'm sorry," he said shaking his head. "I just...well it doesn't matter. Of course, I will give him an autograph. Actually, what are you doing this weekend?" "Well, he's only home from school on the weekends so we normally just have dinner and catch a movie."

"Well if you don't mind, my family and a few guys from the team are coming over this weekend, and I'd love for you and your brother to be my guests." "We wouldn't want to impose," she smiled. "How are you imposing, when I'm inviting you?" "Well, in that case, yes," she smiled. "He'd have a conniption if I said anything other than yes," she laughed.

"Did you just use the word conniption?" Marc laughed. "Man, I haven't heard that word since I was little." "Are you teasing me, Marcus Jackson?" "Of course not," he laughed. "I wouldn't want you to have a conniption." Imani playfully swatted him. "Okay, okay you win," he laughed. "I will text you my address." "Thank you so much," she beamed. "This is going to make his year." "Good, I'm looking forward to officially meeting him."

"Well, I guess we'd better get to it. I don't want anyone to think I am keeping you from your PT." "Well thank you so much for showing me this," Marc said as he followed her down the ramp. As she turned to thank him, she saw a look in his eyes that made her stomach flip. She

realized then that she was in trouble.

CHAPTER 48

Dre wanted to prove to Grayce that he did not sleep with Ashley. He sent flowers to her every day and called her at least 100 times before she finally answered, and when she did, she gave him some excuse about how she was wrong for asking more of him than he was able to deliver.

Dre was devastated. He could not lose her again. Grayce was the first and only woman that Dre had ever opened his heart up to and thinking that he'd hurt her once again was almost too much for him to bear. He decided to talk to the one woman that he knew would understand. Just as he picked up the phone to dial his mother's number the doorbell rang.

Dre jumped up a little faster than he should've and felt a sharp pain. As he continued to rush to the door, he opened it and was disappointed to see that it wasn't Grayce. "Hi Ma," he smiled sadly. "I was just about to call you."

"Are you okay?" she asked noticing the grimace on his face and the fact that he was walking much slower than he was yesterday. "Not really, Ma." "What's wrong?" Gloria asked. "Ma, I messed up," he said leaning his head back on the sofa. "What happened?"

Dre told her all the details about Ashley from her popping up at his home to the day outside the hotel. Gloria rubbed her son's back. "Dre I am so sorry that you are hurting but imagine how Grayce feels right now." "Ma, I have tried everything, but she just won't talk to me. I'm not the same person I was back then ma. I would never hurt her." "I know son, I know," Gloria said, trying her best to console her son. She hated to see him hurting, but she knew there is nothing that she could do to ease this pain. Dre was a grown man, and he'd have to find a way to handle this on his own.

CHAPTER 49

Tony was heading to lunch when his phone started ringing. "This is Detective Weems" he answered. "Hi Tony, it's Drea." "I am so sorry to bother you, but I have a bit of a situation," she said. "Where are you?" he asked before she could tell him what's wrong. "I'm at home," Drea said quietly. "Can you come by?" "Of course," Tony said. "Give me your address, and I'll be right here." Drea gave Tony directions to her condo while she and Angie waited outside.

Angie refused to leave until Tony arrived. Luckily, they don't have to wait long because Tony pulled up with his lights flashing in less than 10 minutes. He jumped out of the car and rushed over to Drea. "I got here as soon as I could," he said. "Is everything okay?" "Tony, I didn't mean for you to rush over. Shawn and I broke up, and I can't prove it, but I think he keyed my car and slashed my tires. He also told my neighbor that we were moving. He took everything out of my condo including the appliances and cabinets."

Tony shook his head. He knew when he saw Shawn that there was something about him that irked his spirit but now was not the time to dwell on that. Tony put his arm around Drea. "This too shall pass sweetie." Drea smiled sadly. "I know, it's just-I…I never saw this coming. It hurts."

Tony did his best to control his anger. He had always loved Drea, and the thought of someone hurting her made him angry. "Well let's go inside and make a report. Do you have insurance?" "I do," she said as they entered the empty condo. "Umm Tony please do me a huge favor." "Sure anything," he said. "Please don't tell anyone about this. I couldn't care less about Shawn, but the family has enough on their plate without worrying about me."

"Of course," Tony said. "But I think it would be a good idea if you found somewhere else to stay for the next couple of days and I would also suggest changing the locks and having someone stay with you when you do return."

"Wow, I didn't even think of that," Drea said closing her eyes and rubbing her temples.

"Let's make a list of everything for the report, and after that, I will change the locks for you." "Thank you so much," Drea said hugging Tony. "I am so sorry to bother you with this." Tony looked at Drea, "It's no bother at all. I would do anything for you, Drea. I hope you know that will never change." Drea smiled. "I do," she said quietly.

CHAPTER 50

An hour after they finished the report, Drea and Tony left the condo with the statement in hand. "So, if you are not busy right now we can go grab the new locks. I'd like to take care of it sooner rather than later." "That's fine," Drea said quietly. Tony looked over at her. It hurt him to see her in so much pain. He had never stopped loving Drea and had always hoped that they would eventually get back together.

He couldn't believe that her boyfriend could be so stupid. He had no idea what he had, but his loss could quite possibly be Tony's gain. A short distance away, Shawn sat in his car fuming. He had pulled up not even 5 minutes ago and planned to talk to Drea and give her one more chance to come to her senses.

When he looked up, he became irate. "I should've known," Shawn mumbled to himself. He was determined that he would not allow Drea or Tony to get away with playing him. Shawn pulled the handgun from under his seat and sat it on his lap as he began following them.

If he couldn't have her, nobody would. Ten minutes into the drive to Home Depot, Tony noticed that they were being followed. "Are you okay Tony?" Drea asked after noticing that he suddenly became quiet and kept looking in his rearview mirror? "I don't want you to turn around or anything, but I think we're being followed. What type of car does Shawn drive?" "It's a white Suburban," Drea said suddenly very nervous.

"Tony, I don't know what's gotten into him lately, but none of this is the behavior of the man I knew and loved." "Don't worry Drea everything will be alright," Tony said as he radioed for backup. Tony gave their current location, route, and description of Shawn's truck to the dispatcher. Luckily two minutes later one unit radioed to inform them that they were nearby and had Shawn's vehicle in sight.

Another car would be waiting for them at the Home Depot. As Tony pulled into the shopping center, he spotted the unmarked car and parked nearby. Before Shawn realized what was happening, several unmarked vehicles surrounded his truck with guns drawn.

"Drea stay here and do not exit the car under any circumstances okay?" he ordered. Drea was in such a state of shock she could only nod as Tony rushed out of the car. The officer removed Shawn from the truck and began reading him his rights as Tony walked over to them.

"We caught him just as he was about to exit the car with this in his hand," the officer said holding up the gun. "Is that right?" Tony said. Yes, and I ran his plates, turns out he also has several warrants out for his arrest for beating his pregnant wife."

"Mr. DeShawn Cooper is a repetitive woman beater," the officer said. Tony couldn't believe it. He walked over to Shawn. "So, DeShawn what were you planning on doing with this gun?" Tony asked looking down at him. "What do you think?" Shawn spat. "I'm hip to your little church boy act. I knew from the second I met you that you were trying to take my girl but trust and believe if I can't have her neither will you," Shawn laughed.

At that point, Tony was beyond angry, and he knew it was only the Holy Spirit keeping him from hitting Shawn. "DeShawn you will never, and I do mean ever see Drea again let alone harm her. You can talk big and bad while these cuffs are on you, but you and I know the truth. You are nothing but a cowardly little woman beater. What you can't hack it in a man's world, so you go home and beat on women to prove how much of a man you are?"

He could tell that his words were getting to Shawn, but he couldn't let up. "What kind of punk hits a pregnant woman? Trust and believe they are going to put you under the jailhouse when you're back in custody." Shawn started cursing Tony out as he walked back over to the officer. "Look I need to go; can you handle this for me?" Tony asked, handing him the report from the breaking and entering. "Yes sir," the young officer said.

Drea was still sitting in the same position that she was in when Tony exited the car. Tony didn't say anything initially; he knew that she needed a moment to process everything. He started the car and began to drive. "I know you must think I'm stupid," she said as they stopped at a red light. Tony looked over at her and turned her face toward him.

"Andrea, you are one of the smartest women I have ever met. I would never think you're stupid." "Did he admit to taking my stuff?" Drea asked. "Not exactly, we didn't get that far. He had a gun Drea," Tony said, allowing his words to sink in. She looked at him in utter shock.

"Oh my God," she cried. "I'm sorry I...," Tony was interrupted by the person behind him blowing the horn to alert him that the light had changed. Tony turned the corner and pulled into the first available parking space that he could find. "Drea, I am so sorry that you are going through this. You have been through so much lately. Drea leaned back on the headrest as the tears fell down her face.

"So, he was planning to kill me, to kill us," she said softly. "The man I loved for the last three years was going to kill me." Drea took a deep breath. "I cannot go back to that house. I won't go back to that house. I don't care about the locks. I want to sell it immediately." Drea knew that she was rambling, but she meant what she was saying. She didn't want any reminders of her relationship with Shawn.

CHAPTER 51

Dre fell deeper and deeper into depression since Grayce had been gone. He had not seen or heard from her since the day outside the hotel. Dre kept replaying that moment in his mind, wishing that he had made a different decision. He called her several times a day hoping that she would eventually pick up the phone or at the very least, send him a text message but that hope was in vain. Dre felt so alone; he went to his parents' home almost daily.

With Grayce's absence, his home felt emptier than ever. The guys all reached out to Dre, but he was inconsolable. He prayed that God would allow the truth to prevail and Grayce would come back to him. He was more determined than ever that if Grayce ever forgave him, he would never let anything or anyone other than God to come before her. The thought that he had broken her heart once again was tearing him apart.

Ashley left several messages apologizing and even offered to tell Grayce the truth. Dre didn't blame her, but he didn't want to hear from her, and she was the last person in the world that he wanted to talk to Grayce. She was just a reminder of his incredible loss.

CHAPTER 52

Eric was exhausted. He was so tired of working late every night, but this company was his baby, and there were specific tasks he just didn't feel comfortable delegating to anyone else. He missed Michelle and the kids so much. They spent almost every day together. He helped her and her children move into an apartment nearby, so they were able to have breakfast together every morning and dinner together every evening.

For once Eric felt like he had a family of his very own. She always made sure to have a hot plate on the table waiting for him when he came over, and he loved having the kids around. There were several times that they called him daddy. Those moments made Eric's heart swell. He couldn't love them more if they were his very own.

Things were really beginning to get serious, but Eric was scared. He'd been hurt several times in the past, and he didn't want to get his heart broken again although he knew it is too late for that. Eric was already in love with

Michelle and would be devastated if she left him. He could

not remember what his life was like before she and the kids

arrived.

CHAPTER 53

After much convincing by Tony, Drea finally informed her family of everything that had been going on with Shawn. She even told them about him being married, and just as she suspected, her parents had already suspected as much. She spoke to her realtor the day after the incident, had the unit repaired, cleaned and put her condo on the market immediately.

Thankfully, Angie was extremely detail oriented and gave the police enough information to find the moving truck. Shawn had not had time to unload the moving truck, so all her items were still on the truck, including the appliances.

Over the last few days, Drea spent more and more time with Tony. She didn't realize just how much she had missed him. Before they started dating, they were the best of friends, and she missed her best friend. Tony felt the exact same way.

He was granted temporary guardianship over Brian, and he loved every second of it. When Tony told Senior and Gloria what he was doing, they volunteered to babysit for him while he worked. They didn't have any grandchildren and loved having a child in the house again, and Brian loved them dearly.

Brian missed his grandmother a lot, but Senior and Gloria made things more comfortable for him. They spoiled him terribly and loved on him every single second. Tony and Brian had dinner with them every evening before heading home. Senior and Gloria also love having Tony around again. They were both secretly hoping that he and Drea would get back together.

One evening after dinner Senior, Tony and Brian were sitting on the front porch having dessert when Brian looked at Tony and asked if he was going to be his new daddy. Tony looked at Senior, unsure how to answer the question.

Holy Spirit help me he thought before he answered.
"I know that I can never take the place of your father, but
yes, I would love to be your dad. Do you want me to be
your dad?" Tony asked. Tony didn't realize until that very
moment just how much he did want to be Brian's dad.

Brian looked up at Tony and smiled so hard that
Tony's heart melted. "Yep you are already my daddy
anyway, but the lady asked me if I wanted you to be my
daddy and I said yes."

Gloria and Drea were walking onto the porch during
the exchange between the two and both were struggling to
fight back their tears. Brian ran over to them both. "Don't
worry, you can be my grandmommy and my mommy," he
said catching them all off guard.

Senior called him over and sat him on his knee.
"Why do you want Drea to be your mommy?" he asked.
Brian looked up as if he was thinking hard and said,
"Because she's pretty and she treats me nice, and my daddy

loves her." Tony almost choked on his ice cream. Senior couldn't help but laugh.

"How do you know that he loves her?" Senior asked. "Because Pop-Pop," he sighed. "He looks at her the same way you look at mama." Tony and Drea stared at each other. "Who wants more ice cream?" Senior asked taking the excited little boy by the hand as he led him back in the house.

Gloria kissed her daughter's cheek and smiled at Tony as she followed them inside. "Well that was embarrassing," Tony said smiling at Drea. "I'm sorry," he apologized. "I know you have a lot going on right now and with everything with Shawn, I promise you that last thing I want to do come on to you when you are vulnerable." "I know that," Drea smiled.

"I would be lying if I said I hadn't noticed the looks though but right now the last thing on my mind is a relationship. I have been wondering more and more lately what would've happened if we had stayed together. If we'd be married or how many children we'd have," Drea sighed.

"Drea I promise you I would never pressure you, but I want you to know that want those things with you; marriage and children. I always have. I believe that you are meant to be my wife, but I will not pressure you just know that I am here waiting for however long it takes because I know in my heart that you are worth it. I love you, Drea". "I know," Drea smiled with tears in her eyes. "I could tell from the moment I saw you the night." Drea swallowed the lump in her throat.

She couldn't bear to finish her sentence. The pain and reality of the situation were still too fresh in her mind. "Shawn saw it too," she continued. "Which was why he got upset. That first night we started to argue on the way to the hospital. I wasn't happy for a very long time, and I think I just stayed because I felt that I have invested so much time and honestly, I didn't know how to leave."

"I'm not hurt because of how much I loved him. I'm hurt because I never expected someone who claimed to love me to do this. I hear stories about things like this happening all the time from co-workers and clients, but I never expected to be in this situation. Everything happens for a reason though; at least that's what they say," Drea smiled sadly.

"For now, I am just happy to be back home with my family and surround by people who love and care for me, and that includes you Tony," she smiled as she watched him blush.

CHAPTER 54

"I think I ate too fast," Jess said as she eased down into the chair at the restaurant. "I don't think she's pleased." "Just sit back and relax ma, and I'll get you some water," LJ said. "Mommy are you alright?" Amir asked concerned. "Yes, I'm fine baby. I think I just ate a little too much. I'm fine baby, go ahead and finish eating." "I'll just stay with you," he responded while rubbing his mother's belly.

Jess suddenly became alarmed. "Sweetie, can you get LJ, please? I think your sister wants to meet us today." Amir rushed over to LJ while Jess pulled out her cell phone. Grayce answered on the second ring. "Is it time?" she asked excitedly. "How in the world did you know?" Jess laughed. "I've had this feeling all day that today was going to be the day."

"Where are you, do you need me to come and get you?" "No, I'm at the restaurant with LJ and the boys.

Would you mind calling everyone for me and just meeting me at the hospital?" "Of course," Grayce said. "I am ecstatic." "Me too," Jess said as LJ returned to the table looking like he'd seen a ghost. "What do you need me to do ma?"

"Well for starters I need you to calm down baby," Jess smiled. "Relax LJ, this isn't my first rodeo," Jess laughed. LJ could be so cute sometimes she thought to herself. "Grayce and everyone will meet us at the hospital, but first we need to get the boys to Senior and Gloria's house." "Mommy I want to stay with you the younger boys pleaded.

"I know sweetie, but children are not allowed in the delivery room. I promise you that as soon as your sister arrives, I'll call Gammy and Papa (the boys' nicknames for Gloria and Senior) and have them bring you and the boys over okay?" "Okay," they say pitifully.

Drea called everyone to let them know that Jess was in labor. Everyone planned to be there for Jess to support her in Jayson's absence. This was a bittersweet moment for them all as the reality that Jayson would never get to see his daughter sunk in.

Dre rushed out of the house as soon as Drea called him. He had agreed to stand in a Jess' birthing coach to welcome his goddaughter into the world. Dre knew that Grayce would also be in the room with them. He was nervous and excited to see her at the same time.

Grayce smiled as she and Jess entered the labor and ward and saw Senior and Gloria, Rico and Kim, Marc, Eric and Dre waiting for she and Grayce to arrive. Jess cried tears of joy and sadness as she thanked God for the support shown by every person in the room.

After Senior prayed over her and her unborn daughter, Grayce and Dre followed the nurses as they ushered her to the delivery room. Jess could feel the tension in the air as Grayce avoided Dre every chance she could.

Jess prayed that Grayce and Dre would be able to resolve

their issue and see that they belonged together.

Four hours later Jess was surrounded by her family

and friends, holding her beautiful baby girl, Jayda Ashleigh

McCall. She was the spitting image of Jayson. Jayda even

shared the same birthmark on her thigh as her father. Jess

felt Jayson's presence as she never had before as she held

their beautiful daughter.

CHAPTER 55

Marcus couldn't wait for the weekend. He had a service come to clean his house from top to bottom, and he even hired Michelle to come up with a menu and do all the cooking. She was thrilled, she loved having something to do. Instead of having a sit-down dinner, they decide to develop a menu where everything could be served buffet style which would be a lot less formal.

Marc once overheard Imani mention that she loved seafood, so Michelle came up with a few ideas that they both thought she'd enjoy. Marcus and Dr. Drew had been texting throughout the week. He sent her a good morning text every day and always checked in with her in the evening asking about her day. Marc knew that he was already gone. Wheelchair or no wheelchair, he had never felt this way about any woman, and if he didn't tell her soon, he was going to go crazy.

Imani couldn't remember a time when she'd been more nervous. She was so excited about seeing Marcus outside of the hospital, but she also had to remember that she could not allow her attraction to him to interfere with her professional relationship with him.

Imani considered texting Marc several times to cancel, but her brother was excited, and she didn't want to disappoint him. He had been talking about meeting Marcus all week. Imani has been getting dressed for the last hour and changed her outfit three times already. She was just about to change clothes once again when the doorbell rang.

She looked out the window and noticed a black Mercedes with tinted windows outside. Imani cautiously opened the door. "Hi, may I help you?" she asked. "Good evening Dr. Drew, my name is Thomas, and I will be your driver this evening courtesy of Mr. Marcus Jackson."

Imani smiled. She needed to be careful. "Umm..okay," she responded. "I am not quite finished getting dressed, could you give me a few moments?"

"Absolutely ma'am, take as long as you need," Thomas smiled before returning to the car.

"Who was that?" Manny asked. "Marcus sent a car to pick us up." "What?!" Manny exclaimed, running over to look out the window. "Sis I can get used to this," he said finally focusing on his sister. "Wow, you look beautiful." "Really?" she asked. "Do you think it's too much?" "Not at all Mani," he said using his nickname for her. "You look beautiful." "Thank you," she sighed. "You like him, don't you? Manny asked.

"Well it doesn't matter if I do or I don't. Marcus Jackson is my patient, and I will never cross that line." "I understand," he said hugging his sister. "But he won't be your patient for much longer," he said as he grabbed her hand and they headed for the door.

CHAPTER 56

Dre tossed and turned all night. All he kept thinking about was Marc's party. He wasn't sure if Grayce would be there or not, but he desperately needed to talk to her. Dre tried his best to get Grayce to speak with him, but nothing worked.

Dre felt helpless. He decided to call Jess. "Hey Dre," Jess said answering the phone. "How are you?" "Not good Jess to be honest. "How are my godchildren?" Dre smiled. "They are absolutely perfect," Jess smiled. "Why do you sound so down?" Jess asked. "Have you talked to Grayce?" Dre asked. "I have," Jess said quietly.

"Jess you know me, I would never have her come back to my life to hurt her. This was all just a big misunderstanding. I really need her to talk to me and let me explain." "Dre, I love you both and you know I want nothing more than to see you both happy, but I really don't want to get in the middle of this."

"Jess please, this is killing me," Dre cried. "The only thing that comes close to this pain is losing Jay…" Dre stopped himself when he thought about what he was about to say. "I'm sorry Jess," he apologized. Jess smiled as her eyes misted. "Dre you have nothing to apologize for. I know how much you loved him. You have known him longer than I have. This is going to be a process for all of us," she said, softly rubbing her daughter's head.

Dre nodded his head and closed his eyes. Jess felt awful for him. "Sweetie look I will see what I can do to get her to talk to you, but I can't make any promises. Are you coming to Marc's party tonight?" "Yes, I don't really feel up to it, but I am going to support him." "Good, Grayce and I will be there as well." "Thank you so much, Jess," he sighed.

"I'm so sorry to drag you into this, I just don't know what else to do. I love Grayce so much." "I know that and so does she, but she needs to feel like you are all in." "I really am Jess. I don't want anyone but her." "Good, I will pray that things work out for you two tonight," Jess said. "Can I come to get the boys one day this week?" he asked. "Of course," Jess smiled. "I think they would love that." "Good, I feel like I have been the worst godfather lately." "Dre you've had a lot on your mind, and you are still recovering yourself, don't try to be Superman. They understand." "Okay, well I will see you tonight Jess, I love you." "I love you too sweetie."

Jess hung up the phone as she looked over at Grayce as she wiped away the tears running down her face. "He's really hurting Grayce. It's none of my business, but I think you should at least hear him out. Dre is not the same man he was back then. I saw it from the moment he looked into your eyes." "I'm afraid Jess," Grayce cried. "I know baby, but fear is of the enemy. Don't let fear stop your destiny," Jess said hugging her best friend. "Now come on, let's find you something that'll make Dre's mouth drop to

the floor," Jess laughed.

CHAPTER 57

Marc couldn't wait until everyone arrived, but he was especially excited for one guest in particular. He checked his watch every couple of minutes and sent Thomas several text messages. Marc wanted everything to go perfectly tonight. Michelle was busy putting the final details on dinner. "Bro if you check that watch one more time," Eric laughed, walking out of the kitchen.

"I know man, I'm just nervous." "For what, we do this all the time, and you know my girl can burn." "Oh, I don't have any worries there and thank you so much for allowing her to help me out. I don't know what I would've done. I just need everything to be perfect tonight. I invited Dr. Drew," Marc said. "Ahhh, so that explains everything," Eric laughed. "Yep, I'm gone E," Marc sighed.

"I really like her and its crazy because one minute it's the best feeling in the world and the next I am terrified." "Why?" Eric asked. Marc shook his head. "Look at me E; realistically what beautiful, accomplished woman is going to want a man in a wheelchair?"

Eric didn't miss a beat before responding, "One who realizes a man isn't defined by the fact that he currently can't stand on his own two legs. Marc, I am not making light of your situation at all. I pray every day that God heals you totally and restores you, and I believe that He will. As a matter of fact, I pray that he makes you better than before."

Eric shook his head laughing. "If nothing else, this situation has made me pray more than I ever have in my entire life." Marc nodded his head. "You and me both. God will grab your attention one way or another." "Yes, He will," Eric laughed.

"So how do I look?" Marc asked. Eric looked Marc up and down. "Well you're not my type, but I guess you're okay." Before Eric could process what was happening Marc had him in a headlock. Michelle walked out of the kitchen drying her hands on her apron. "I can't leave you two alone for a minute. You are just as bad as the children."

Eric laughed when he finally broke free. "Man, that physical therapy is definitely working, but I decided to let you win." Marc laughed. "Sure big brother, whatever you say." "Michelle thank you so much for your help today. I really appreciate everything you've done."

"No problem at all Marcus, it has been my pleasure. Cooking is my passion. I used to dream of opening my own restaurant." "Me too," Marc said. "Maybe that's something we can do together," he suggested. "I didn't tell him anything I promise," Eric laughed. "What did I miss?" Marc asked. "Since we've met she's been telling me how she wants to open her own restaurant." "Are you serious?" Marc asked.

"I've wanted this for so long." "Well it's a deal then," Marc said. "I don't know anything about cooking, so I think it's only fair that we split the profits 60/40. I'll call my realtor on Monday so we can start scouting locations. Then we'll need to think of a name," Marc added. "Ooohh and I have some new recipes I've been wanting to try," Michelle said excitedly.

"Maybe we can have a little get together once a month to try them out on everyone, Marc suggested. "Oh my gosh, Marc I don't know what to say. Thank you so much," she said hugging him tightly. "God works in mysterious ways," Eric said. "Yes, He does," she said, looking at Eric. "I love you so much. If it weren't for you seeing past my circumstances, none of this would have been possible, and I wouldn't be completely in love with one of the greatest men in this world. You saved me." Eric held her close and kissed her softly. "We saved each other." Marc smiled as he left to give them some privacy.

CHAPTER 58

People finally started arriving, and Marc was more nervous than he was before. Michelle was placing a tray of hors-d'oeuvres on the table when she noticed Marc checking out his outfit for the hundredth time. She smiled and walked over to him and lightly touched his shoulder.

"Marc you look amazing. You could wear dirty sweats and a holey tee shirt, and you'd still be fine as wine," she teased. "Thank you so much, Michelle," Marc said laughing. "For everything. People have been raving about the food. I am so happy that we're starting a business together. "Me too," Michelle said smiling.

"Mr. Jackson, I think you have an admirer," she said. As Marc turned around, he locked eyes with Dr. Drew. He was speechless. "Hello Mr. Jackson, thank you so much for sending the car. That was very sweet of you." "No problem at all," Marc responded, but since you're a guest in my home, please call me Marc."

Imani smiled. "In that case, please call me Imani."

Marc smiled back. "So, this is your LITTLE brother?"
Marc asked looking at the tall young man standing beside
her. "Yes, I'm sorry this is my brother Manny." Manny
could not believe he was standing in the home of one of his
biggest idols. "I am your biggest fan, I've watched every
game you've ever played. College and professional. Man,
my boys are not going to believe this," he said, not trying to
control his excitement at all.

Imani just shook her head laughing. "Manny please
do not embarrass me." Manny realized that he must sound
like a grade-school groupie. "I'm sorry man. I just got
excited." "No need to apologize. You should've seen me
when I met Joe Montana," Marc said. "I thought I was
about to pass out. I was smiling so hard my cheeks hurt for
two days."

Marc turned his attention back to Imani. "You look
beautiful Imani." "Thank you, and you look very nice

also," she blushed. "You have a beautiful home," Imani

said looking around and trying to change the subject.

"Thank you, I'll have to give you the tour before you

leave." "I'd like that," she said. "Good, come on I'd like to

introduce you both."

CHAPTER 59

Dre sat in front of Marc's house for almost an hour. He watched Grayce and Jess arrive 20 minutes ago, but he could not control his nerves enough to get out of the car. Dre finally took a deep breath before walking to the door. Dre was just about to turn around when the front door opened.

"Hey Dre," Eric said hugging his cousin. "I was wondering if you were going to come." "Me too," Dre said. "I'm sorry I haven't returned any of your calls. There has been a lot going on," Dre sighed. "I heard," Eric said. "If you need to talk you know I'm here right." "I know Eric," Dre said. "Grayce and Jess just arrived. They are around here somewhere," Eric said as he spotted Michelle talking to Cortez.

"Come on, I want you to meet my baby." Dre couldn't help but laugh. Dre had never seen his cousin so happy. "Excuse me, Baby," Eric interrupted, "This is my cousin/brother Dre. Dre this is Michelle." "Hello Michelle, it's very nice to meet you. I've heard a lot of great things about you." "Thank you so much, it's nice to meet you too," she said shaking his hand.

"Everything looks great," Dre said looking at the buffet table. "Well on that note I need to get back to the kitchen. I have something that I need to get out of the oven," Michelle said. "Of course," Dre said. "Hey D, I'm going to go help her out," Eric said. "Okay bro, I'll talk to you later," Dre said. making his way to the buffet table.

Dre didn't realize how hungry he was when he smelled the food. Everything looked so good; Dre didn't know what to try first. He was reaching for a plate when Michelle and Eric exited the kitchen.

"Michelle, did you really make all of this?" Dre asked. "Yes," she smiled shyly. "I love to cook." "Everything looks amazing." Dre popped the mini crab cake in his mouth and closed his eyes as he enjoyed the delicious appetizer.

"You really cooked this?" Dre asked again. "Yes," she laughed. "Oh man, you better keep her," Dre laughed. "I plan on doing just that," Eric said with a wink. Dre loaded his plate up before making his rounds. He still hadn't seen Grayce yet, but he thought of that as a blessing in disguise.

He was nervous. As he turned the corner, he saw Marc talking to a woman who looked very familiar to him. "Hey Dre, what took you so long?" Marc asked. "I was beginning to wonder if you were still coming." "I had some stuff to deal with, but this is a nice turnout," Dre said looking around. "Michelle did an amazing job with this food," Dre said. "I know bro. We're going to partner up and open a restaurant."

"Really?" Dre and Imani asked at the same time. "Yep and I'm sorry Dre, you remember Dr. Drew from the hospital?" "I knew you looked familiar for a reason, I do remember, nice to see you again Doc." "You too," Imani smiled. "It's good to see you up and around. Thank you," Dre smiled. "How's our boy doing?" Dre asked.

"He's getting better and better every day," Imani smiled. "That's great," Dre said excitedly. "I'm so happy that you both came out of this okay." "So are we," Dre said. "If you two will excuse me, I need to find Grayce." "I just saw her go out by the pool," Marc said. "Good luck." "Okay, thanks. "Nice to see you again Dr. Drew," Dre said, shaking her hand. "Please call me Imani." "Imani…" Dre smiled.

CHAPTER 59

Dre took a deep breath before walking toward the patio door, but he made a mental note to talk to Marc about the doc. As he stepped out onto the patio, he couldn't help but think how beautiful Grayce looked. She had always been beautiful, but now there was this glow about her.

Her back was to him so she could not see him as he approached her, but as soon as he got within arm's reach, she quietly said, "Hello Dre." "How did you know it was me?" Dre asked, his throat suddenly dry. "I felt you," she said turning around, not trying to hide or wipe away the tears that fell from her eyes.

Dre held his head down. To know that he was the cause of her pain hurt him to his core. He blinked back his own tears and cleared his throat. "May I speak to you for a moment?" "Sure," she sighed. It was the perfect spring evening. The sun was just beginning to set, and the scene looked like something out of a movie.

Dre led her to the dining table and sat across from her. "Grayce, I need to start by apologizing for giving you any cause whatsoever to doubt me. Grayce, I love you, and I promise you that I would never do anything to ruin what we are rebuilding. I made a foolish decision, but I give you my word that nothing happened."

"Ashley called me that morning and told me that her mom passed away. She'd been battling cancer for a few years. I felt sorry for her because it was just the two of them. Even as my better judgment advised me not to do so, I met her at the restaurant in the hotel where she was staying, and we had lunch. I called your cell phone twice, but it went straight to voicemail."

"In hindsight, I probably should've left you a message. You don't know how many times I beat myself up because I didn't. I did not go to her room. I give you my word on that, and you know that I have never ever lied to you. She apologized for popping up unannounced and other than that the conversation was solely about her mother."

Grayce, I know that I messed up in the past, but I promise you that I am not that person anymore. There is not a woman on this earth that would make me risk what I have with you. You are everything to me, Grayce." Dre knelt before her as tears flowed from his eyes.

"Grayce Karen McDaniels, I love you more than I ever thought it was possible to love anyone. If you do me the honor of being my wife, I promise that I will love and cherish you every second of every day for the rest of my life in this world and the word to come. Dre opened the small box as Grayce gasped in surprise when she saw the massive diamond ring. Grayce nodded her head yes as the tears continue to flow down her face. They both held each other and cried together as the sunset.

CHAPTER 60

Dre and Grayce could not contain their happiness. As soon as they returned to the party holding hands, Jess spotted the ring immediately. "Oh, my gosh…congratulations! I can't believe it. My baby is getting married." Everyone cheered for them especially Rico who had arrived while they were on the patio.

"That's my man," Rico smiled as he walked over and hugged Grayce and Dre. "Now we gotta get these other three on board," Rico laughed, referring to Marcus, Eric, and Tony. Everyone made their way over to congratulate Dre and Grayce, and Marc's party immediately turned into an impromptu engagement celebration for Dre and Grayce.

Jess did not waste any time talking about wedding dates and dresses. Dre watched Grayce as she and the other women discussed wedding ideas. This was where he belonged.

CHAPTER 61

Dre couldn't wait to pick his godsons up for the game. He had missed them so much. As soon as he pulled up, all four of them rush out to greet him and tackled him to the ground like they always did. Dre loved being their godfather. He always said that he never wanted kids, but ever since Grayce's returned, he totally changed his viewpoint.

They've been talking a lot about children recently, and they both wanted to start a family soon. "Congrats Uncle D," LJ said hugging Dre. "Thank you, I can't wait. I also wanted to ask you if you would be my best man." "Of course, Uncle D," LJ smiled. "I'm happy that you are marrying Auntie," LJ said as he made sure his little brothers were strapped into their booster seats.

Dre smiled. "Me too." "Jayson would be so proud of the man you have become, LJ." LJ fought back the tears as he looked out the window. "How have you been doing with everything?" "I'm good," LJ said quietly. "Well you know if you ever need to talk, I'm right here." "LJ smiled at his uncle, "I know Uncle D. I just hate watching Ma go through this."

"She cries herself to sleep every night. I just wish things could go back to the way that they were." "I do too," Dre said. "I miss your father every single day." "Uncle D can I ask you a question?" "Of course," Dre said. "Do you think my dad knew something was about to happen to him?" LJ asked. "What do you mean?" Dre asked.

"Well a couple of nights before everything happened we were talking about college and life, and he said if something ever happened to him he wanted Ma to get married again and for me to be happy for her and support her. I keep replaying it over and over, and I'm just wondering why he would say that and two days later...".

Dre fought back his own tears. "Honestly LJ I don't know. All I do know is that your dad loved you, your brothers and your mother. Don't focus on anything else right now. We all miss your dad. I can't tell you how many nights I still cry myself to sleep. I do know that he loved your mother and would want her to be happy if that time ever came around. "I just miss him," Little Jay said quietly. "I know man, I know," Dre said as they rode in the car crying together.

CHAPTER 62

Grayce and Jess decided to play matchmaker with Tony and Drea, and Marcus and Imani. They planned a bonfire at the beach. Dre purchased a beach house on the outskirts of Virginia Beach a couple of months before the shooting, and this was the perfect time for all of them to get away.

Grayce suggested that Jess make the calls because none of them would say no to her. They all enjoyed the ride to Virginia Beach. Instead of everyone driving separately, Dre rented a minibus so that they could all ride together. Senior and Gloria happily agreed to babysit the children while they are away. They couldn't wait to become grandparents.

The gang arrived at the beach shortly before noon. Marc was so excited because, after much hesitation, Imani and Manny agreed to join them. Since the party, Marc and

Imani had gotten a lot closer. Marc could tell that she was still a bit guarded, but he felt that there was a definite connection between them.

He decided that he would pursue a relationship with her regardless of the outcome. He didn't want to have any regrets about what could've happened. Everyone loved Imani and Manny, and they loved the tight-knit group. They fit in perfectly.

Dre, Tony, Eric, and Rico had just finished setting up for the bonfire when Marc suggested that they go swimming before lunch. They all looked at Marc like he had lost his mind. "What?" he asked when he noticed that no one was moving. Everyone looked from Marc to Imani to Marc and back to Imani. She smiled and explained that part of Marc's therapy involved swimming. "He's actually a great swimmer and in even better shape than he was in before. We'll just need some help getting him into the water."

Eric rushed over and hugged his brother. "I'm good E, but you need to hurry up and change because I'm in the water in 5 minutes with or without y'all." They all headed off to get dressed, leaving Marc and Manny alone on the deck. "I love the beach," Manny said. "Me too," Marc smiled as he took off his tee shirt. "I could live at the beach," Marc said. "My sister loves the beach too, she said the water soothes her."

"Marc, may I ask you a personal question?" Manny asked. "Sure," Marc said turning to look at him. "Do you really care about my sister as much as I think you do?" Marc smiled. "Is it that obvious?" "Yeah pretty much," Manny laughed. "I really do," Marc sighed. "I care a lot about your sister, more than I have ever cared about any woman I've ever dated." "Okay," Manny nodded.

"Are you okay with that?" Marc asked. "Absolutely, I really like you, and I think you're a good guy. I just don't want my sister to have her heart broken again. I have never seen her so happy, not even when she was with her ex-fiancé. He hurt her really bad, and she's finally in a good place now, and I just want it to stay that way."

"Manny, I have never really had a girlfriend. To be honest, my life has always been about two things: my family and football. I mean I dated women here and there, but I have never had a serious relationship. When I met your sister, there was this instant connection that I couldn't explain. I'm actually a little nervous saying it out loud especially when we've never even been on a real date, but I feel like I am falling in love with her."

"She is one of the most amazing women I have ever met. I want to date her, but I am not comfortable doing that right now. I want to be the perfect man for her, and right now she deserves more than a man who uses a wheelchair. "I know how you feel," Manny said. "Well not exactly how you feel, but I can't have kids. I have always wondered what woman would want to be with a man who cannot give her children, but I have to trust and believe that God has a plan for my life that's bigger than whether or not I can father a child."

"Marc, I know she'd hurt me if she heard me say this, but I know my sister, and she loves you. I can see it in her eyes. I think her biggest issue is the fact that you are her patient. She will never cross that line no matter how much she likes you. "So, you think I have a shot?" Marc asked. "I know you do but don't tell her I told you that." "My lips are sealed," Marc laughed.

"What are you two up to over here?" Imani asked, walking up to them. "Not much," Marc said winking at Manny. "Yep just relaxing and enjoying the view," Manny smiled. Imani looked between the two of them and shook her head.

Kim walked out onto the deck, "Y'all know I am way too big to be out there. I am going to stay right over by the pool" Kim laughed. "Good, we can waddle on over to the pool together," Jess laughed. "I need to start working out to get this baby weight off."

"Look at them, they are bigger children than the boys," Jess said looking over at the guys. They were dunking and splashing each other in the ocean. "Speaking of children, we should bring the boys back next weekend," Drea chimed in. "Brian has never been to the beach before. It's so sad that he has been deprived of so much." "That baby has been through hell," Jess said, shaking her head.

"Yes, he has," Kim agreed. "He and the boys hit it off immediately," Jess smiled. "Jackson, Aaron and Amir are already asking when he can come over and spend the night." "How is he adjusting to everything?" Jess asked. "You would never know that Tony was not his father. They are two peas in a pod." "That is so sweet," Kim said.

"Sooooo…speaking of Tony, is he seeing anyone?" Jess asked not so subtlety. "Well, that is somewhat of a long story," Drea sighed. "What's a long story?" Grayce asked as she and Imani walked over to the pool. "Tonyyyy and Dreaaaaa," Kim teased. "Stop it," Drea blushed. "Well after everything with Shawn we had a long talk, and he told me that he was engaged a year ago, but it didn't feel right, so he broke it off.

He then told me that he never stopped loving me and would wait as long as he had to wait to be together again." "Awwww that is so sweet," Grayce said. "You two are cute together," Imani added. "Speaking of cute missy. I see you and my cousin are getting pretty close," Drea said, directing the attention to Imani.

It was now Imani's turn to start blushing. "I'm his doctor. He doesn't look at me like that and besides it goes against the code of ethics." "Well, you are not his doctor anymore so do you like him?" Drea asked, happy to have the focus on someone other than she and Tony. Imani began stuttering.

"Yeah, how does it feel when the shoe is on the other foot," Drea laughed. "Touché," Imani smiled, "touché." "I guess if I am being honest, I have to admit that I like him way more than I should. I was in a relationship with a colleague at work, and when it ended, I was the last one to know. One week later he was dating a nurse at the same hospital who is now pregnant."

"I felt like such a fool; but most of all, I have never been so hurt by anyone. I met my ex shortly after I lost my parents. I thought he was a blessing from God. I'm just so afraid of being hurt again," Imani said wiping away a tear. "I have heard all the rumors about Marc never dating the same woman twice, and as much as I like him, I'm not looking to be a notch in someone's belt."

Grayce hugged her tightly. "Well I have known Marc for a very long time so let me start by saying what you see is what you get with him. You never have to wonder where you stand with Marc. While on the outside he may appear to be a womanizer, I promise you that he is anything but and I think everyone here can attest to that.

He may have dated a lot of women, but I can guarantee that not one of them can say that he has ever hurt them. "He really is a good man Imani," Kim added. "Don't allow his false reputation to keep you from what could be your blessing. Had I done that with Rico, I would've missed out on the love of an amazing man."

Imani smiled as she wiped away her tears. "Thank you all so much. He must be a good man if he has all of you vouching for him." "He really is, they all are good men, although you wouldn't be able to tell they are men the way they are behaving right now," Jess said shaking her head.

The trip to the beach is just what Drea needed. She was happier than she'd been in a very long time. She sat by the fire watching her family and friends. Drea had never felt more grateful as she looked around at everyone laughing and having a good time.

"Penny for your thoughts," Tony said breaking her focus as he sat down beside her and handed her a bottle of water. Drea smiled, "I was just thanking God for this moment. It wasn't long ago that I wasn't sure we'd all even end up together like this and now look at us."

"I know," Tony said. "I have been on some bad calls, I mean really bad but when it hits home…there is no feeling to describe it. When I saw Jayson, I lost it for a second. I know God kept me that night. Jess is so strong," he said looking over at her and Imani laughing with Marc. "She truly is, I pray to God I never have to walk in her shoes. This day has really made me think about all my blessings, and that includes you. With everything that's been going on, you've been a rock for my family and me. I hope you know just how special you are to all of us." "I love you all, you're my family," Tony smiled.

CHAPTER 63

Dre was so happy to be back with Grayce. He had never been happier in his entire life. They held hands and stood quietly along the shoreline. "This is perfect," he said skipping a small rock in the ocean. "I know," Grayce sighed as she laid her head on his chest. "I could live like this forever." "Good because I plan to get a lot of use out of this house. It's so amazing how God works because after I signed the deed I came back here and just sat on the deck for hours watching the water. I didn't even tell anyone that I bought it."

"As I sat there, I thought of you more than once." "I saw us on the beach. Who knew a few of months later you'd be back in my life, and we'd be right here." "God knew," Grayce smiled into his chest as she listened to the beat of his heart. "By the way, mom and dad are coming up this weekend and want to have dinner with your parents and us." "Sounds good," Dre said. "Soooo have you given any more thought to a date?" he asked. Grayce looked up at him and smiled. "You really want this don't you?" "Grayce, I have never wanted anything more. If I could, I'd marry you right here, right now." Grayce hugged him tightly. "Good because I've been thinking, and I don't really want a big wedding."

"Except for our parents and the boys, everyone that I truly love and care for is right here. "I'd like to get married right here on this beach as soon as possible." "I don't think I can love you any more than I do right now. So, is next weekend too soon?" Dre asked trying to control his excitement. "It's perfect baby," Grayce smiled.

The next week flew by so fast. Everyone planned to head down to the beach the night before to avoid the possibility of getting caught up in traffic. The past six days had been surreal. Grayce sipped her tea on the deck as she watched the sunset. "By this time tomorrow I will be Mrs. Andre Jackson III," she said to herself shaking her head.

Grayce smiled as she thought about her life with Dre. For so many years, it was nothing more than a fantasy, and now here she was, hours from marrying the man of her dreams. The knock at the patio door broke her train of thought. "Hi," she said softly. "I thought I wasn't supposed to see you before the wedding." Dre smiled. "We don't need luck baby, we've got the grace of God.

"Hi, my love," Dre blushed. "Want to go for a walk with me?" "I'd love to," she said. "I was talking to LJ a couple of weeks ago, and he said something that I haven't been able to shake." "What did he say?" Grayce asked as they sat in the sand.

"He said that the days leading up to the shooting Jay had been acting a little different." "He said Jay basically told him that if something happened to him and his mother met someone new, to be happy for her. It's like he knew something was about to happen. It just really made me think. What if he did know? How do you prepare to leave the people you love?" "I don't have an answer for that baby, but I do believe that God is in control of everything. Some people say that God doesn't give us more than we can handle but that doesn't really make sense because if we could handle it on our own, we wouldn't need Him."

"God's timing is divine, even though we don't comprehend it." "I know you're right, baby; it just feels so strange not having him here standing by my side. I always thought he'd be here when we got married." "You thought about us getting married?" Grayce asked.

"Of course, you are the only woman I ever thought about marrying." "And you are the only man I ever thought about marrying." "I love hearing that," Dre smiled. "It's the truth. Any last minute jitters?" Grayce asked. "None at all...I am so ready for you to be my wife." "Do you have any last-minute jitters?" Dre asked. "Actually, I do she said turning to look at him."

Grayce could see the panic in his eyes and grabbed his face in her hands. "Not about marrying you, Dre. This is new territory for me. I'm not as experienced as you are," she said nudging him with her shoulder. Dre started to blush.

"Babe it will be perfect because our union is perfect." Grayce smiled. "Tomorrow I am giving you one of the two most valuable gifts that I possess." "Why can't I have both?" Dre pouted. "Because you had my heart a long time ago," she responded. Dre's heart swole as tears welled up in his eyes. "My only regret is that I cannot say that you can't say the same about me," Dre said.

"That's where you are wrong. I was your first love. It took me some time to fully get it but as jealous as I was of those women I realized that they may have had your body, but they never had your heart. Deep down I always knew that. I love you, Andre Jackson." "And I love you Future Mrs. Andre Jackson."

CHAPTER 64

It was just about 6:00 PM Dre and the guys finished getting dressed. As Dre walked into the living room, the smell of his mother's homemade mac & cheese and Grayce's mom's shrimp and grits hit him hard. Grayce didn't want a traditional reception menu. She had been away a long time and wanted to have all their favorite dishes.

Their moms had been prepping for days. In addition to the macaroni and cheese and shrimp & grits, they'd prepared a ham, fried chicken, pork chops smothered with gravy, crab cakes, BBQ ribs, deep-fried fish, greens, potato salad, sweet potatoes, fried cabbage, pound cake and banana pudding.

"It smells amazing in here," Dre said looking at the full spread they'd prepared. "Look at my baby," Gloria said hugging her son. "I am so proud of you Dre. I thank God every day for the man that you have become. Grayce is a wonderful woman, and I love her as if she were my very own daughter. You don't know how long I've prayed for this day."

"I can imagine mom," Dre laughed. "I'm just so glad that God brought her back to me." "There will be obstacles Dre, but I promise you that if you keep God first in your marriage, you will overcome them all," Gloria said hugging her son. "Thanks mom," Dre said hugging her back tightly.

"We are both so blessed to have parents with more than 60 years of marriage experience combined. You all have set excellent examples to us about what a godly marriage consists of, so we can't fail. I love and appreciate you and Pop so much. I know I don't tell you as much as I should, but I really do love you." "I love you too baby. You just show your appreciation by giving me some grandbabies," Gloria laughed.

"Momma, can I have her to myself for a week before you start up about the grandbabies?" Dre laughed. "I guess if you must," Gloria laughed. "Is everyone all set?" Gloria asked. "Just about, Tony and Rico are helping the boys get ready now." "Have you seen Grayce yet?" Dre asked with a smile. "Yep, she looks absolutely beautiful Dre." "I cannot believe that I am going to be a husband in less than an hour." "Are you nervous?" "Mom, I am excited. I feel like I have been waiting my entire life for this one moment."

CHAPTER 65

Dre waited for what felt like an eternity. He blinked back tears as he thought about Jayson's wedding; wishing that his best friend could be here standing by his side. The last wedding he'd attended was Jayson, and Jessica's just a little over a year ago.

He was caught up in his memories when he heard one of the most beautiful sounds he's ever heard. As Grayce walked down the "aisle" toward him, she sang one of her favorite songs to him by *CeCe Winans*.

I could tell by the way you smile

I could feel it in your touch

And I knew this heart of mine

This time would fall in love

All the hopes and promises given

And the pain that life can bring

Will build our will and commitment to face anything

I will love you faithfully, forever unconditionally

And my love I promise

Everything I have is yours

You're everything I prayed and waited for

And my love I promise you

Now we begin our life today

And though we've only just begun

The quest until we're old and gray is the vow to live as one

Through the desert winds that blow

I'll walk you through the winters cold

I'll be there to keep the fire alive

And when each passage we endure

We will stay strong, we can be sure

Our love survives

Dre felt like he was seeing Grayce for the very first time. She was the most beautiful woman in the world to him. She looked like an angel. Senior cleared his throat and wiped his tears as he smiled at Dre and Grayce.

"First and foremost-we give honor to our Lord and Savior Jesus Christ on this blessed day. "I have officiated over hundreds of weddings in my lifetime, but today I not only stand here as a pastor. I stand here as a proud and loving father. I have known Grayce since she was just a wee little thing with her pigtails and dimples."

"Grayce you've always been like a daughter to me, and on this day, I am so very honored that I get to welcome you into our family officially. We are gathered here today in the sight of God, and in the face of this company, to join together Andre and Grayce in holy matrimony; which is an honorable estate, instituted of God, since the first man and the first woman walked on the earth."

"Therefore; it is not to be entered into unadvisedly or lightly, but reverently and soberly. Into this holy estate, these two persons present come now to be joined. If anyone can show just cause why they may not be lawfully joined together, let them speak now or forever hold their peace."

Senior looked around and smiled. "Alright then, let's get to it. Who gives this woman to be married to this man?" "We do," Grayce's father said with his voice breaking. When her father placed her hand in Dre's, he felt like he was giving him the most precious gift in the world.

Grayce kissed her father on his cheek. He smiled at Dre and patted him on his back before he took his seat. Grayce wiped the tears from Dre's eyes as he kissed her hand. "Dre and Grayce wanted to write their own vows, so I will let them begin," Senior said looking at Dre. Dre nodded his head. "I started writing my vows, but for some reason, I couldn't accurately relay what was in my heart on paper.

It was then that I noticed that the only word that kept echoing in my head when I think of you is a blessing, so I looked it up. Webster's Dictionary describes a blessing as help and approval from God or something that helps you or brings joy. I had to smile because that's what you are to me, a gift from God that brings me joy. Grayce, you have made me happier in the last few months than I have been in my entire life. I don't know how I would've made it through these months without you by my side. You have always been that Proverbs 31 woman."

"I promise to love you, protect you, be kind to you and honor you for the rest of my life. I don't feel worthy of you, but I am going to work hard to prove to you and myself that I am. We are so blessed that we've had parents that have led by example. "They have shown us how to love through the love of Christ, and I am so grateful for that. Grayce, I never really knew love until God sent you back to me. He loved me enough to give me another opportunity to love and cherish you, and for that, I humbly thank you both. You are my heartbeat…my rib. I love you."

Senior was so proud of Dre. Gloria passed tissues to all the girls. Grayce dabbed her eyes trying not to mess up her makeup. "You would do that to me wouldn't you?" she smiled as the group laughed.

"Andre…my Dre, my heart, my man. For so many years I tried to forget about you. "I told myself that we were just two kids with a case of puppy love, but deep down inside I knew better. I knew from the moment I met you that I'd love you for the rest of my life. Back in high school, Jess and I would write out the characteristics we wanted in a husband, and even back then I knew you were the one. The more I tried to get over you, the more I'd think about you."

"You are the man that I prayed for; the man that God promised me, and I am so thankful that He did not allow me to stray but helped me to remain steadfast in Him. It's in Him that I'm able to love you truly and I do love you. My heart is so full of joy right now. I pray that I will be a wife and mother that you will be proud of and on this day in front of God and our family I give you the most precious gift that I have to give, my heart. I vow to love you, support you, honor you, encourage you, respect you and cherish you for the rest of my life. I love you."

Senior wiped his eyes with his handkerchief. "Praise God." "The Bible says that when a man finds a wife, he finds a good thing. Son, you have a good thing. Andre Joseph Williamson III, do you take this woman to be your lawfully wedded wife, to love and to honor, to have and to hold from this day forward in sickness and in health for the rest of your life?" "I do," Dre said with tears flowing down his face as his voice cracks.

"Grayce Karen McDaniels, do you take this man to be your lawfully wedded husband, to love and to honor, to have and to hold from this day forward in sickness and in health for the rest of your life?" "I do," Grayce cried.

"Mark, chapter 10, verses 6 through 8 says, *at the beginning of creation God made them male and female. For this reason, a man will leave his father and mother and be united to his wife, and the two will become one flesh. So, they are no longer two, but one.*"

"It is my absolute pleasure to pronounce you man and wife. Son, you better kiss your bride," Senior smiled. Dre lifted the veil and gave Grayce a gentle but passionate kiss. "I love you baby," she whispered. "I love you too," he smiled. "We did it!"

"May I present for the very first time…Mr. and Mrs. Andre Williamson III". Dre hugged his father tightly. "I love you pop." "I love you more son."

CHAPTER 66

Dre and Grayce continued to pose for pictures for the next hour. "I don't know about y'all, but I am hungry," Marc said. "Me too," Brian said. "Me three," Amir and Aaron giggled. "Well come on two and three" Gloria laughed. She and Patricia walked behind the boys as they ran to the table.

"I know if anyone touches that table without washing their hands there's going to be trouble," Patricia threatened. Marc and the boys froze instantly as everyone laughed.

They enjoyed a long casual dinner. Grayce pushed her plate aside. "I didn't fully think about this meal selection before I put on this dress." "Tell me about it, I feel like these buttons are about to pop at any moment," Dre laughed. Grayce smiled at him as she rubbed his hand.

"I still cannot believe that we are married." "Me either," Dre said. "All these years I felt like marriage would hold me back from something but right now I feel like I can conquer the world with you by my side." "And you can baby," Grayce said kissing her husband.

Their parents were happier than they'd been in a very long time. Gloria shivered as the memory of seeing her son lying in that hospital bed reemerged; Now here he was on his wedding night looking happier than she'd ever seen him. LJ stood up and tapped his fork on his glass.

"Excuse me may I have your attention please." Dre sat back and smiled as he looked at his godson. He reminded him so much of Jayson. Grayce smiled at Jess as LJ pulled a sheet a paper out of his pocket. He cleared his throat.

"Good evening friends and family. I am so happy to be here on this special day. On this special day, I want to honor the best godparents in the world. I love both of you very much, and I am so happy that we all finally get to witness this union." "Amen baby," Gloria said causing a few chuckles.

LJ smiled before he continued. "I hope that you will both love each other the way my mom and dad loved each other." Every adult at the table immediately starts to tear up. "I wish you both a lifetime of love and happiness, and I pray that when I get older, I am blessed enough to find a woman like the women sitting here this evening. I love you."

Dre stood and hugged LJ tightly. "I love you man. That was the best speech ever." "Thank you," LJ said. Grayce stood behind Dre with tears in her eyes. "I am so proud of you baby. Thank you so much." "You're welcome," LJ blushed.

Jess walked to the head of the table and hugged her son tightly. "Baby that was amazing. I am so proud of you." LJ smiled all the way back to his seat. "My heart is so full as I stand here today," Jess said." "You two don't know how many nights Jayson and I have prayed for this. I know that he is here with us in spirit, praising God. If I am honest, I didn't know how I would handle today, but last night there was an overwhelming presence of peace. I thank God that we are all able to witness this beautiful union."

"Dre you have always been like a big brother to me. You were my ace from the moment we met. I knew exactly why you and Jayson were such great friends. I love you, and there is no doubt in my mind whatsoever that you will be an excellent husband to my best friend."

"Grayce…wheewww. I promised myself I would not cry. Grayce, you've been my best friend, my confidant and my sister for as long as I can remember. During the best and worst times of my life, you have been right there, and I thank God for you every single day. You are my right hand, and I wish you and Dre a lifetime of happiness," Jess said as she hugged Grayce and Dre and walked back to her seat.

Imani stood and helped Marc to the front of the table. Marcus shook his head, wiping the tears from his eyes. "I've cried more in the last six months than I have in my entire life but today these are tears of joy. Dre and Grayce. I have known you both for almost as long as I've been alive."

"It's crazy because I always knew you two would get married. There was always something about you two. When I look at the two of you, I see Senior and mom; I see Grayce's parents; I see longevity. The love you both have for each other surpasses time. I pray to God that I have an opportunity to share that type of love," Marc said thinking of Imani.

"I love you both more than anything and wish the absolute best for you." Dre smiled at his cousin. He knew from the look in Marc's eyes that it was just a matter of time before they'd be seated at his wedding. Grayce's parents stood. Her father cleared his throat before he began to speak.

"Dre you know that I have always been very fond of you. I love you as if you were my own son and I speak for her mother and me when I say that we are so happy for you and Grayce. You are the son that I never had, and I am so grateful that God chose you to be my daughter's help mate."

"In the good and bad times, never lose sight of this moment. There may be times when you two may not like each other very much but hold strong to the love that you both share and God will guide you through it. Baby, you want to say anything?" Grayce's mom tried to speak, but she was overcome emotional. "Aww mommy," Grayce said, blowing her a kiss. "I love you, baby," she said before taking her seat. Senior and Gloria stood last. "Well, I pretty much said all I had to say," Senior said. "Baby," he said turning it over to Gloria.

"Lord knows I have been waiting forever for this day, but I thank God for rewarding my patience."

"Patience?" Dre asked with a smirk. Grayce tapped his arm while everyone else laughed. "Well, be that as it may, I am overjoyed today. Son, I love you so, so much and I have never wanted anything more than for you to give your life to Christ and to be happy. I cannot ever remember seeing you so happy."

"Grayce thank you for loving and taking care of my son. Marriage is work, but you two will survive because you have a praying family right here supporting you both every step of the way. I challenge each one of us seated here to help them along the way by praying for them and continue supporting them."

"Continue to keep God first and always love each other, even when you don't like each other. Stay in love. "To Grayce and Dre." Everyone stood and lifted their glasses to Grayce and Dre.

Marc was unusually quiet on the ride back home. "The wedding was nice," Imani said trying ease the tension in the car. "Yeah, it was," Marc said quietly looking out the window. "Is everything okay Marcus?" Imani asked. Marc looked at her. "Yes, I was just thinking. Don't get me wrong I am so happy for Dre and Grayce. I love them both more than I can even express. I guess the wedding has me thinking about my life and wondering if I will ever have someone to love me unconditionally."

"Marcus you are an amazing man and any woman in this world would be lucky to have you." "Even you?" Marc asked as his heart beat out of his chest. "Imani, I think I fell in love with you the first time I saw you. During these last few months, we've gotten a lot closer, and I feel like there is a connection. If I am wrong, I sincerely apologize, but I feel like if I don't get this off my chest, I am going to explode."

"Imani, I love you so much. You're the first thing on my mind when I wake up and the last thing on my mind before I go to sleep. If you say no I will completely understand and respect your decision, but I'd like to take you out on a date. Not as friends but a real date."

The seconds that tick by felt like forever. "I'd love to go on a date with you," Imani smiled. "Are you serious?" Marcus asked. "Yes, I am. I just really need us to take things slow. I would be lying if I said I don't feel the same. There is definitely an attraction between us that I cannot continue to deny. The girls even called me out on it last week". "Wow?" Marc laughed.

"So, what happens next?" she asked. "Well I was wondering if you'd like to come to church with me tomorrow and I was thinking we could go to brunch after and just play it by ear the rest of the day," Marc suggested. "Sounds good to me," Imani said. It had been so long since Imani had been on a date. She was looking forward to it. She and Marc were on cloud nine the rest of the ride back to the city.

CHAPTER 67

"Dre and Grayce looked so happy," Michelle said. "It was such a beautiful wedding." "Yes, it was, and yes they did." Eric smiled as he kissed her hand, keeping his eyes on the road. "Eric, I could never thank you enough for everything that you've done for us. I literally cannot remember what my life was like before you came along, and I thank God for you. I am happier than I have ever been in my entire life."

"I love you too. Before you came along my life revolved solely around my family and work. I was so lonely, but Dre and Marcus were the ones who got the looks in the family." "Pull over Eric," Michelle demanded. "Baby what's wrong? Are you okay?" Eric asked as he turned off on the next exit into a convenience store parking lot and looked at Michelle with concern.

"Eric Christopher Jackson you are one of the most handsome men I have ever seen in my life. I don't like it when you say things like that. It hurts me that those women made you feel that way. They didn't value or deserve you, but I am glad that they didn't see you for who you truly are because I would not be here with you right now."

"Michelle this isn't how I planned to do this but now just seems to be a perfect time." Eric reached into his pocket and pulled out the tiny blue box. Michelle began to bounce up and down. "Eric please don't play with me." Eric smiled. "Michelle, you and the kids, have brought so much joy to my life; will you please marry me?"

Michelle covered her mouth as the tears fell down her face. "Yes," she finally said through her tears. Eric exited the car, ran around to her door and pulled her out of the car. He kissed her softly as he placed the ring on her finger. "Thank you, thank you, thank you. This is the best day of my life."

All the excitement woke up the kids. "Mommy what's wrong?" they asked when they saw her crying. Eric opened the door and helped them out of the car. "I love you both very much. You both know that right?" he asked. "Yes," they both said, with tears in their eyes.

"What's the matter, why are you crying? Eric asked Kiara. "We don't want to move out," she cried. "What?" Eric asked confused. "Who said you were moving out?" Eric asked. "I saw mommy crying that I thought you wanted us to leave," the little girl said.

"The last time mommy cried is when daddy put us out." Michelle hated that her children had endured so much in their young lives. Eric cried as his heart broke for the children he'd grown to love so much.

He pulled them both close to him. "Kiara if you, Kevin and your mom ever move out it will break my heart. I love you all so much that I want you to live with me forever. Your mom was crying because we are happy. I asked mommy if she would be my wife and she said yes and if it's okay with you and Kevin, I want to be your dad."

Kiara jumped up and down with excitement.

You and mommy are really getting married?" she asked. "Yep, we are so you guys can't ever leave me okay?" Kiara nodded her head and hugged her mom. "Kevin is that okay with you?" Marc asked. "Yep," he said, grinning at Eric.

"So, you gonna be my daddy now?" he asked. "Yep, so now we all will live together okay?" The children started jumping up and down with excitement. They loved Eric and his family, and they loved having other children to play with. Eric looked up to the heavens and said a silent prayer, thanking God for blessing him with a family of his very own. He'd never be lonely again.

CHAPTER 68

Jess was beyond exhausted as the car slowed to a stop in front of her house. "Okay, boys we are home," she said gently shaking them. "Manny I cannot thank you enough for driving us home," Jess said stifling a yawn. "It's no problem at all," Manny said. "If you ever need anything at all please let me know."

"Thank you so much, Manny. You and Imani have been a blessing to all of us." "We feel the same way, it's been Imani and me for so long that I think we both forgot what it felt like to have a family." Jess smiled. "Well, that's what you both have become; family. I have never seen Marc as happy as he is when Imani is around, and you have been a godsend.

"Don't forget about tomorrow Manny," LJ said as he exited the car. "I won't," Manny said. I'll be here at 10:00 AM. "Okay cool, goodnight," LJ said as he carried his brothers in the house. Manny and Jess watched as LJ tended to his younger brothers.

"He reminds me more and more of his father every day. Thank you so much for getting him out of the house tomorrow. He wants so much to be the man of the house that he's forgetting about being a teenager. This will be his last year of high school, and I really want him to enjoy it." "He is a remarkable young man," Manny said. "That he is," Jess smiled.

CHAPTER 69

Dre woke to the sound of the ocean. He smiled as he looked down at Grayce thanking God that yesterday hadn't been a dream. He kissed her softly on her shoulder as she smiled with her eyes closed.

"Good morning Mrs. Williamson." "I love the sound of that," Grayce said turning to face Dre. "Good morning Mr. Williamson, I love you." "I love you more," Dre smiled. "I was so scared that yesterday was just a dream."

"Nope, no dream," she said snuggling into his chest. "You are stuck with me, buddy." "I can't imagine another person in this world that I'd rather be stuck with," he winked. "Are you okay?" he asked. "I am amazingly wonderful," she gushed. "Are you hungry?" No sooner than Grayce asked, Dre's stomach began to growl. "I'll take that as a yes," she laughed.

"What are you smiling about?" Grayce asked. "I can't believe how much I love being your husband. "I know it's only been one day, but I have never been this happy in my life." "I know what you mean," Grayce smiled. "And this is only the beginning."

CHAPTER 70

Tony had just finished a double shift at work when he received a call from Brian's school. Brian was being rushed to the hospital. Tony felt as if his knees were going to buckle. "What happened?" Tony asked the school's administrator while rushing out the door.

"I don't have all the details sir, but he's being taken to Kingdom Hospital." "Okay, I'm on my way." "What's going on T?" Curtis asked. "I'm not sure, but they are rushing Brian to the hospital." "Okay man, come on I'll drive." Tony nodded as he looked down at his shaking hands.

He had come to love Brian as if he were his very own son. Tony nervously dialed Drea's phone number. "Hey you," Drea answered when she saw his name come across the caller ID. "Drea something happened to Brian, and the ambulance is taking him to Kingdom. Can you please pray with me?"

"Of course," Drea said as she began to pray, grabbing her car keys and heading out to meet them at the hospital. "Tony, I know you're concerned, but Brian will be okay, whatever it is," she said after praying. "He's a tough little boy." "I know," Tony said nodding.

"I can't believe how much I love that little boy." "He's easy to love," Drea said as she stopped at the light. "All will be well Tony, trust in the Lord." "Thank you, Drea. I'm sorry to bother you. Were you busy?" Tony asked. "No, I was just reading over some papers." "I hate to ask but..." Tony began." I'm already in the car sweetie," Drea interrupted. Tony smiled. "Thank you, Drea. I love you so much."

That admission shocked everyone including his partner who looked over at Tony. Before he could retract his statement, she said, "I love you too Tony. I will see you in a few." Tony could not believe his ears. All his fears immediately disappeared. "Everything is going to be just fine," he said out loud as he hung up the phone. His partner smiled as they arrived at the hospital. This was Déjà vu all over again. Tony shook the memories out of his head as he rushed into the hospital.

The ER staff knew why Tony was there. They quickly escorted him to the room where they were prepping Brian for surgery. "Dr. Baxter, what's going on?" Tony asked nervously. "Brian's appendix ruptured, and we need to get him into surgery now." "Is he okay?" Tony asked, his voice cracking with emotion."

"He's in a bit of pain, but he will be fine, I need you to sign these consent forms, so we can get him into surgery." Tony quickly signed the forms and handed them back to the nurse. "Let's pray," she said as they held hands with the doctor.

Tony loved that just about every doctor he'd met at the hospital was a Christian. He was pacing in the waiting room when Drea arrived. She ran to him and hugged him tightly. "How is he?" she asked. "His appendix ruptured.

He's in surgery right now." "Aww my little man," Drea

said.

"He's going to be fine Tony. We're going to have to

spoil him when he comes home," she said, trying to ease

some of his worries. "Yes, we will" Tony smiled. "We

should have a movie night and invite Jess and the boys

over. I think he'd love that!" "He definitely will," Tony

smiled. "Thank you for being here Drea." "Where else

would I be?" she asked. "In case you haven't noticed, I

love you both very much," she smiled. Tony couldn't hide

the joy on his face if he tried.

CHAPTER 71

Grayce left the doctor's office in a daze. She knew that there was a possibility but hearing the doctor say the words made it a reality. Her cheeks hurt from smiling so much but Grayce could not stop herself. "I'm going to have a baby," she whispered to herself. She and Dre had discussed having children soon, but neither of them expected it to happen this soon.

She knew in her heart that Dre would be just as happy as she was, but she was still nervous. Grayce picked up her phone to call Dre with the good news when she had a second thought. She wanted to surprise him, and she knew just how. Grayce stopped at several stores to ensure that she had everything that she needed.

The phone rang as soon as Grayce stepped into the house. She dropped her bags on the sofa and rushed to answer the phone. "Babe are you okay?" Dre asked concerned. "Yes, I'm fine baby, I was just running to answer the phone." "Oh, okay. Well, the conference ended early so I will be home in a few hours. Would you like me to pick up something for dinner?" he asked. "No baby, I'm cooking dinner.

What time will you be home?" she asked. "I should be there by 6:00. Do you need anything?" "Just to have my baby in my arms. I've missed you so much," Grayce sighed. "Me too baby. It's taking everything for me not to speed home to you." "Dre, don't you dare," Grayce warned. "I need you back here in one piece." "Okay baby," he smiled. "Well let me concentrate on the road. I will see you in a few. I love you." "I love you too," she said, hanging up the phone. Grayce was grinning from ear to ear as she started preparing their dinner.

CHAPTER 72

Tony exited the precinct and saw a familiar woman standing outside. A couple of the younger officers were harassing her and telling her to leave the area. "Now you both know better," Tony lectured. "Is this how the academy trained you to deal with the public that you swore an oath to protect?" he asked angrily.

"Detective this is just some crackhead," one of the young officers laughed. Tony grabbed him by his collar. "This woman who you call a crackhead is my mother and if I ever see you speaking to anybody the way you just spoke to her I can promise you that you will never work at this precinct again."

The young officers apologized as they hurried off sheepishly. Tony's heart was beating a mile a minute. He hadn't seen his mom in years. Theresa Weems had been on drugs ever since the loss of her youngest son and has been homeless for the last five years. It had been an on and off again struggle for her.

She finally decided to give her heart to the Lord and wanted to give up the drugs and alcohol. She had done unspeakable things as a means of soothing her pain, but nothing worked.

"Hey mom, how are you?" Tony asked. Theresa began to cry as she looked at Tony. He had become such a handsome man. He reminded her so much of his father who died before Tony was born. Tony tried to hug his mom, but she backed away. "No, I smell," she cried. "I don't want to get you dirty." Tony cried as he looked at his mother and pulled her close to him.

He hugged her tightly. "I love you, mom." Theresa wept. "I love you too Anthony." Tony smiled remembering that his mother was the only person who called him Anthony. "I am sorry Anthony. I just want this pain to go away." Tony held her tightly in his arms.

"Mom I can't promise you that it will happen overnight, but I promise you that God will make it right. How did you know where to find me?" Theresa smiled. "You are my baby. I always keep track of you." She reached into her ragged bag and pulled out a tattered Ziploc bag filled with newspaper articles about him.

"I want you to come to stay with us," Tony said. "Baby I can't do that." "Yes. you can, you are my mother, and I know Brian would love having you around." "Who's Brian?" Theresa asked.

Tony pulled out his phone to show her a picture of he and Brian at Dre's wedding. "This is my son Brian, I'm in the process of adopting him." "Really?" Theresa smiled. Anthony was always such a loving young man. "Baby, I don't want to hurt your chances. You know those people are strict and look at me. I couldn't even keep my own son alive."

Theresa cried, thinking about her own son. "I need to go. I'm sorry I bothered you." "Mom I'm not going to allow you to leave me again. I can't lose you again, and whether you realize it or not, we need each other. I need you, mommy." Theresa cried as she hugged her son. Tony wiped her tears. "Come on mom, let's go home."

CHAPTER 73

Michelle loved every second of starting a restaurant. Marc's real estate agent chose the perfect location for the restaurant. Michelle was at the restaurant every day, overseeing the renovation and making sure that everything was just right. Marc gave her full authority to purchase everything that she needed for the restaurant.

She wanted to make both he and Eric proud of her. She hated living off Eric. She was so used to providing for herself, and now this would give her an opportunity to be independent. Everything was coming along flawlessly. She was working with a designer and the chef that she and Marc chose to help her design the perfect kitchen.

The grand opening was less than two months away, and things were hectic. Michelle's only regret was that her mom hadn't lived long enough to see her accomplish her biggest dream. She knew that her mom would be so proud of her and she would love Eric. He was the type of man that her mom always told her that she deserved.

Some days it all still felt too good to be true. Michelle's life literally changed in the blink of an eye. She smiled thinking about the last sermon at church. The favor of God can accomplish more in one week and a lifetime of hard work.

"Baby this place is amazing," Eric said as he entered the restaurant. "Thanks babe, I am so excited." "I'm so proud of you Michelle." "That means the world to me, baby. It feels so good to be walking in my purpose. I know that this is what I was born to do. I just want everything to be perfect, the grand opening is going to be amazing.

Marc has a ton of his NFL friends coming, and I just don't want to let him down." "Baby relax, everything will be fine. The restaurant looks amazing, and you couldn't let Marc down if you tried. He's been bragging to anyone who will listen about you." "You're right, I know that fear is from the enemy and I will not allow fear to steal my joy." Michelle hugged Eric tightly. "I don't know what I did to deserve you but to God be all the glory."

CHAPTER 74

Dre was excited as he drove into the driveway. Two days away from Grayce felt like a lifetime. He didn't even bother grabbing his bags from the car. He just wanted to see his baby. Grayce watched from the window as he arrived and anxiously rushed to the door to greet him. He kissed her as soon as she opened the door.

"I missed you," he said. "Not as much as I missed you," Grayce said hugging him tightly. "Something smells good." Grayce smiled, helping him out of his jacket. Grayce could barely contain herself. Dre laughed at her. "Babe, what's going on? You're really giddy today."

"I'm not used to being away from you, I guess I just really missed you." "I missed you too baby." "Good, why don't you go take a shower and dinner will be ready when you finish." Dre kissed her and shook his head as he headed off to shower.

Grayce was just putting the dinner on the table when Dre entered the kitchen. "This looks amazing babe," Dre said as they sat down. Grayce blessed the food before they began to eat. "Oh, I almost forgot that I have a present for you in the car. I'll grab it once we're done with dinner," he smiled.

"You are too good to me, and I actually have a present for you as well." "Oohhh what is it?" Dre asked anxiously. "You'll see after dinner," Grayce said. "Aren't you going to eat?" Dre asked looking down at the plate that she'd hardly touched. "I'm not very hungry right now." "You haven't been eating much lately babe, are you feeling ok?" "I'm feeling great baby," Grayce smiled rubbing his hand as he continued to eat.

Dre shook his head again. "I am truly blessed. God could've easily let me die, but He didn't. Not only did he give me my life back, but he also gave me you." Grayce's heart swelled. "Dre, I love you so much. Being your wife is one of my greatest joys." "And I am grateful to be your husband," Dre smiled.

"Had someone told me three years ago that I would be married and loving it I would've thought they were crazy, but here I am happier than I have ever been in my life. Oh yeah, your gift. I'll be right back."

Grayce put the dishes in the dishwasher and walked into the living room to get her gift for Dre. "Yayyyy," Grayce said clapping her hands when he walked in with the small bag. Grayce opened the tiny box and in it was a beautiful platinum bracelet with their wedding date engraved on it. "Oh my gosh Dre it's beautiful. I love it!" Dre put the bracelet on as she admired it.

"Thank you, baby. This is one of the best gifts I have ever received. Okay, now it's your turn," Grayce said, beaming as she handed the wrapped gift over to Dre. "I think you're more excited about this than I am," Dre laughed. Dre took the top off the box and looked at the photo album.

Grayce had the photos from the bonfire and wedding placed in a beautiful photo album. She and Dre sat back looking at the pictures, reminiscing about their wedding ceremony. When Dre turned to the last page, he looked at Grayce in shock before looking back down at their baby's first sonogram picture.

"Babe is this for real?" he asked. "Yes," Grayce says nervously. She was hoping that he'd be as happy as she was about their new arrival. Dre dropped to his knees and kissed her belly. He looked up at her as the tears fell down his face. Thank you, baby. Thank you so much." Grayce laughed at Dre. "Babe I think you had a little something to do with it too," she smiled.

Grayce sat on the edge of the sofa and wiped away his tears. "I was hoping you'd be happy." "Why wouldn't I be happy?" Dre asked. "Well I know we were planning this, but I didn't expect it to happen so soon." "Baby this news just gave me life. I'm about to be a father." Dre picked her up and spun her around. "Thank you, God," he yelled. Grayce was so relieved that Dre was happy. He stopped abruptly and put her down.

"You know our moms are going to lose it right?" "I know," she laughed. Dre looked lovingly into her eyes before he softly kissed her. "We can tell them tomorrow," he said as they sat on the couch. Dre laid his head on her lap and fell asleep talking to their baby. Grayce smiled as she continued to rub his head. She drifted off to sleep, envisioning the smaller version of Dre growing inside of her.

CHAPTER 75

After praying long and hard, Imani decided to put her reservations aside and fully open herself up to loving Marcus. The last few months had been heaven on earth, and they were both on cloud nine. Marcus was a good man, and she was so in love with him. Imani and Manny had become a part of the group, and she loved them all.

She could easily see why he loved his family so much. Manny entered the room, watching his big sister smiling. Manny was so happy that she had found someone who truly deserved her. There was no doubt in his mind that Marc loved her every bit as much as she loved him. They were a match made in heaven.

"I don't think I need to ask what you are smiling about," Manny said sitting down next to his big sister. "What are you talking about?" she blushed. Manny laughed. "Sis you may be able to fool a lot of people, but I am not one of them." "Is it that obvious?" Imani asked.

"Yes, sis. Anyone can see that your nose is open from a mile away. It's good though. I love seeing you happy again."

"I have never, ever been this happy Manny," Imani smiled. "I have never had any man treat me the way that Marcus does. This almost feels too good to be true. I don't want to move too fast. I love Marcus more than I have ever loved any man, but I cannot take being hurt again.

"Well, why are you talking about being hurt then? You said yourself that no other man has ever treated you the way that Marc does. Enjoy it, sis. You deserve to be happy. What are you so afraid of?" Imani laid her head on her brother's shoulder.

"If I am honest, I am afraid that when he walks again, he will change his mind. I'm afraid that right now I am a comfortable infatuation and when he's back to his old life, this boring old doctor won't be enough for him." Manny didn't know what to say, so he just held his sister close, praying that Marcus was the man that he appeared to

be.

CHAPTER 76

Kim was excited as she and Rico left the doctor's office. Rico looked as if he'd seen a ghost. Babe, I'm scared. Kim stopped and turned to Rico. "Why baby?" "Kim, the thought of raising a daughter, scares me. The thought of raising two terrifies me." "You didn't want girls," she asks slightly disheartened. "No baby it's not that at all," Rico quickly said.

"It's just that before I met you, I wasn't the type of man I would want my daughters to date. If some guy treats my daughter that way I treated women back then, I am going catch a charge." "Baby you won't have to worry about that," Kim smiled as she pulled him close and placed his hand on her belly.

"Our daughters will recognize true love, and you will love them in a way that they will never even look twice at a man who would treat them in any manner less than how their daddy treats them and their mommy." Rico kissed her softly.

Kim was the best thing that had ever happened to Rico. He sighed deeply. "You're right, I love you baby." "I love you too," she said kissing him softly. "Now come on feed your girls, we're hungry." "What else is new?" Rico mumbled and immediately felt a light smack to the back of his head. "I'm just playing baby," he laughed hugging Kim.

"You better remember for better or worse," she smiled. "I wouldn't have it any other way baby. So, what's on your agenda for the rest of the day?" Rico asked as he helped Kim fasten her seatbelt. "Jess and I are going shopping for baby clothes." "How's she doing?" Rico asked. "I've been meaning to drop by to see her."

"She's a remarkable woman, I will give her that. I can't even begin to think about losing you, but I trust and believe that God has a purpose for everything. I think even in the worst of tragedies, there is an underlined blessing somewhere." "I truly hope so babe," Rico said. "Babe God does not make mistakes, never forget that. Everything that He does is always for His glory." Rico nodded his head.

"Babe you can find the light in any dark situation." "We have to baby because darkness is all around us and if we allow it to, it will consume us. The enemy has stolen enough, I will not freely give him anything else. Every time we sit here and wallow in self-pity and sadness he rejoices. I'm not saying that there will not be days where we will be sad, because we're human; but it's those times where we have our most amazing moments with God. Just look at Dre and Grayce." Rico smiled thinking about his friends.

CHAPTER 77

Dre and Drea were busy preparing for their parents 50th anniversary. They had been planning for months. Senior was a well-respected pastor, and people from all around wanted to come and celebrate with them. The guest list had grown to almost 300 people, and people were still sending their RSVPs. "People really love Ma and Dad," Drea said as she and Grayce sorted through photos for the slideshow.

"I can't believe how much you like your dad," Grayce smiled at Dre. "If I didn't know any better I would swear this was you." "I know, everyone says that," Dre smiled. "At least you know I'll still be fine when I get older," Dre winked. "You are silly," Grayce laughed. "Grayce please stop encouraging him," Drea laughed.

"On another note, I cannot believe I am finally going to be an auntie." "This baby is going to be spoiled rotten," she said touching Grayce's belly. "Tell me about it," Grayce smiled. "I thought our moms were going to pass out," Drea laughed. "That makes two of us," Grayce said. "They are already planning the baby shower," Grayce added. "They are happier than children on Christmas morning" Drea laughed, "but they are finally getting their grandchild, so we can't really blame them."

"It's good to see them so happy," Dre smiled looking up from the guest list. "Well, you two better enjoy your privacy now because you are not going to be able to get rid of them when the baby comes," Drea laughed. "When the baby comes?" Dre asked. "We can't get rid of them now. You need to hurry up and marry Tony and get them off my back," Dre said watching his sister blush.

"Tony and I are taking things slow." "I am so happy that you guys are back together, you are the cutest couple," Grayce smiled. "I don't know how I would've gotten through all of this without him," Drea said. "I am just so fortunate that he was still single," Drea said. Grayce placed her arm around her sister-in-law, "God was saving him for you." Before Drea could respond her phone began ringing. "I wonder who that could be," Dre laughed as Drea tossed the throw pillow at his head.

CHAPTER 78

"Baby, I really enjoyed the movie but 2 ½ hours is too long for any movie," Kim said stifling a yawn. "I know babe it took everything in me to stay awake. I kept dozing off," Rico yawned. "I know," Kim laughed. "But thank you for making time for our date night." "Of course," he laughed. "We better get all the date nights in that we can while we still have the time. In a couple of months, it's going to be over."

"Tell me about it," Kim agreed, rubbing her belly. "But I can't wait." "Neither can I baby," he smiled. "I was talking to Dre earlier it's crazy that we're about to be fathers. I know one thing I am going to be a much better father to my kids than my father was to me." "You already are baby," Kim said rubbing his hand that rests atop her belly.

"It's unfortunate for him that he didn't get to know the amazing man that you have become, but you're here to ensure that that cycle ends with you. I can't count the number of girls I went to school with who are raising children on their own. I take my hat off to them because I know that's not what they envisioned when they thought about having a family." "True," Rico agreed, nodding his head as they stopped at the red light.

"You still want ice cream?" he asked, looking over at Kim. "You know we do," she giggled. Rico shook his head. "How do you eat ribs, shrimp, a huge piece of cheesecake and popcorn and still want ice cream?" "Umm…daddy did you forget that I am eating for three now." "Three what?" Rico laughed.

As the light turned green a speeding car lost control coming around the corner and plowed into the passenger side of the vehicle. The force of impact split the car in half and ejected Rico from the car even though he was wearing his seatbelt. Neither he nor Kim them saw it coming.

CHAPTER 79

It was one of the worst scenes the paramedics had ever seen. Several of the medics were visibly shaken by the sight of the accident. Rico was found three blocks from where the crash had taken place. Surprisingly he still had a slight pulse. He and Kim were both rushed to the hospital via helicopter in grave condition.

Time was of the essence if they were going to survive although no one expected either of them to survive. Tony arrived on the scene after getting the call while at lunch. Tony immediately recognized Rico's personalized license plate and rushed over to the wreckage.

Tony's knees buckled from under him as he got closer and realized just how bad the accident was. In less than a year he'd lost one of his closest friends and now this. He immediately began to pray for Rico and Kim. The other officers in his unit realized that this was someone Tony knew and rushed to his side.

Several of the officers prayed with him. Tony finally composed himself before heading over to view the scene. Although he didn't want the images in his head, Tony knew that before he could tell anyone he needed to be confident that Rico was in the car.

Tony prayed the entire walk over that it was some sort of mistake. Maybe Rico had loaned his car to someone he hoped, but in his heart, he knew the truth. The scene was chaotic. There were news cameras and people everywhere. Several times he heard the words horrific and heartbreaking.

Tony noticed a female officer that he was acquainted with crying. Tony took a deep breath before he headed over to speak with the officer in charge of the scene. One of Tony's friends from the academy noticed that Tony was distraught and walked over to him before he could get any closer.

"Tony, I don't think you should be here," the sergeant said. "I have to be here," Tony said, his mouth suddenly dry. "Do you have a positive IDs?" Tony asked feeling like he was going to be sick to his stomach. "Yes, the driver has been tentatively identified by his driver's license as one Ricardo Antonio Durant. We are still trying to notify his next of kin." Tony closed his eyes. "His wife is his next of kin. Both of his parents are deceased."

The officer cleared his throat. "We couldn't make a positive identification on his passenger, but it does appear that she was pregnant. We're praying that the baby survives." "Babies," Tony corrected. "We found a purse nearby with documents for a Kimberly Ashley Durant, but we need to confirm that." Tony held his head and dropped to his knees. "I cannot believe that this is happening."

Tony looked down at his phone as it began ringing. It was Drea. The last thing Tony wanted to do was deliver any more bad news to her. Tony knew that she'd immediately tell that something was wrong if he didn't answer since he was supposed to pick her up over an hour ago.

Tony sat down on the ground with his head in his hands. "Lord, please help me," he begged. His phone began to ring again. Tony took a deep breath before answering the phone.

"What's wrong Tony?" Drea asked. Tony's mouth moved, but nothing came out as the tears flowed down his face. All he could manage to say was "Rico and Kim." Drea's stomach dropped. "Baby where are you?" Tony cleared his throat, trying to find his voice.

"There was an accident. Someone hit the car." "Oh God nooo," Drea screamed. Senior and Gloria ran into the living room after hearing Drea scream. "Where...how are they?" Drea asked holding her breath. Tony knew that it didn't look good, but he was taught to think beyond natural

sight and know that God doesn't always work in the
forefront.

"We need to pray," he said quietly. Drea nodded her
head over the phone understanding what he meant. "I love
you, Drea." "I love you too baby. Be safe." Drea told
Senior and Gloria what happened, and they all began to
pray.

After praying Drea contacted the group to inform
them of the accident. Everyone headed over to the hospital
while praying for Kim, Rico and their babies.

CHAPTER 80

Two days later, everyone was still gathered at the hospital. Rico and Kim both suffered massive brain trauma. Rico was undergoing his second surgery in as many days to relieve the swelling on his brain. Although Kim was in a coma, the doctors had to deliver the babies prematurely via Caesarean the day of the accident.

Miraculously both preemie babies were doing very well. Grayce held Dre tightly as she shed tears for Rico and Kim. She subconsciously rubbed her belly as she thought about Kim and the babies.

Dre did his best to keep Grayce calm. The doctors were not letting anyone see Rico, Kim or the babies right now but they all still wanted to be there. Dre had never felt this helpless in his life. He wondered if this was how his family felt as they sat around when he was shot. The thought of losing another friend terrified him. "We need to pray," he said, wiping away his tears.

They all stood in the middle of the waiting room and clasped hands. There were even a few other people in the waiting room that they didn't know who stood to pray with them. Dre bowed his head and waited for his father to lead the prayer as he always did.

After a few moments of silence, he lifted his head and looked to his father. "You've got this son," Senior said, nodding at his son. Grayce squeezed his hand tightly as a show of support. Dre looked at his wife and smiled.

"Father God we come before you right now as respectfully as we know how standing in intercession for Rico, Kim, their daughters and everyone in this hospital right now Lord. Father, we know that you love them more than we ever could, and we ask that you touch the hands of the doctors and surgeons throughout this hospital right now Lord God."

"We ask that you work through their hands and show your ultimate power Lord. "We know that you are in

control right now. I stand here as a living testament to your

grace and your glory father. Lord, we ask that heal them

from the top of their heads to the soles of their feet. You are

the ultimate physician. Lord, you are Jehovah Rapha, our

healer and we declare their healing in the name of Jesus,

Amen."

Grayce hugged Dre tightly. She had never been prouder of him. Senior beamed. He always knew that there was a calling on Dre's life, but he had to let Dre realize that for himself. "I see he was listening after all," Gloria smiled. Senior kissed his wife's forehead. "Yes, he has…yes he has."

CHAPTER 81

The guys sat staring at Rico lying in the hospital bed. It had been months, and he still had not come out of the coma. The twins, known around the hospital as the miracle babies, were released from the hospital and are getting better every day. Since Rico nor Kim's biological parents were still living, Senior and Gloria were granted temporary custody of the babies.

Everyone took turns visiting Rico and Kim daily, and they all gathered together to visit them every Sunday after church. The doctors agreed to allow them to share a room in ICU. Marc had an eerie sense of Déjà vu looking at Rico and Kim lying unconscious. It brought back the memories he had tried his best to forget.

It had been months since the day of the accident, but the doctors were still holding out hope that Rico and Kim would recover. Dre felt like he was going to be sick. "I need some air," he said walking out of the room while

Marc continued to talk to Rico and Kim, telling them about his trip to the Hamptons with Imani.

They all believed that they could hear them. "I'll see you guys tomorrow," Tony said after saying a quick prayer. Dre was leaning on the wall outside of the room loosening his tie. "Are you okay Dre?" Tony asked. Dre nodded. "I just felt like I couldn't breathe." Dre stared at the wall in front on him. "It felt like somebody was sitting on my chest. Tony, I can't lose anyone else, I can't," Dre cried.

Tony shook his head. "Honestly Dre my mind cannot even fathom the idea of losing them. I will not let myself think anything other than complete recovery for them. They didn't expect Kim to make it through the night when she was brought in but two months in, look at her. When they come out of this, they both are going to need us."

"Just focus on that Dre. It's easy for us to look at the here and now but the hard part is using our faith to see beyond that. Thinking back, it's a miracle that they are even alive. If you had seen the car, you would not think anyone survived, but there they are in one piece. God is moving, Dre. Just stand back and watch Him work," Tony smiled.

CHAPTER 82

Seven months to the day of the accident, Senior received a call from the hospital informing him that Rico was awake. Senior praised God as he relayed the message to everyone else. Drea called and updated everyone, and they all agreed to meet at the hospital.

After a few moments with the doctor, Rico looked around at the unfamiliar surrounding, totally unaware that he'd been in a coma for the last seven months. "What's going on?" he tried to ask as the nurse asked him not to speak.

Another nurse rushed in carrying a pitcher of ice water followed by the doctor. Rico immediately had a flashback of Dre and Marc. "Just one second Mr. Durant," the doctor instructed as Rico attempted to sit up. "Slowly sip this water before you try to speak, okay?" the doctor asked. Rico nodded his head. He hadn't realized that he was so thirsty.

"Okay Rico, do you know what year it is?" the doctor asked. "2016," Rico responded. "Why am I here?" he asked. "Rico you were in a car accident, and for the last seven months you were in a coma." "Where's my wife?" he asked immediately looking around the room.

He tried to get out of the bed when he saw Kim lying in bed across from him. "Kim, Kim," he called. "Why isn't she answering?" he asked. The look on the doctor's face told it all, Rico immediately knew that something was wrong.

"Please tell me what's wrong with my wife? Please tell me that she is okay," he said looking from the doctor to the nurse. The same nurse who took care of Dre and Marc could no longer hold back her tears as she walked over to Rico.

"Mr. Durant, I need you to be strong for your wife and your daughters. "Your wife is in a coma Mr. Durant," the doctor informed him. Rico just shook his head. It takes a few seconds before Rico truly realized what the doctor

was telling him.

Rico tried to get out of the bed again to get to his

wife. "Mr. Durant you have to calm down sir. Your body

is still healing." "I need to see her," Rico said. The nurse

looked to the doctor for approval. The doctor nodded his

head and had the nurse help him carefully move Kim's bed

closer to Rico.

Rico began crying as he watched the machines

breathe for his wife. "I know it looks bad Mr. Durant, but

the surgeons were giving both of you less than 10% chance

of survival when you came in, but seven months later you

both are still here," he said.

Rico tried to sit again when he saw the image of his

wife lying helpless in bed. The nurse helped the doctor

restrain him while the doctor gave him a shot of something

to calm him down when Grayce entered the room. "Rico

sweetie I need you to listen to me okay?" Rico nodded his head as the tears rolled back onto the pillow.

"Sweetie this is going to be a rough road ahead for all of you. The doctors are doing everything that they can to help Kim. The best thing that you can do right now is pray for her and continue to get better yourself. Kim is going to need you. Rico closed his eyes and nodded again." "The girls are really okay?" Rico asked.

Grayce smiled. "They are better than okay. They are beautiful and full of energy just like their mommy," Grayce laughed. We have tons of pictures and videos. I don't think it would be a good idea to bring them here right now, but you can FaceTime with them a little later if you're up to it. Rico bit his bottom lip, nodded his head and wept for his wife. The effects of the medication started working immediately, as Rico drifted off thinking of his family while the tears fell down his face.

CHAPTER 83

Rico was officially released from the hospital two weeks after he regained consciousness. Although he was free to go home, he refused to leave his wife's side. Rico sat by her bed and prayed for her every day. Rico felt numb. He didn't want to live without Kim, but the only thing that kept him going was thinking about his daughters, and he knew that would not be fair to his daughters and it wasn't what Kim would want.

Rico wiped the tears and took a deep breath as Dre walked into the room. "How are you holding up Rico?" "Not good," he responded defeatedly. "I understand but do me a favor and stop burying your wife." Rico looked up at Dre in shock. "Why would you say that?" "Rico look at you man, sitting here praying and reading the bible but you're not believing. If you are going to trust God, trust Him."

"I believe with everything in me that Kim will be fine, but you need to believe that too. What do you think Kim is going to do to you when she finds out that you have not been to see your daughters man?" Rico smiled and shook his head. "You're right Dre. I just don't want to leave her here alone." "She's not alone," Jess said as she, Grayce, Imani, Michelle, and Drea entered the room.

"Rico sweetie, we know this isn't easy," Grayce said. "Trust me watching Dre lay in that bed was one of the hardest things I've ever had to endure but I had to be strong for him just like you have to be strong for her. She can't fight right now, so she needs you to stand in intercession for her. What would you do if some guy tried to hurt her?" Grayce asked. "I would kill anybody that tried to hurt her," Rico responded boldly.

"Well guess what sweetie? The devil is trying to kill your wife, and your faith is the only thing that can defeat him so are you going to sit here wallowing in pity or are you going to go do battle for your wife?" Rico stood and hugged Grayce tightly. "I get it sis. Thank you so much. I need to go see my girls and show them pictures of their mommy." Come on Rico, I'll take you," Dre said hugging his friend, "but we need to hit the barber first. I don't want you to scare them."

Rico and the girls laughed as Rico looked at himself in the mirror. His usually neatly trimmed beard has grown so much that he barely recognized himself.

CHAPTER 84

Rico had butterflies the entire ride to Senior and Gloria's house. "You okay?" Dre asked as she watched Rico continuously shift in his seat. "I'm nervous Dre, I don't know the first thing about being a father. Welcome to the club man. I think I've read every baby book ever written in the last few months. You will be fine Rico, babies are easy. Just love them, feed them, change them and play with them and they are good."

"It's crazy that all of this is happening now. One of our last conversations we talked about everything that's been going on and her exact words were, God has a massive blessing coming our way, and the devil is just trying to distract us."

"She told me to stay focused and never stop praying." Dre nodded his head. "Bro I'm not even going to say I understand any of this because I don't at all, but I am praying for you man. I love you, Rico." "I love you too D."

"You ready to do this?" "As ready as I will ever be," Rico said as he opened the door.

Dre called his parents when they left the barber to inform them that he and Rico were on their way. Senior opened the door as they walked up the walkway to the porch. "Well it's about time," he said as he pulled Rico close to him and hugged him. "How are you son?" Senior smiled. "I'm good Dad, how you been?"

"I'm great. Your daughters have been prepping me to be a grandfather," Senior smiled. Rico smiled as he walked into the house and saw his beautiful daughters playing together on the blanket on the floor. Gloria got off the floor and walked over to hug Rico.

"Go head over there and meet your daughters baby." Rico slowly walked over and sat on the floor next to the girls as they were totally distracted by each other. Rico cried as he watched his daughters marveling and how much they looked like a perfect combination of he and Kim.

He felt guilty for being away from them for so long. All the apprehension that he felt before they were born was gone. Rico was in awe of the fact that he and Kim created these beautiful little people. As if one of the twins were reading his mind, she looked over at Rico and began bouncing and laughing, causing the other little girl to do the same.

Rico had never felt such joy in his life. He looked over at Dre, senior and Gloria. "Do you think they know who I am? "Of course, they do," Senior beamed. "They feel your love and your spirit." Rico smiled as only a proud father can while Dre started taking pictures of Rico and his daughters. Rico was more determined than ever to totally trust God for Kim's healing. He would not allow his daughters to grow up without their mother.

CHAPTER 85

Another month had passed, and while Kim had shown definite signs of improvement, her overall condition remained the same. Rico was true to his word. He prayed life and recovery over her like never before. He even made a point of taking the girls to church every Sunday.

Rico sat at the foot of his wife's bed massaging her feet thinking about how much he'd changed since the accident. Physically he walked with a slight limp that only someone who knew him would notice, but spiritually he has changed his life completely. Rico went to church with his grandmother often when he was a child but stopped going as he got older.

He hated the idea of religion, but since the accident, he discovered that God didn't focus on the religion. He focused on the relationship. Rico smiled thinking how happy Kim was going to be when she found out that he gave his life to God and joined Senior's church. "What are you smiling about?" Jess asked as she entered the room.

"Hey Jess, I was just thinking about Kim and how shocked she will be when she finds out I got saved." Jess smiled. "You know she might start shouting," Jess laughed. "It just feels good to be able to pray over her the same way she's been praying over me all of these years." Jess nodded. That's why it's so important to be equally yoked. "There's nothing like the power of prayer, and when a husband and wife can come together on one accord, there is not a demon in hell that can penetrate that union."

"That's why the enemy is trying so hard to destroy the family unit. I am so proud of you Rico. I know Jayson is up there rejoicing too." Rico held his head down and tightly closed his eyes to keep the tears from falling. "He always talked to me about God. Talking about how he wanted all of us up there together. I miss him so much, Jess." "So, do I," she said quietly. "But I am comforted knowing that I will see him again. So, how's our girl doing today?" "She's good," Rico smiles. "I was telling her about her girls showing out in church yesterday," Rico laughed. "Yes. they are something else, and I thought my twins were active," Jess laughed.

CHAPTER 86

The last year had been heartbreaking for them all.

Drea sat in her car outside her parents' home and wept.

"God, I know that everything that you do is for your divine

purpose, and I trust your process; but this hurts. It hurts so

much. Please help me."

Drea was laying her head on the steering wheel

when she heard a tap at her window. It was Tony. She

exited the car and fell into his arms. "It's okay baby. I'm

here," Tony said comforting Drea. "Tony, I just don't know

how much more I can take. How much more any of us can

take?" Tony held her tightly.

"Baby I don't understand it. I don't understand any

of this. I've been seeking God like never before trying to

gain some type of clarity, but at the end of the day, God

doesn't owe us anything. Every second of every day that

He allows us to breathe is a blessing in itself. He needed

Jay more than we did and Kim...well I don't know baby, but she's alive."

"No matter what we see, she is alive, and for every beat of her heart, we need to give Him thanks. We can't dwell on the loss. If we do it will drive us crazy. For our own sanity, I must think about the treasures that Jay left behind and think about those beautiful baby girls waiting for Kim. I don't think it's a coincidence that all of this is happening. God is shifting some things around. We just have to be patient and await the outcome."

CHAPTER 87

Rico was asleep when he kept hearing this faint sound in the distance. He sat up confused until he realized that Kim was awake. Rico tripped over his chair running to alert the nurse. "Mr. Durant please just wait here. I promise as soon as we know anything we'll tell you, but we need to attend to your wife right now okay?"

Rico nodded his head. He had been praying for this day for so long. He dropped to his knees and began to thank God. Rico didn't care who was watching or what they thought about him. God gave him his wife back, and he wasn't going to let anything or anyone stop his praise.

Marc and Imani were getting off the elevator when they saw Rico laughing and praising. Rico looked over and saw them. "She's back Marc, my baby is back," he said hugging Imani. "Praise God," Imani said. Marc immediately called to let the others know as they begin to praise God with him.

The doctor exited the room 20 minutes later. "Mr. Durant, you can see your wife now" he smiled. Rico rushed into the room. The sight of Kim made his heart beat faster. He walked over to the bed and softly hugged her. "I love you so much baby," he smiled. "For so long I didn't think I would ever see your smile again."

Kim smiled weakly, softly touching his face. "You know I am not going anywhere, Rico. I felt myself leaving when I saw someone pointing telling me to go back. I could hear your voice, and I heard my babies' voices," Kim cried. "Thank you Jesus for bringing me back to my family."

For the next hour, Rico laid beside his wife in the bed showing her pictures of their beautiful daughters. "They look just like us," Kim cried. "I know baby, that's the first thing I said when I saw them. I missed you so much baby," he said showering Kim with kisses allowing his tears of joy to flow.

"I never really realized just how much I love you. I am going to cherish you every second of every day. Thank you for loving our beautiful daughters and me." Just then the door opened and Senior and Gloria with the twins. "Hey baby," Senior smiled at Kim, "I think these two have been waiting to meet you."

Kim's face lit up as she saw her beautiful daughters in the stroller. The tears streamed down her face as Rico stood to take the girls out of the stroller. "Thanks dad," Rico smiled. "This is Hope," Rico said holding the first little bundle, "and this is Faith," he smiled, sitting back down next to Kim as Senior placed her in his other arm.

Kim could not find the words to express her feelings as she held the tiny hands of her beautiful daughters. Senior and Gloria prayed with Kim and Rico before departing to the waiting room to give the two of them some much needed time with their daughters.

Kim wept as she looked at her beautiful, very vocal daughters. "I cannot believe that so much time has passed. How old are they?" "They will be eight months tomorrow," Rico said quietly. "I've missed so much of their lives, Rico." "Baby please don't focus on that. We're both here now, and we will never leave their side again." Kim nodded. "Babe we'll get to watch them take their first steps, and we can throw a huge birthday party when they turn one. We will cherish every moment from this day forth, and I will never, ever take my family for granted," Rico said as Hope smiled at her mommy.

CHAPTER 88

Dre was sound asleep when Grayce softly kissed him on his cheek. "Baby wake up," she said softly. Dre turned on his side and slowly opened his eyes. "Baby my water just broke." "WHAT?!?!?" Dre jumped out of bed so fast that he knocked the lamp from the bedside table on the floor. Grayce shook her head. "Baby come here please," she said calmly.

"Sweetie I need you to calm down okay. Take slow deep breaths." Dre nodded as he sat down on the edge of the bed taking deep breaths. "I am fine right now. I called the doctor and our parents. They are calling everyone else, and they will meet us at the hospital, okay?" "Okay," Dre said nervously. "Are you ready daddy?" She smiled. "I have never been readier for anything in my life," he nervously laughed, kissing her softly. "Good now get dressed and get me to the hospital. Your little one wants to meet you."

By the time Dre and Grayce arrived at the hospital, everyone else was already there. Marc rushed over to him. "Man, what took y'all so long? I thought something happened," Marc said concerned. Grayce laughed. "Probably because your cousin drove 20 miles an hour the entire way here."

Gloria prayed before they ushered Grayce into the delivery room. They were all so excited. There had been so much tragedy around them the last year. Everyone was ready for a new chapter.

Ten hours later, Dre ran into the waiting room with the biggest smile on his face. "My wife and handsome son are doing great." Everyone was overjoyed, especially Gloria and Patricia. Dre and Grayce had decided not to have a baby shower considering everything that had happened in the last few months, so Gloria and Patricia were looking forward to more shopping for their grandson.

Dre linked eyes with Rico and Kim. "Hey man I am so happy to see you," Dre said hugging his friend. "Congrats man," Rico said with tears brimming in his eyes. Wishing he'd had an opportunity to witness of birth of his daughter. Thanks man. "So, what's his name," Marc asked.

"Andre Williamson IV of course," Dre beamed. "The nurse said if we're really quiet she will let everyone come in for 5 minutes." Drea clapped. "Yayyy…I'm an auntie." "Me too," Jess said laughing. "Me three," Imani and Michelle say in unison. They all laughed as they headed off to meet the newest member of their family.

CHAPTER 89

Marc exited the shop with the biggest grin on his face. Eric smiled. "So, you're really going to do it huh?" "Yep," Marc smiled, holding the small bag tightly. "I'm just praying that she says yes," he said thinking about the 4-carat engagement ring that he'd just purchased for Imani.

"Marc are you serious? You don't see the way that woman looks at you?" "I know she loves me E, but I also know that she's a little scared of being hurt again too. Remember she was engaged before and it didn't work out." "Yeah, that's because God had a plan for both of y'all." "True," Marc said nodding his head.

"I used to think that it was his loss and my gain but then I thought about it, she was never his. I know that this is the woman that I am supposed to spend my life with. I knew that something good had to come out of all of this and it has. Think about it, I never would've met Imani, and you most likely would not have met Michelle. You hate

Popeye's. You only went for me." "Wow, I never thought about that," Eric smiled. "I never thought it was possible to love anyone the way that I love her."

"Trust me E, I know that feeling all too well. Hey, what do you think about us having a double wedding?" Eric asked. "I love that idea, but we better run it cross the girls first," Marc laughed. "You're right about that. I know Michelle would love to have someone else helping with the wedding plans though.

"I can't believe that we're both getting married. Momma would be so happy right now." Eric said tearing up. "I am sure she is happy. I believe that she watches over us." "I hope so Marc, I really hope so."

CHAPTER 90

Tony locked the door to his apartment so happy to be home. He was thrilled to have his mom back in his life. She adored Brian, and he loved having her around. Gloria had even convinced her to come to church. Theresa eventually joined Senior's church and sang on the choir. With all the loss that they'd endured, Tony was relieved that they were all finally experiencing some happiness.

"Is he in bed?" Tony asked his mom as she exited Brian's room. "Yes, that boy is a slick one. He reminds me so much of..." Theresa couldn't bring herself to say Andrew's name. Tony walked over to his mother. "Mom you can say his name. Not saying his name doesn't change the fact that he was here."

"Tony, I am sorry. I don't know how you can even look at me. I can't stand to look at myself. I was a horrible mother. I allowed one son to die and turned my back on the other one." "Mom, I know that this can't be easy for you, but God has forgiven you already and so have I, now you are going to have to forgive yourself."

"I think of about Drew every day, but it gives me comfort knowing that he's watching over us and we will see him again. The enemy tried to use that guilt to destroy you. Don't let it mom. It doesn't matter who you were or what you did. All that matters is that right here, and right now you gave your heart to Jesus."

Tony held his mother as she wept in his arms. He knew that she would have a long road ahead of her, but he was determined to help her through every step.

"You're right Tony. I am so glad that God gave me another chance." "So am I mom," Tony smiled. "Something smells great," he said just as Drea exited the kitchen with his plate. "Babe I didn't know you were here," he said softly kissing her. "I wanted to surprise you," Drea said looking into his eyes.

"Well on that note, I am going to turn in. Thanks again for the shopping trip and dinner Drea. You turned out to be such a beautiful woman. I can't wait until Brian has a little brother or sister running around here," she mumbled as she left the room.

Tony shook his head and laughed. "What is it with parents and grandbabies?" "Tell me about it," Drea laughed. "Mom has been dropping hints about us getting married and having kids too." "Are you serious?" Tony asked. "Yes," Drea laughed. Tony smiled at her while continuing to eat his dinner. "What are you smiling at?" Drea blushed. "My future," Tony responded quietly.

CHAPTER 91

Marc and Michelle were overjoyed at the success of the restaurant. They knew it would be huge, but they were surprised at just how big it had become. Their financial advisor informed them that the restaurant had made more in the first two months of the opening than in the first-year projection. They could not believe their ears. Michelle hugged Marc tightly.

"Marc I cannot thank you enough. You have no idea what this whole thing has meant to me. God sent your family to save us." "Michelle you saved us too. I have never seen my brother happier, and I love being an uncle. The unconditional love of a child is an amazing thing, and you've given us that."

"You are all such good men. I could not have prayed for a better group of people to call my family. God is faithful." "Yes, He is," Marc agreed.

"Now come on we need to get to the ceremony before Imani kills me for making us late." Imani was being honored as the Businesswoman of the Year. Marc was so proud of her. He never imagined having a woman like her by his side, but she gave him a strength that he never knew he had. She made him a better man. They prayed together every morning and every night. She was the very definition of a helpmeet and Marc couldn't wait to make her his wife.

CHAPTER 92

Manny finally received his teaching degree and the entire family was there to celebrate with him. Manny loved children and thanks to Senior's recommendation, he was able to secure a job as a freshman coordinator at a new junior high school.

Teaching was one of his greatest passions, and it brought him so much pleasure. Although he'd never be able to have children of his own, he loved being around them. He'd recently taken over as head coach for Jackson, Aaron and Amir's soccer team.

The entire team loved "Uncle Manny." He was a big kid himself. He took them out to eat after every game and even tutored a few who were having trouble in school. Manny had also become good friends with Jess over the last few months, and if he was honest with himself, he had a major crush on Jess; but Manny was also respectful of the fact that she was newly widowed and the last thing he wanted to do was make her uncomfortable.

Manny decided to talk to his big sister. Imani answered the phone on the second ring out of breath. "Hey big head," she answered breathlessly. "Hey, did I catch you in the middle of your run?" Manny asked. "Nope, I actually just finished. How have you been? We haven't talked in a while." "I've been great," Manny said quietly.

"The new job is amazing, and I love the kids." "Aww, I am so happy for you Manny. I feel like there's a but somewhere though." Manny sighed deeply. "I am in trouble sis." "What's wrong..talk to me." "Are you still at the park on Lincoln?" Manny asked. "Yes, I'm walking to the car now." "Okay perfect. I am at the coffee house around the corner. I'll be there in five minutes. Do you have a few minutes to talk?" "Of course, I'll be here waiting." "Okay sis, see you in a few."

Imani sat on the bench waiting for Manny, thinking about how different their lives had become. It went from being just the two of them to a huge family. Imani never realized just how much they were missing. The sound of Immanuel's motorcycle interrupted her thoughts.

Imani walked over to hug her little brother. They both had been so busy the last few weeks that they haven't really had time to see each other. Imani missed him terribly. "Hi Manny," she said hugging him tightly. "I miss you," he said looking at his big sister. "You look happy." Imani couldn't hide the smile if she wanted too. "I am happy Manny. I'm so happy that it scares me. I keep expecting something to go wrong, but I know it's nothing but the enemy but enough about me, what's going on?"

"Well you know I've been spending a lot of time with Jess lately right." "Yes," Imani said quietly already knowing where this conversation was heading. "Sis I like her. I mean really, really like her." Imani remained quiet while he talked, knowing that right now he just needed to get out everything that he'd been holding inside.

"I feel so bad because she lost her husband and I feel so...I don't even know the right word to use. I just feel bad. What kind of man pushes up on a woman who just lost her husband?" "How did you push up on her exactly," Imani asked. "I mean I didn't really do anything, but whenever I am around her I just feel like a little kid on Christmas morning, and I love her kids. If I could have children, I'd want them to be just like them."

Imani smiled. She'd never heard Manny speak about any woman like this and she really felt for him and the position that he was in. Imani linked his arm in hers as they walked along the lake. "First off, you've done absolutely nothing wrong. Jess is an amazing woman. I'm sure she has her share of admirers." "Wow thanks Sis," Manny laughed. "You know what I mean," she smiled.

"I do agree with your decision to not share this information with her, at least for right now. Pray on it, sweetie. If she's meant for you, God will work it all out."
"You're right big sis. Thank you for not judging me."
"Sweetie there is nothing to judge. Just seek God-He will work it all out one way or another."

"You're right. Thank you for being the best sister ever." "Aww, you're such a good man. I am so proud of you Manny. I wish there were more men in the world like you." Manny blushed at his sister's compliment. "Come on I'll fix you lunch." "Okay, but I don't want a salad," Manny laughed. "If you feed me another piece of lettuce I am going to scream."

CHAPTER 93

Eric was so happy to be home. It had been a very long week, and he has missed Michelle and the kids terribly. Michelle rushed to light the candles. She knew that Eric would be tired, so she dropped the kids over to Jess' house before heading to his home to cook him a nice candlelight dinner.

Eric smiled when he entered the house and saw candles everywhere. "Hi baby," Michelle said, hugging him from behind. "Hi yourself. Where are the kids?" Eric asked. "They're at Jess' for the night" Michelle smiled.

"I wanted you all to myself tonight." Eric smiled. "It smells good in here. Is that your famous seafood stew I smell?" Michelle cocked her head and looked at Eric. "I love the fact that you are so perceptive. It means so much to me that you take time to notice the little things."

"Baby you are one of the most important people in this world to me. There are no little things when it comes to you." Michelle held him tightly before she helped him out of his suit jacket. "I hope you're hungry." "I'm starving, I didn't get a chance to eat lunch today." Michelle turned to look at him. "I know baby, I didn't mean to skip lunch. Things were just intense for a while, and when I looked up it was almost 4, and by that time I just wanted to finish and get home to you."

"I understand, and things will be a lot better now that we've hired the new chef." "Congrats baby. I'm proud of you and Marc is thrilled." "I think that has more to do with Imani than the restaurant," Michelle giggled. "You might be right about that. They are too cute together." "Marc said the same thing about us. I wanted to run something by you. Last week Marc and I went ring shopping. He is going to propose to Imani."

Michelle could not contain her excitement. "Oohhh wouldn't it be so cute if we could have a double wedding?" Eric laughed shaking his head. "Actually, I wanted to discuss that with you." "Are you sure you wouldn't mind baby?" "Eric, I would love it. Your family means the world to the kids and me. I've never in my life seen them happier. They love you all so much. Thank you for sharing your family, your home and your heart with us. We don't take it for granted."

Eric held her close as the tears fell from his eyes. All the money in his account could never compare to the feeling of being loved. "I still feel like I am dreaming," Eric said laying his head on her shoulder. I never in a million years thought that I'd end up with a woman like you and now that I have you I won't ever let you go."

CHAPTER 94

Manny thought he is dreaming until the ringing continued. "Hello?" he answered groggily. Marc laughed. "Man, they must've worn you out last night if you are still asleep." Manny laughed as he stretched and looked at the clock. "No, they were pretty chill, I just had some trouble sleeping." "Everything okay?" Marc asked. "Ye..yes everything is good," Manny stuttered

"Come on Manny you are family now. You can talk to me." "I don't think I can talk to you about this Marc." "Are you in some kind of trouble?" Marc asked concerned. "Not really but hey I know you didn't call to talk about my problems. What's up with you?" Marc noticed how quickly Manny changed the subject. Little did he know that this was far from over. He'd drop it for now, but Marc was determined to get him to open up to him.

"I was wondering if you have plans for lunch. I wanted to talk to you about something." "Um sure, what time and where?" "Can you meet me at the restaurant in an hour?" Sure, see you in a few." Manny hung up the phone feeling a little uneasy. For a moment he wondered if Imani mentioned anything to Marc, but then he realized that his sister would never do that.

Manny arrived at the restaurant seconds after Marc. "Wassup Manny?" Marc asked as he exited the van. "Not much," Manny said closing the van door behind Marc. "I see you're picking your weight back up." "Yeah man, thanks to you sister and Michelle," he laughed as they made their way to the table.

After they place their drink orders, Marc suddenly became serious. "I know you're probably wondering why I asked you here." "It did cross my mind," Manny smiled. Marc shook his head and laughed.

"Well, I am here to ask for your sister's hand in marriage." Manny laughed aloud out of joy and relief. "I hope that's a good laugh," Marc said looking at Manny.

"I'm just trying to imagine how bad Imani would beat me if I say no." Marc laughed. "She doesn't know. I know you both grew up leaning on each other and I just want you to know that you both have become such an important part of our family."

"Everyone loves you both so much, and I know you are a blessing to Jess and the boys. She talks about you all the time." Manny couldn't help but blush. "Hold up-was that a blush?" Marc asked teasing Manny. Manny shook his head. "I don't know what you're talking about," he said trying to hide his smile.

One look at Manny and anyone could clearly see that that has had fallen in love with Jess. "Manny let me just say that Jayson was one of my best friends and one of the best dudes you would ever want to meet. I wish you'd had an opportunity to meet him. I think you two would've gotten along well. You both have a lot in common like the fact that you both love Jess."

"Marc, I didn't plan this. It's like in the blink of an eye before I even realized what was happening, I fell in love with her." "Manny, love happens when you least expect it. Look at your sister and me. I was going through one of the worst ordeals in my life, and there she was. I wasn't looking for love or a wife before I was shot and now I want both of those things more than anything else in this world.

All of this has taught me one thing," Marc said as he picks up the menu. "God has a plan for all of us, and it doesn't always line up with what we planned. You can fight it all you want but at the end of the day He knows what's best and He is gonna do what He's gonna do."

Manny nodded his head and smiled. "You are going to make a great brother-in-law." "Let's hope your sister feels the same way," Marc said signaling the waitress.

CHAPTER 95

Tony fell onto the sofa after removing the last box from the truck. "I hate moving," he said. "I know babe but just look at it like this. You won't ever have to do it again" Drea said as she leaned over and kissed his forehead. "I know you are exhausted babe, but if you don't get in the kitchen, they are going to devour the pizza and wings."

Grayce laughed as she continued to feed her son AJ. Tony pulled himself up off the sofa and walked over to Grayce. "He is adorable Grayce. I can't wait until we have a little one," Tony said smiling. He winked at Drea before walking into the kitchen.

"Well well well," Grayce smiled. "Looks like there will be another little one in the family soon if Tony has his way." "Girl yes, that's all he's been talking about." "How do you feel about that?" Grayce asked.

"I would love to have a child. Brian is my heart and joy, and I must admit that having him around has stirred up some maternal feelings. I never thought in a million years that Tony and I would be back together but look at us now," Drea smiled, watching Tony in the kitchen.

"Thank you all for helping with the move," Tony said while fixing his plate. "I really appreciate all of your help." There were murmurs of thank you around the table while everyone had their mouths full. "Eric, I noticed that Michelle isn't here, is she okay?" Tony asked. "Yeah, she's fine. She's checking out a new location for the second restaurant, and this was the only time that the realtor had available."

"That is great," Tony said. "Congrats Marc." "Thank you man, but I can't really take any credit. Michelle has done an amazing job with the restaurant. I think she even surpassed her own expectations." "This is really a nice spot," Marc said as he looked around. "I love that yard." "Me too," Brian beamed. "I never had a yard before, and dad said we're going to build a treehouse."

"That sounds like a lot of fun," Dre said. "Yep," Brian said looking proudly at Tony.

They had finally become a "real" family. The adoption process went through without a hitch. Brian was officially Tony's son. Tony was happier than he'd been in a very long time. He had his mother, Brian, and Drea in his life and he was never going to let them go.

CHAPTER 96

Marcus, Imani, Eric and Michelle's wedding day finally arrived. The wedding was held in one of the largest venues in Maryland. The hall was almost filled, and they still had another hour to go. 'Man, it's packed out there," Dre said. "I know," Tony laughed. "I bet you're glad you had a small ceremony, aren't you?" Tony joked.

Rico stepped away to call to check on his daughters. As he turned the corner, he stopped in his tracks as he locked eyes with Kim. "Hi beautiful," Rico said pulling her close. "Hi handsome," she smiled back. "Did I tell you how beautiful you look today?" Rico asked. "Only 100 or so times," Kim laughed, "But I never get tired of hearing it. Thank you, baby," she blushed.

"How are the girls?" She asked. "They are great, Mrs. Mary says they are sleeping right now." "Do you regret not having a big wedding like this?" Rico asked. "This is beautiful, but I wouldn't trade our wedding for

anything in the world. It felt like we were one with God.
Nothing can ever replace that."

Rico smiled as he hugged his wife, careful not to
wrinkle her dress. "Alright, places everyone," the wedding
coordinator called. Imani immediately felt butterflies in her
stomach. In less than an hour, I will be Mrs. Marcus
Jackson she thought. Imani sighed and held her head back
to keep her tears from ruining her makeup.

"Okay girl, none of that, we've got two of the most
handsome men in the world waiting for us," Michelle said
hugging her soon-to-be sister-in-law.

The wedding was beautiful. Neither of the brides'
fathers were still living so Senior walked them both down
the aisle together while thanks to Marc's connections, India
Arie sang *Beautiful Surprise.*

They all wanted a traditional wedding with a twist.
Instead of writing personal vows, each couple decided to
come up with joint vows for the minister to read. They also

asked Tony to perform their ceremony. He was so honored. This was the first wedding he's ever officiated, and he was more than a little nervous.

Marc smiled at Tony calming his nerves. Marc cried throughout the entire ceremony. He couldn't believe that he is marrying the woman of his dreams. His life was different from this time last year.

He was getting better and better every day. He had started feeling light sensations in his legs and believed that he would be able to walk again. He was happier than he'd ever been in his life. Marc didn't know what he would've done without having Imani by his side, praying with him and for him throughout this entire ordeal.

He thought back to a conversation he'd had with Dre the night before. They'd suffered much loss, but it seemed like it God still had the last say.

CHAPTER 97

"I cannot believe I am Mrs. Marcus Jackson," Imani smiled. "Believe it baby, because I am never, ever letting you go," Marcus smiled. He had never been so happy in his life. He watched as Eric and Michelle danced together. His brother had finally come out of his shell. He was no longer the shy big brother that he'd known all his life and Marcus was so happy for him.

"Penny for your thoughts," Imani said as she watched him watching Eric and Michelle. "I just can't believe how much Eric has changed," Marc smiled. Imani smiled watching the two on the dancefloor, slow dancing to Ribbon in the Sky by Stevie Wonder. "The love of a good woman can completely change your world," Marc said kissing his bride.

"I am so blessed to call you my wife," Marc beamed. "And I am honored that you chose me to be your wife," Imani smiled as she kissed him softly. "I have never felt so loved in all of my life, Marcus. Everything that I endured led me to this very moment, and it was so worth it." Marcus felt like he was on top of the world. "I feel the same way baby. It's like God hit the reset button on my life. I feel like I can do anything." "You can baby," Imani smiled at her husband.

"Welcome to married life," Dre said as he walked over to Marc and Imani. "If I had known that being married felt this good, I would've gotten married a long time ago." "Tell me about it," Dre laughed, looking longingly at Grayce. The highlight of the entire reception was Senior and Gloria doing the wobble dance. Dre laughed until he was in tears.

CHAPTER 98

It had been two months since the wedding and Eric was still on cloud nine. He and Dre were just finishing up their workout when they saw Grayce rushing toward them. They immediately knew that something was wrong as she raced over to him. "What's wrong?" Dre asked as he ran to meet her.

"Your mom just called. Dad had a heart attack, and they are rushing him to the hospital now." Dre felt his stomach drop. "Where's the baby?" Dre asked. Jess had just arrived when your mom called; she and the boys are at the house with him.

Dre nodded his head solemnly thinking about his father, his best friend, as they all ran to the car. Dre always prayed that if he ever he had a son they would have a relationship just like his relationship with his father. Grayce softly held his hand as she began to pray. She knew that Dre was scared. They all were. Senior was one of the greatest men that Grayce had ever known and she would not fathom the possibility of him not being in their lives.

As she parked the car in the hospital parking garage, Grayce was finally able to take a good look at Dre. It broke her heart to see him look so defeated. "Baby it's going to be okay," she said hugging Dre. "God is in control of this and Senior is a strong man and in great health."

Dre nodded his head again as the tears fell from his eyes. He kissed his wife before running into the emergency room to find his mom. After what felt like an eternity Dre found her sitting in the waiting area reading her bible. "Mom is he okay?" Dre asked. "He's just fine Dre, the doctors are still with him, but I know my husband, and more importantly, I know my God. Your father's work isn't done. I keep telling him that he needs to slow down. It's a shame that this is how God had to get his attention."

Gloria's calm demeanor helped to ease Dre's fears. Dre looked up as the doctor walked toward them. "Hello," the doctor said addressing Dre and Eric before looking at Gloria. "Ma'am your husband is going to be just fine. He had what's called a Coronary Artery Spasm. Basically, when the artery wall tightens and blood flow through the artery is restricted it leads to chest pain or blood flow issues, causing a heart attack."

"The spasms come and go, but we did an angiogram, and there are no blockages, and there are no blood clots or plaque build-ups. I'm going to prescribe a couple of medications and monitor Mr. Williamson for the next six months, but I think your husband is just fine. We would like to like to keep him overnight for observation just as a precaution though. We've also put him in a private room, so you all are more than welcome to see him whenever you like. He's in room 3C, it's the first door on your right, you can't miss it."

"Thank God," Dre said hugging his mom. He didn't realize that he'd been crying until his mother wiped his face. "I told you Senior would be fine," Gloria said kissing her son on the cheek. "Now get yourself together so we can go see your father." Dre took several deep breaths and wiped his face before grabbing the hands of his mother and wife as they walked to Senior's room.

"Come on Eric," Dre said when he noticed Eric still standing in the doorway of the waiting area. "I can't Dre," he said slightly above a whisper. "It's too soon." Dre nodded his head. "I'll stay with him," Grayce said. "I need to call Jess anyway. "You guys go on and give Dad my love." "I will," Dre smiled. "What would I do without that woman?" Dre said as Gloria smiled.

CHAPTER 99

Dre's father was released from the hospital the next day which happened to be the week before Father's Day, so the girls got together and decided to host a Father's Day brunch. Senior had been a surrogate father to them all at one point or another, and they all love him dearly.

"I'm glad you're doing okay Pop," Rico said as he hugged Senior. "I don't know what we'd do without you keeping us in line." "Tell me about it. Dad didn't play at all. He put the whoop in whoopings," Marc laughed. They all laughed and murmured in agreement.

"Remember that time we took his car without permission to go to the Coliseum, and somebody stole the car while we were in the club." They all bust out laughing. Pop laughed so hard he had tears streaming down his face. "Yeah…he beat the skin off me," Dre laughed. "I knew we were going to get it good that night because Pops was way too calm," Marc added. "Those calm whoopings were always the worst ones. He beat my yellow butt til I turned red." They all start laughing even harder.

Dre suddenly became serious, "Dad, I thank God that we can sit around and laugh right now." "When Grayce told me the news, I had never been more scared in my life." "The thought of losing you," Dre tried to hold back the tears in his eyes. "Dad the thought of losing you was more than I could bear." Senior allowed the tears to fall from his eyes. "You know different people have different thoughts about life and death, but I tell you one thing before I lost consciousness all I could think about was the people in this room."

"I love each one of you so much, and the thought of not being here with all of you or watching my grandchildren grow up wasn't an option. I'm so thankful that God chose to spare my life." "So are we baby," Gloria smiled hugging her husband.

CHAPTER 100

"Drea I was wondering if you'd help me out with something?" Tony asked nervously. "Sure, what's up?" she asked, taking off her glasses and closing her book. "Um this is a little awkward, so I am not sure where to begin." She pulled Tony down on the sofa beside her. "What's going on babe? Talk to me."

"Well as you know the youth pastors meet twice a month and tonight we were discussing some of the young ladies in the church and I was thinking about having some type of teen forum where we could get together with them and talk about the issues they face, and I was wondering if you'd mind talking to them."

"I'd love to," Drea smiled. "Thank you so much, babe." "The pastor and I thought it would be good for them to hear from someone other than us and I thought you'd be the perfect person to talk to them. You're young and fly enough where they can relate to you and old enough for them to respect you."

"I really appreciate your confidence in me," Drea smiled. "That means the world to me, and I think that may be my purpose. I see so many of these young girls, and I want to pull them aside and just talk to them, but you never know how people are going to react; so, something like this would be the perfect forum for me to talk to them."

"Great," Tony beamed. "Thank you so much for agreeing to do this. I truly believe that your testimony will have a great impact on them." "I hope so," Drea smiled. "I wish I had someone to talk to when I was younger. It's easy to tell them to just focus on Jesus, but at the end of the day that's not realistic today."

"Teens are going to date and like it or not, they will have sex. The least that we can do is inform them of the repercussions and prepare them to make conscious decisions," "I totally agree with you babe," Tony said hugging Drea. "This is going to be great," he smiled as he

and Drea began planning the event.

CHAPTER 101

Drea and Tony had been working with Pastor Mike for weeks preparing for the youth summit, and now that the time had finally arrived, Drea was so nervous. Tony hugged her tightly and kissed her forehead. "Babe you are going to do great, you have nothing to be nervous about." "Is it that obvious?" she smiled nervously.

"Only because I know you," he said assuring her. "Baby, you are going to be fine," Tony said, kissing her forehead. Drea nodded and took a deep breath as Pastor Mike introduced her. "Well, I guess it's now or never." As she walked to the podium, she cleared her throat and smiled nervously. "Okay, I need you all to bear with me. Public speaking has never been my strong suit which should tell you just how much this means to me."

"First, I want to thank every one of you for coming out today, especially my family and friends. Your support and constant love mean everything to me and I thank God for all of you. As Pastor Mike said, my name is Drea, and as I look around at many of you I am reminded so much of myself. Let me start by saying that I am not here to preach to you. I think people need to do more conversing and listening than preaching."

"We should live our lives in a manner that every moment is our sermon. I can show you God much better than I can tell you about Him. I can also show you the bruises that my ex-boyfriend gave me when he beat me because of his insecurities, and he couldn't understand why I believed in God."

"I've always heard my father preach about being unequally yoked but I never truly understood until I dated a man who didn't believe in God. I knew deep down that it would never work because you can't build a house and have the home and the garage set on different foundations. It just won't work. It's not our job to try to convert anyone or judge them. The best thing that we can do for them is to pray for them."

"You have to know that God loves you and that's one thing that I have never, ever doubted. I dated several men who expressed their anger by abusing me, physically and sexually; there were also times when the devil would tell me, well you should not have said this or did that. Then one day it was like someone had turned a light on. My earthly father nor my heavenly father ever talked down to me or put their hands on me in any unloving way so why would I ever let any other man do that to me."

"I have never told anyone this, but when I was 16 years old there was this guy that I fell in love with, and he was a couple of years older than me, but I loved him with everything in me. He kept pressuring me to have sex, but I am the daughter of a pastor, no matter how many urges I had, I always planned to save myself until marriage. The thought of giving my virginity to my husband was something that I desired more than anything at that time."

"One day, that guy that I loved so much raped me. Drea could not look at her parents as the tears fell down her face. I was a virgin, and he took something that I planned to save for my husband, something that I could never get back. I felt horrible, but I blamed myself. I felt like it was my fault. I told myself that I should've known better and it was my fault for allowing it to happen."

When he was done, his only response, after he slapped me and told me to stop crying, was wow you really were a virgin. I left his house shortly after that as I walked alone to the bus stop, sore and embarrassed, all I could think about was who's going to want me now. I felt like my life was over and to add insult to injury later that day he called me and put his friends on the phone with me to prove that I was a virgin. I had never felt that low in my life."

"The man that I loved; didn't love me. I disappointed myself, God and my parents. Several of the girls in the audience wiped away tears. I felt so worthless and used. From that point, I had the lowest self-esteem.

The following year I met Pastor Tony, and we dated for two years. As much as I loved him, I consistently found myself pushing him away because I felt so unworthy of him. For years after that, I found myself running from relationship to relationship searching for something that can only be found in Jesus."

"Every single one of those men reminded me of that first man in some way which didn't help the self-esteem issues that I already had. I didn't feel pretty. I felt stupid for even allowing myself to entertain men that would beat on me or cheat on me and as much as I knew that it was wrong I overlooked it because I just wanted someone to ease the loneliness. I didn't realize that although they were there with me, I was still alone which is why I never felt whole."

"I didn't feel whole until I stopped running from God. Drea looked over at Dre as she blinked back tears. About two years ago I had one of the worst experiences of my life. I lost a very dear friend and almost lost my brother and cousin. Not too long after that, two other very close friends almost died in a car accident." Drea wiped her eyes with the tissue that Pastor Mike handed her.

"Let me tell you I didn't think I could handle anything else. I felt so broken because, in the midst of all of this, that ex-boyfriend that I told you about earlier who beat me, still did everything he could to make my life miserable. He entered the home that we shared and took everything that I owned and eventually tried to kill me. I've always known that God loved me, but in the middle of the chaos I couldn't hear him and definitely didn't feel him."

"Then, while at my lowest point, I cried out to God because I felt doubt creeping into my spirit and I immediately went to my bible. *Proverbs 3:5-8 says to trust in the Lord with all our heart, and not to lean on our own understanding. That scripture says to acknowledge him in all our ways, and he will make our paths straight.* I realized then that it wasn't about me or for me to understand. God was in control.

So, with that, I sucked it up and continued to trust God. We will never know what lies ahead for us, but one thing we can bank on is that God loves us beyond measure. His love for us cannot be defined, he proved that on Calvary and continues to prove it every day that he wakes us with new grace."

"God loves you in and out of your sin. Never, ever stop trusting Him. Even when you don't feel Him, trust Him. Even in the midst of your sin, trust and know that He loves you and He will show you the way. I promise you He will show up and show out. God can use any situation to grab your attention and totally change your world."

"The worst thing you can do is allow someone else to tell you how God feels about you. God loves every one of us, and no sin we commit will ever change that. We don't need the world's validation. God has already validated us. The bible is full of sinners who God used for His glory when the world wanted to shut them out."

"If you are truly tired just pray. Pray daily without ceasing and ask God to remove those people and things from you. I stopped praying that God would make me stop loving crazy men. Instead, my prayer became Lord place the desire in me to fulfill your will for my life. I want to live my life totally for you. I want my deeds to be your deeds, my thoughts, your thoughts and my words to be your words. Now things won't change overnight, at least it didn't work that way for me, but eventually God rewarded me."

"So, stop focusing on the negative things and focus on the positives. Good always trumps evil. Always. I love you all, and I hope that this has helped you in some way. My contact information is in the brochure Pastor Tony passed around earlier, so if you ever need to talk, please feel free to call, text, DM or email me-day or night. Thank you all so very much for coming and for being so patient with me today."

The group stood and applauded as Tony hugged Drea. "Baby you did it," he whispered in her ear. Drea hugged him tightly. "Thank you so much for everything, Tony. Everything seemed to be falling into place." Tony smiled. "It was God's timing baby. Speaking of timing. I cannot think of a better time than right now to do this."

"Excuse me, may I have everyone's attention." Drea started to walk off stage when Tony gently pulled her back to him. "As most of you may know Andrea Williamson has been the love of my life since I was still wet behind the ears and before I truly knew what love was." Turning to Drea, he smiled nervously.

"I'm not very eloquent but Andrea I love you more than you will ever know. I knew immediately the second that I saw you two years ago that you would be my wife, so I stand here now in this house of God, in front of our family and friends, asking you to be my wife. Will you marry me, Drea?" Tony asked. "Yes Tony," she cried, "yes." "Amen," Senior yelled, hugging his wife who sat next to him drying her eyes.

CHAPTER 102

"Mom, Manny did you see me?" Amir asked as he and Aaron ran over to the sideline after making the game-winning touchdown. "Of course we did," Manny smiled, picking him up. "You guys were awesome," Jess beamed. "I am so proud of you."

"Thanks mom, thanks Manny," Amir said excitedly before rushing back to his friends. "Manny you've done an amazing job coaching them this year," Jess smiled as she watched Jackson, Amir, and Aaron celebrating with their teammates on the field.

"It's been my pleasure," Manny smiled looking down at the beautiful little girl in the stroller. "I love children, and this is the closest I'll ever come to having my own, so I treasure this." "I'm sorry Manny," Jess said, rubbing his arm. "Thank you, Jess. I'm just so fortunate that God has allowed me to work with children. I love being a part of their lives." "They love you too," Jess smiled. "I'm so grateful to God for allowing us to meet you. This has been a rough few years, but your presence has been such a blessing."

Manny started blushing. "Jess I am so sorry to do this, especially right now but I was wondering if I could take you out for dinner." "I'd like that," Jess smiled to Manny's shock. "Okay, great! Umm, how about next Friday?" "Next Friday is perfect Manny," Jess smiled. "Okay great, I'll see you guys on Wednesday." Manny smiled before hugging Jess before walking over to the team. This is the best day of my life Manny thought as he swooped Amir up on his shoulders and celebrated with the boys.

CHAPTER 103

The group all sat at the dinner table delighting at the beautiful view of the Aspen Mountains. Their flight was long, but they enjoyed every second of it. Marc looked around at everyone and shook his head. "God has really brought us all full circle." "Yes, He has," Drea smiled with tears in her eyes. "My baby girl is getting married," Gloria cried. "I prayed for this day." "Me too," Tony smiled as he looked at his bride-to-be.

"Thank all of you so much for being here for us, and Eric I can't thank you enough for flying everyone out here. On my salary, it would've taken me forever to afford a trip like this." "Don't think twice about it Tony," Eric responded. "It's my pleasure. Besides I'm happy that you guys agreed to use it, it'll be a while before we can travel so this was the perfect excuse for a getaway Eric smiled looking at his pregnant wife.

"Everything feels so surreal like this is a dream, and I am going to wake up at any moment. I know that sounds crazy, but I can't shake it." Dre put his hand on his cousin's shoulder. "Eric that is nothing but the enemy. There has been so much craziness going around that I felt fear creeping in. Fear comes from the enemy. I refuse to sit back and be afraid of the maybes and the what-ifs. I know that God has a plan for everything. I don't know what that plan involves but I am just going to ride shotgun and let Him take complete control."

Eric smiled and shook his head. If nothing else I must admit that all of this has brought us all back to God and closer to Him than we've ever been. "Amen to that," Dre said kissing his wife. "There is no way that I would've believed that I would be a pastor, husband and now a father of two kids but here I am."

"That makes two of us," Marc laughed. "I have always known," Senior said with a gleam in his eye. I knew what I saw it in all of you, even when you were younger, but I couldn't force that on you. You had to choose for yourselves. I am so proud of you."

"The last few years brought forth tragedies that bring out the true character of people but every one of you stood strong, and your faith brought you to this very moment. We've all lost our way at some point, but the bible says that if we train up a child in the way he should go when he is old, he will not depart from it. You will always return to your roots. "Just like the prodigal son," Marc smiled. "So, you were listening" Senior laughed as he prepared to bless the food.

"Father we thank you for the keeping us, and we thank you for the gift of those that are no longer with us. Lord, we love you and honor you this day and every day. Lord as we sit at this meal that you have prepared, we thank you, Lord. Not only for the food on this table but we thank you for the people at this table Lord. We thank you that those who were lost, are now found. To God be the glory, Amen."